Violently ¹

Nikki,

Thank you again for
all the online support!

Love

all the online support!

Also by Christine Winston

Cooped Up

Acknowledgements

This book has been my most challenging so far and on the days when I wanted to give up, my best friend was there, as always, encouraging me to push ahead with Joanna and Davis' story. Thank you Nicole, for yet another amazing book cover and for the endless brain-storming sessions. If it wasn't for you, Joanna and Davis' story would never be told.

To Orla, my beautiful, amazingly talented cousin and friend. Thank you for editing Violently Undone and for giving me the kick in the ass that I needed, when I was dragging my heels. This book would not have reached its full potential without you painstakingly going over every word. We are so happy to have you on board team undone.

To Patricia Essex, I am truly grateful to you for proofreading Violently Undone. You too have helped to ease my mind about putting this book out into the big bad world.

To my beautiful daughter Isabelle, who makes me smile every day, reminding me why I do this. I love you with all my heart.

To my parents Breda and John, for your unconditional love and support. I'm going to take your advice and just keep on writing.

To my aunty Dee, who taught me to always look inward. Without this advice, I don't think it would be possible for me to connect with my characters. I love you.

To Jay, our male model, for being so photogenic. Absolute professional, #four.

To all my family and friends, who have been there for me, listening and offering words of encouragement. Thank you all. I truly appreciate your time and kindness.

There have been many people who have read and reviewed my book, giving an unknown indie author a chance. So, I'd like to say a big thank you to the following people;

Stef (British book binge), thank you for rallying support and helping me to get reviews. I appreciate all the work you continue to do online to support me. Nicole Mc Curdy (Red Cheek Reads), you have been my biggest online support and I truly appreciate all the work you do to help to push out Desperately Undone. I am so grateful to you, it's beyond words. Jade (Reflections of a book geek), for loving Michael and Bree's story and for all of your online pimping. To Diane (Give me books), Shanoff Say's, Clare, Lisa & Ikira (Book ramblings of a neurotic mom), Kathy Savage, Lynn Smith, Nikki M, Michelle Chen and everyone else who has taken on Desperately Undone for review. I hope that you will also enjoy reading this one.

Last but not least, to everyone who has read my book. Thank you for taking a chance on me, you are the reason that I continue to write.

Dedication

When darkness takes hold, of all that we know,
No light can enter, nothing can grow.
In our hour of need, we cease to exist,
The temptation of freedom, too hard to resist.
We leave behind those, who held us so dear,
And search for the light, without any fear.
We know how much you loved us, we felt it every day,
We're sorry we can't be there, to take your pain away.
Know that we are now smiling and watching you from
above,
Distance won't stop us, from feeling your love.
And when you are consumed, with fear and with dread,
Take comfort in the knowledge, you're loving angels now
instead.

Christine x

Dedicated in memory, to Phil "Skinny" James.

PROLOGUE

I lie on the cold, wet ground, staring up at a thick white smoke, billowing out from the overhead aluminium air ducts. The rain continues to pelt against my trembling body, but I feel nothing; I am in a state of desolation. I release a jagged breath and watch, as it passes through my blue lips. I'm not entirely sure at what point I left my body, separating myself from the relentless onslaught of violence he was inflicting, but I have felt no pain for some time now. My feet are bare; my heels grazed, having been dragged from his van to this spot behind a dumpster, in a dark alleyway. My wrist pulses and I know I should be in agony, since he twisted it behind my back during the initial attack; but again all I feel is a dull thud.

My eyes are wide open, but I see nothing, except the white smoke that pumps out above me, like a dark cloud hanging over my head. Footsteps and the sound of clinking bottles draw near, and I hear them dropped into some trash cans close by. I want to call out for help; beg someone to rescue me but I can't find my voice. If I could just close my eyes, I would sleep forever and never have to recall tonight's awful events; yet I lie here, on the cold, wet ground, with the rain against my skin and I know that tomorrow *will* come. The memories and horror will follow, and despite this fear; I know that somewhere inside, I am here, screaming at myself to move and willing myself to find the strength I need.

"Oh shit......is she dead?" A deep male voice echoes around me.

"Her lips are moving; she is trying to say something," a second male voice fills the air, and a shadowy figure appears through the smoke and leans over me. He bends closer, putting his ear next to my lips, attempting to understand my mumblings.

"I can't understand what she's saying, call the police," he instructs the person behind him.

"You're going to be ok, helps on the way," his calm voice reassures me softly.

He shrugs out of his jacket and covers my half naked body. His words and actions are comforting; reminding me that there is good in the world. A few hours ago a monster robbed me of my dignity and a stranger has returned it. I will be forever grateful to him for his kindness.

"What's your name sweetheart?" He prompts, softly.

"She won't tell you man, working girls don't give their real name," his friend snaps, sounding impatient. My throat is dry and it hurts to swallow, but I make and attempt to speak again.

"Joanna," I croak, when my lips part to allow my name through and I taste blood.

"Speak up," he urges.

"Joanna Carmody." I cough out once more.

"Help is here Joanna, don't you worry, help is here," he pats my hand, the warmth of his touch breathing new life into my body. A moment later, flashing blue lights and police sirens flood the alleyway just as he promised.

Davis

I sprint to my car, trying to avoid the heavy downpour. Throwing my gym bag onto the back seat, I switch on the wipers, before pulling out of my apartment complex. I feel buzzed, despite the shitty weather. I haven't been to the gym all week and regardless of the early start, I'm looking forward to getting into the ring with Michael. My mission is to put him on his back today, he has gotten one too many over on me lately. It kills me to admit that he has knocked me on my ass more than a few times, but I give him a good run for his money. The time on the dash reads 5.45 a.m. which means I should get a good session in, before heading to work. I lean forward, wiping the steam from my windshield just as my cell phone begins to buzz. Pulling into the parking lot, I grind my teeth before answering; I already know I will be missing my workout.

"Davis," I say curtly, not caring if I offend Roche.

"It's Roche," he answers and I squeeze the steering wheel a little harder. I haven't had sex in months and Roche is beginning to sound more and more like a nagging wife these days. I really needed to work off some of this pent up frustration.

"What's up?" I take a steadying breath.

"Look, we have a situation, it's not really our jurisdiction but I thought you might want to be involved."

"My work load has doubled in the last three months; we have too many open cases, pass it on to Marks or Jules." I'm about to hang up, but his silence compels me to enquire a little further.

"What is it anyway?"

"There has been a rape close to Fenway," he pauses.

My stomach twists as a strange knowing comes over me. "Who is it?" I rasp. My throat constricts and I swallow past the wave of nausea.

"It was Joanna Carmody."

"I'm on the way."

CHAPTER 1

TWO MONTHS EARLIER

Jo

I pull with all my might, holding on with every ounce of strength. Fear courses through my veins, seizing me, taking my breath away and rendering me powerless. I need to hold on; I need to forget the tingling sensation in my body that tries to convince me that my grip is weak. I look into angry, determined eyes and fight for my friend, she needs me. They want her. "Help," I yell out, twisting my head in search of a saviour, despite my current struggle. "Help," I screech violently, looking back with my own fierce resolve. "You will not take her," I grind through clenched teeth. My eyes are focused on the man, whose face is masked, peering out through the slit in his balaclava, with amused disinterest. I don't see his friend step out of the black van. Bree continues to hold onto me, screaming with me for help and then the fight is lost. A fist, triple my strength, takes aim and finds its target, my cheek. My head snaps back with such force that I am catapulted away from the van; I'm mid-air, listening to the tyres screech away, when I hit the ground. "Bree," I release her name in an unmerciful scream.

"Jo, wake up." I push away the hand that gently rocks me, disturbing me from my slumber. "Jo, you're having a bad dream." Jakes groggy voice moans in my ear, shaking me harder. My eyes flutter open.

"What?" I ask, rubbing my tired eyes, irked at having been woken.

"I'm in work tomorrow Jo, you woke me, shouting help." He flops back onto his pillow, covering his eyes with his forearm. Sitting up, I pull my mussed hair from my eyes and yawn.

"Sorry, I must have been dreaming," I say, looking towards the alarm clock on my dresser. I only have an hour before I need to get up and decide to take full advantage. I flop back down and snuggle into Jake, wrapping my arm across his bare chest.

"Jo, I can't sleep with you sprawled all over me," he moans and I roll my eyes before fluffing my pillow and hugging that instead. It's not long before I hear the familiar sound of Jake snoring and curse him for waking me. We have been together for almost a year now and in all that time, I have never woken him when *his* snoring interrupted *my* sleep.

After thirty minutes, I resign myself to getting up earlier and decide to take a long shower. I have a full diary today; hopefully this will make up for my scattered sleep. The hot water wakes me fully, washing away my sleepy haze. I begin to recall my dream and make sense of why I might have woken Jake.

I stay under the water for a long time before finally stepping out. I dry myself, wrapping the large white cotton towel around my body, securing it at my chest. It's a little after 6.00 a.m. so I decide to leave my hair to dry naturally, until it's a decent time, to fire up my hair dryer. Jake's not a morning person, he is grouchy, bordering on rude at times, but after a few hours, he settles into his laid back self. Our first date had been the night Bree and Michael left for Hawaii, after the trial. It was a momentous day for everyone. I smile now, remembering the relief we all felt that Seamus Lynch was finally behind bars, for good. With bare feet, I tip toe across the wooden floor of the bedroom, to select an outfit for today. Slowly, I slide the mirrored wardrobe across and select a mint green blouse and my high waist, black slacks to wear, before creeping back to the bathroom to dress.

"Oh no, this can't be happening," I suck in a mouthful of air and hold my breath. Pulling my tummy in, I try once again to secure the button on my slacks. Putting up a fight, the button continues to slip from my fingers before finally; I manage to slip it through the slit. Sweating a little too much from this simple task, I release the trapped oxygen and watch, as my small, but noticeable belly, rolls over the waistband. I feel the trousers slacken before, *pop*, the button flies across the room. My eyes widen in horror, I knew I was gaining a few extra pounds but clearly, I was oblivious to just how bad it was getting. I pull open my bathroom cupboard and take out my scales and hop on. Holy cow, a stone! I stare down at the needle, as it points at the double digits and gasp. Bree and Michaels wedding is less than two months away and I've already paid for my bridesmaid dress, which is a size smaller than I am now. Frustrated with myself and not caring for Jakes precious few extra minutes of sleep, I stomp to my wardrobe and pull out my stretch fabric, pencil skirt and pull it up my legs, whispering cuss words at myself and stuffing my blouse into the band, with undue force.

"Jesus Jo, get the hell out," Jake whines from the warmth of *my* Egyptian cotton sheets and I'm not in the mood for his doom and gloom, on top of my expanding waist.

"This is my apartment Jake, I need to get ready for work," my irritated voice snaps, without apology.

"I'm going to my own place, I need to catch up on my sleep," he barks, hurling himself out of bed and pulling on his shirt and slacks. I remain firm in my standing.

"Funny that an hour ago, you had to be up early," I hiss. He forgets his anger at having been disturbed again for a moment, replacing it with a bewildered look.

"Oh, well I forgot I had the morning off," he finally says, sheepishly.

"Well I don't have that luxury, I have been working flat out for two weeks and you disrupt my first full night's sleep, for nothing." I prop my hand on my hip, thoroughly pissed off at him and myself now.

"You were shouting, help, all over the bloody apartment, I was afraid the neighbours would call the cops," he defends himself, as he pulls on his socks.

"That's bullshit and you know it!"

"I don't know what's gotten into you, but call me when you've chilled the fuck out," he shakes his head, pretending to be disappointed in me, before walking out of my room. I quickly run after him.

"Oh and by the way, you snore," I yell, as the hall door slams.

The traffic around the courthouse is insane. There are roadworks which have disrupted the flow, forcing one lane to close and pushing all the vehicles into the same lane. With every parking space taken, I have no choice but to circle around again, but thankfully, I'm lucky enough to scoop a spot, just across the street from the Supreme Court. Grabbing my brief case and handbag, I rush up the steps to meet Eric, my associate, at the entrance. He looks down on me from his 6ft 2 tower, his eyes questioning my tardiness. Ignoring his disapproving stare, I throw him my own, don't even ask, look. Eric is my closet work colleague, he is tall and slim with jet black hair and beautiful olive skin. He is the epitome of what an Italian stallion might look like, if he was Italian.

Unfortunately for him, his roots are a lot less exotic and more country bumpkin, which he hates. He tends to spice up his upbringing, for fun, on nights out, with tales of barn brawls and cowboy courting. The truth is, life as a gay man growing up in Douglas, Wyoming, had been tough. His parents, devout Christians, had shunned him once he came out, which would break most young men. Instead, it pushed Eric to make something of his life. When I first met him, I asked him why he had chosen to move to Boston. "For the sexy accent," he'd replied, his Western accent leaking all over his attempt to mimic the Boston one. It made me laugh hard. He was good natured enough to take my teasing about his massive fail and we hit it off from there.

"Cutting it tight," he says, looking at his watch and keeping one hand behind his back, as if holding some authority over me. I nudge him in the stomach playfully, to keep him in check.

"I've had a bad morning," I warn him and he gives up the angry pretence, pulling two coffees out from behind his back.

"Trouble in paradise with the good doctor?" He queries, passing me the white, to go cup.

"Its times like these," I say, tipping the coffee up at him, "that I wish I were either a man, or that you could be straight," I sigh, sipping the tasty brew.

"That bad huh?" He smirks and I roll my eyes, confirming his suspicions. "Try to hold onto him Jo, you wouldn't be my type, male or not," he laughs, his chocolate brown eyes shining, mischievously, at me. Taking my briefcase to help lighten my load, he pulls open the heavy brown door, leading into the court house.

"I think my grip is slipping," I laugh, walking through the door and we both cross the large marble floor, to check the location of the courtroom we will be in today.

CHAPTER 2

"This scumbag could get off," Eric sneers, grinding his teeth, as Fergus Sanders takes a seat to our right, directly across from me. He looks presentable, despite having spent months behind bars and I hope that it won't fool the jury. His beady eyes run up my body, before finding my face. Ugh, disgusting pig! I recoil. With no DNA evidence, our case hindered on his three victims taking the witness stand. Two followed through but the third, too afraid to face her rapist, pulled out, two days before trial. I had interviewed these women, listened to their horror stories and promised them justice, and I'm praying that my two witness testimonies and corroborating timeline of events, will be enough.

"Court is in session," the court officer bellows out and the room falls silent. Judge Mary Wright, comes out from her chambers and takes her seat, looking over everyone. She gives a short speech before turning to the head juror.

"Have you reached a verdict?"

The slight blonde female stands. "We have, your Honor." She looks nervously to the Judge before continuing. "On the charge of sexual assault, we, the jury, find the defendant, not guilty, on both counts."

I hear Jennifer Morgan, one of his victims, wail in horror, but I keep my head forward, waiting for the rest of the charges to be read out.

"On the charge of intent to cause grievous bodily harm, we, the jury, find the defendant, not guilty, on both counts."

I hang my head now, anger and disappointment, welling up inside.

"On the charge of possession of illegal, class B, narcotics, we, the jury, find the defendant, guilty," she finishes.

I take a deep breath, trying to wrap my head around their grave mistake. Eric pats my shoulder in support.

"Mr Sanders, you will be remanded in custody until sentencing," the Judge throws down her gavel, ending the hearing and the courtroom erupts, as angry family members, curse the jury.

"You did your best," Eric tries to soothe me.

"This is bullshit, we had two victims point him out and CCTV footage of him at both crime scenes, but because I couldn't prove penetration, they ignore the testimony," I growl.

"He will get time for the drugs, at least," Eric shrugs, trying to make me feel better. He had worked hard with me on this case, gathering evidence and preparing the witnesses for trial.

"The judge will knock off time served, that scum will be out in a couple of months," I sigh, stuffing my case files into my briefcase before seeking out his two victims, to apologise.

****

Michael and Bree bought their new house in a gated community, in Salem. It takes me an hour in the car to visit them, but the risk is too big for them to live in Boston. When they first told me that they planned to move back to Massachusetts, I had my concerns. Seamus Lynch and his gang are finally off the streets, but he could still have some pull on the outside. My expressed worries were met with a steely resolve to live their lives on their terms. I admire their fearlessness; I just wish I was that brave. Lynch has been behind bars for almost a year now and there have been no further attempts on Bree or Michael's lives, yet I think there will always be a niggling doubt at the back of my mind. I disembark from the train and follow the red painted line down Washington Street, towards Bree's house. Salem is the most beautiful and quaint town. It is steeped in history and attracts tourists from all over the world, who come to visit the witch house, or to re-enact the witch trials. The painted red line on the sidewalk, is designed to help them get from one attraction, to the other. It's an especially enjoyable walk on summer evenings, and I enjoy the fifteen minute walk to their home. Walking pass the witch house, I, as always, pick up my pace. The grey structure is the only remaining building that is directly linked to the Salem Witch Trials and was owned by the infamous, Judge Jonathon Corwin.

It creeps me out and a cold shiver runs down my spine. I relax when I'm passed it and continue down Chestnut Street, until I come to the guard shack at the entrance to Bree and Michael's estate. I don't recognise the guard on duty; he steps out to meet me.

"Mam," he tips his hat, "what can we do for you this evening?" He says, as a cocky side grin, creeps up his right cheek. He's slightly taller than me, but he has a friendly face.

"I'm here to visit with Bree Richards and Michael Ryan, they are expecting me," I smile back.

He leans into his hut and pulls out a clipboard.

"You're not on the list Mam, I'll need to double check," he insists.

I nod, knowing Bree's need for security is important and I'm happy that he is double checking. Our plans were last minute, so I'm sure she just forgot to inform the guard. I watch him pick up the phone and just as he is about to dial the number, a large, familiar black SUV, pulls up at his window, beeping.

"Open up Dick," Davis' cocky tones, bellow from the SUV.

"Agent Davis, nice to see you, go right ahead," Dick smiles back, lifting the barrier and allowing him access.

"Hey," I begin, before narrowing my eyes at Davis, who just laughs and drives off.

"Agent Davis is on the pre-approved list Mam, you'll need to wait one more moment," he continues to make his call. I wait patiently for another minute, seething inside. Davis will just love this. He fancies himself as Bree and Michaels best friend, while I look like the clinger on. *Uuuggghhhh, Bree, of all the nights to forget, he has to be coming over*, I curse her.

"I just spoke with Ms. Richards; you are free to go up to the house. I'll need to see some identification first please," Dick, aptly named, looks sternly at me, exercising his power.

I begin to laugh at his absurdity, but quickly realize he

is being serious.

"You're kidding right? Bree just told you it was ok," I quip.

"Yes, she informed me to allow access to Joanna Carmody, but I've never met you before, you could be anybody. Agent Davis didn't seem to recognize you either," he finishes.

"Agent Davis didn't see me," I lie.

"Agent Davis just told me on the phone he didn't recognize you," he corrects me.

I swallow the anger that is beginning to bubble up inside me. It's been a long day and all I want, is to eat Bree's spaghetti, drink wine and chill out. Davis is such an asshole at times. I begin rummaging through my bag to find my driver's license. It's in here somewhere, but the bloody bag is oversized and stuffed full of make-up and god knows what else. Frustrated, I plop it on the ground and get on my hunkers, in search of my ID. I hear Dick's phone ringing and he returns a moment later, red faced.

"Seems Agent Davis was winding you up Mam, go ahead," he coughs. I pick up my belongings from the footpath and march towards the house, *I'm gonna kill Davis!!*

When I arrive, Bree, Michael and Davis are all sitting out the back. Michael stands to greet me as I come out.

"Hey Jo Jo," he growls, capturing me in a bear hug. I giggle at his pet name for me and slap his muscled bicep.

"Put me down, you big gorilla," I tease.

"Hey, you didn't greet me like that," Bree pouts playfully and Michael drops me, in favor of his beautiful fiancé. I smile as he pulls her into the crook of his arm and instead of kissing her, he messes her hair. I adore Michael, he is perfect for Bree. He isn't overly affectionate in public, but I know he gives her everything she needs. I turn to Davis, who is lounging in Bree's garden furniture and sipping beer from a brown bottle. He looks, as usual, self-assured and cocky, leaning back into the white metal chair. One foot is propped on the small round table, blocking me from reaching the free seat. He looks up from under his mirrored sunglasses and cocks a smile.

"Joanna," he says, taking another sip from his bottle.

"Davis," I reply, kicking his legs out of my way as I pass. I'm rewarded when his drink sloshes down his face and onto his clean white shirt. I can't help the giggle that escapes; my evening is beginning to look up.

"Fuck," he curses, standing quickly to grab a towel, which only gives the dribbling alcohol, more freedom down his shirt. He throws me a dirty look.

"Oops," I say, unapologetic.

"I'll let you get away with that, considering I had you begging for entry," he reminds me of his annoying prank from only moments ago.

"No need to apologise, I got to check Dick out a little longer," I lie and watch his face redden, in disgust. Davis sits back in his seat, defeated, and I turn my attention to Bree.

"Do you want me to help with dinner?" I ask, as she pours me a glass of white wine.

"No, you guys sit here and relax, I have everything under control. Just a few minutes and it will be ready," she beams, handing me the wine and entering the kitchen. The large, French doors are open, leading onto the patio. I watch as she scurries around, preparing the dishes and listening to Michael and Davis' conversation.

"Are you coming in for a work out in the morning?" Michael asks Davis.

"Yeah, I'm still sore from yesterday," Davis moans and I roll my eyes, he's such a wimp.

Michael begins laughing.

"You're losing your touch, how many times did I pin you down again?"

"I was having an off day."

"There has been a few of them lately," Michael continues to goad him.

"You mean to tell me, the almighty Agent Davis, had his ass handed to him?" I smirk at Davis. Michael and I, both enjoying ourselves now continue to laugh. Davis purses his lips in annoyance, its great fun goading him and most of the time, he asks for it, so I never have to feel guilty.

"Joanna, looks like you could do with joining us there once or twice a week," he quips and before I can reply, both Michael and Bree jump to my defence.

"Whoa, whoa, whoa, Davis, that's a bit too far man, Jo Jo was just kidding," Michael shakes his head, with a disappointed look on his face. Bree, however, looks angry.

"Davis! Jo is beautiful, that's a hideous thing to say," she scolds, and I swear, if I could capture the look on his face and frame it, I would keep it forever. He is mortified and what's more, I was taking his remark in jest. I should ease the tension, laugh it off and help him out but, nah, I think I'll let him squirm.

"Sorry Joanna, I was only joking, obviously you look great," he splutters and it's too much, I laugh out load. He narrows his eyes, as it dawns on him just how much I enjoyed it all.

"That's ok Davis and thanks for the compliment; I never knew you thought so highly of me."

"On a serious note Jo, Davis has promised to teach me some self-defence moves at the gym, a couple of nights a week, you should do it with me, it'll be fun," Bree suggests. I contemplate having to be around Davis more than once a week and graciously decline.

The smell coming from Bree's kitchen is mouth-watering. A mix of tomato and garlic aromas, waft towards me and compel me indoors. Bree has been teaching herself to cook and since Michael is getting home late most evenings, I'm her Guinea pig. Last week, she even dropped cheese cake to my office for me to critique.

"Bree, you need to stop feeding me, I've put on a stone and I'm afraid to try on my bridesmaid dress," I groan, when I'm out of ear shot of Michael and Davis.

"Don't be silly, you look stunning," Bree scowls, as she stirs her large pot of spaghetti sauce, creating a cloud of new smells which disperse through the air.

"I'm not too concerned about the extra weight at the minute, I can lose that but I don't want to gain anymore," my words are a complete contradiction to my actions, as I lean over and grab some bread from a bowl, placed neatly in the middle of her dining table.

"Why don't you train at the gym, it's not far from your office, that way you can eat what you want and I can keep feeding you," she laughs. Bree has always been naturally slim and I envied her growing up. As I got older, I learned to appreciate my curves and even fell in love with my shape. Sure my butt is bigger than most but in general, men seem to love it. The gym is something that I have comfortably managed to avoid for years, I hate getting all sweaty and sticky, but I think my luck is running out. I let out a little moan, I'm useless at dieting and it's impossible when all my socialising, revolves around food and drink. I tap my fingers on my wine glass before taking a deep breath and making the commitment.

"Ok, well, I usually see Jake a couple of nights a week, but I could cool that until after the wedding." Bree reaches into the cupboard, removing the dishes and eyes me cautiously as she sets the table.

"Surely he could just come by later?" She asks, leaning over the table, but keeping her eyes on me. I shrug off the question and move to take out the cutlery.

"When is Michael free to train me?" I quickly move on. I'm not ready to admit my relationship doubts to anyone yet, once I say it out loud, I'll need to make a decision. Bree looks sympathetically at me.

"Aww, sorry Jo but Michael is too busy right now. He has classes every evening with the boys from the youth clubs and after those, his 8.00 p.m. Adult MMA training starts. I could see if he could squeeze you in in the morning, before work?" She kindly offers and I wonder how Michael would feel about being dragged out of bed an hour earlier. His schedule is already jam packed and I would never allow that.

"No, don't do that, I am not getting out of my bed

earlier than I already do. Is it ok if I come down and use the equipment?"

"Why don't you just work out with me and Davis? He's there most nights helping Michael with the boys, it will be fun, plus Michael is adamant I learn self-defence."

I look out onto the patio at Davis, who is laughing with Michael, his white teeth gleaming in the evening sun. He looks like he fell out of a male model calendar for the FBI. I hate that he is so good looking and the idea of seeing him all sweaty and manly, does something funny to my insides. I haven't completely forgiven him for rejecting me that night in the warehouse, my feminine ego would love to make him regret ever turning me away. Facing Bree again, I contemplate if I really want to punish myself with hours of gruelling workouts? The memory of my popping pants settles my inner battle, I have no choice really.

"I'll do it, but don't start pressuring me to go faster or work harder when I'm lagging behind, my butt is bigger than yours, so I take longer," I laugh.

"Wahoo, I'm more excited to do it now too," she smiles. "Michael, Davis, dinner's ready," she bellows over her shoulder and we all sit down to eat.

"Davis, Jo has agreed to do the workouts with us," Bree announces straight away and I roll my eyes, he will love torturing me. I catch a glimpse of him and I'm surprised to see something else cross his face, dread. I must admit, it stings to see him look so disappointed to be around me. I know we argue back and forth a lot but, if I'm honest, I enjoy being around Davis. He is so easily wound up and I love the banter we have.

"Oh, ok, will you be ok to do it, with work and everything?" He asks, clearing his throat.

"Not every night, obviously, but most, what about your job?" I return.

"Yeah, I'm there, unless I'm working late or get called out of town, are you sure you want to do it?" He stalls.

"I'm sure, are you sure it's ok with you?" I ask, sounding affronted, but I'm not going to do something if I'm not welcome. I reach forward and load my plate with more salad than spaghetti, suddenly feeling more insecure than before. I hate that he is making me feel this way; it's ridiculous, *why do I even care*? The table goes quiet before Davis hisses, his face scrunching in pain. Bree just kicked him under the table and I want to laugh at my friend for caring so much.

"I'm sorry Joanna, for the second time," he says, through clenched teeth, like a bold child forced to apologise. "It's just that I thought with your job and what's his name, it would be too much, but you're more than welcome, it will be good for both you ladies to learn."

"Yeah and then you can kick his ass for being such a dick," Michael puts in and I laugh.

"It's Jake! I don't know, I'll think about it," I shrug and change the subject. We settle into lighter conversation and before I know it, it's time for me to catch the last train home.

"Ok guys, I'm off," I announce, standing and moving my dishes to the sink.

"Hold on, Michael will give you a lift into the city," Bree comes up behind me, clearing the dishes.

"No way! It's too late for him to do that drive, I'm happy to take the train Bree, or else I'll stop visiting." Every time I come to visit and leave my car at home, poor Michael is forced to drive an hour back into the city.

"I'm heading to the city now," Davis sighs "I'll drop you."

"Great," Bree excites, before I get the chance to refuse the offer and within a few minutes, I'm in the front seat of Davis' car, waving goodbye to Michael and Bree.

CHAPTER 3

Davis

The wind catches Joanna's hair as we drive away from Salem, blowing it into her face, causing her to giggle. She struggles to contain the wild bundle of blonde curls and finally, closes the window.

"I'll put on the ac, if you're warm?" I offer, speaking for the first time since we left Bree and Michael's. Things between Joanna and I, have been strained over the past few years, to say the least. We are rarely alone and when we are, the conversation doesn't flow too easily.

"Yes please," she smiles warmly at me, her eyes still alight with humour. "It's really warm this evening," she reaches over to figure the ac out for herself.

"It's that one," I begin to point to the correct buttons for her to press, but stop myself, when air blasts throughout the car, blowing Joanna's hair again. A light vanilla smell floats towards me; the familiar scent of Joanna, is strangely comforting. She turns to me, lifting her eyebrows and smiling. I'm not sure if the look depicts pride at having worked the ac, or if it says, don't be silly, of course I know how to do it!

"Theatre District, Boylston Street, right?" I look to her, confirming her address.

"That's it, thanks for giving me a ride," she sits back, looking out the window and I take the opportunity to look at her. Joanna is a beautiful woman. From the first moment I met her, she oozed sex appeal and despite our rocky relationship, she still manages to draw my eyes to her fine curves. No man could help but admire her figure, especially when she is dressed like she is tonight. The tight, black dress, clings to her body in all the right places and yet, revealing nothing. The only skin on show is her long legs. *How is it possible to tempt a man with nothing on show?* I wonder to myself. When Bree announced that Joanna would be doing the self-defence lessons too, I almost choked on my salad. It's tough enough to hide my boner when she is in a pant suit; the idea of her in Lycra, gives me an instant hard on. Fuck! It's happening again. I quickly try to banish those thoughts from my head. I pull onto the Newbury Turnpike before she speaks again.

"You should have taken Highland Avenue onto the 129, it's much quicker at this hour," she whips her head around, eyeballing me, as if I have ten heads.

I try to bite back my smile at her expression, she looks so bewildered at my decision to take this route, but I break and a broad grin crosses my face.

"But I prefer this route," I say, innocently. She drives me crazy and I often wonder if she is this argumentative with just me, before remembering her chosen career.

"I'm just saying, the other way is faster," she shrugs, trying to shake it off but her eyes are unmoving, her expression remaining.

"I'll remember that next time," I laugh now, bringing one hand to my mouth to hide my delight at her. I won't ever tell Joanna, but I love that she challenges me; it makes our every encounter, interesting. Yes, there are times when I want to strangle her but for the most part, I enjoy the unspoken competition between us, especially because I usually gain the upper hand.

"So, about the self-defence, are you coming along tomorrow?" I ask and watch her cute button nose wrinkle in disgust.

"I need to get fit for the wedding but, ugh, the idea of working out, I feel tired just thinking about it," she shivers.

I imagine her breathless, her damp hair matted to her forehead, as she pants after a work-out and my pants twitch, again. *Oh please say you can't do it*, I pray.

"But I need to do something, I'm getting fat," she pats her flat tummy, playfully.

"Hardly Joanna," it's my turn to eyeball her as if she's an alien.

"Obviously not Davis," she laughs, "I just want to get a handle on it." She punches my bicep gently and the light contact causes my stomach to flip. The feeling catches me completely by surprise; I need to get Joanna home, fast.

I drive straight through the easy pass toll, my hands firm on the wheel, trying to concentrate on the road ahead and not what Joanna's hands all over my body, would feel like. *She has a boyfriend, she has a boyfriend, she has a boyfriend,* I repeat over and over to myself. I turn onto Boylston Street and sigh with relief. The windows have fogged up despite the ac; the air thick, with my sexual frustration.

"Ok, I will see you tomorrow," she mutters, her face hidden by hair as she bends to pick up her handbag from the floor. She is about to get out of the car, but turns back, her hand comes up pinning her hair behind her ear before finding her earlobe and tugging it gently.

"You are ok with me doing the class, right?" Her face is flush, her eyes, glazed, search mine intently and I nod.

"Of course," I shrug, dismissively, longing to free her hair from behind her ears.

"Night," she smiles once more before disembarking and I suck in a lungful of air, tasting her vanilla scent. I watch her walk away, her round ass swaying seductively. I groan in agony and look down at my cock "down boy" I warn, before pulling away.

Jo

My phone buzzes in my handbag and I scramble to get it as I walk towards my apartment, the cool air a welcome change, from the thick sexual chemistry I felt around Davis. I manage to find my vibrating phone and catch the call.

"Hey," I bite my bottom lip, feeling guilty. Jake is silent for a moment before he speaks, which only deepens my sense of disloyalty. I shouldn't have been so attracted to Davis.

"Have you calmed down?" He eventually mutters.

"Yeah, sorry about this morning, I was stressed," I say sheepishly, turning the key in my front door.

"You just getting home now?" He asks, sounding surprised.

"Yeah, I was at Bree's for dinner."

"Oh, who was there?" He tries to sound indifferent, but I know better. I narrow my eyes, knowing exactly where this is going. Jake doesn't like the idea of me dining with Bree, Michael and Davis alone; he feels that it's too intimate.

"Bree, Michael and Davis," I reply honestly, refusing to buy into his insecurities. *He isn't completely wrong this time,* my conscience butts into my thoughts. His disapproval is clear, in his silence.

"Jake, I told you before, we're all just friends," I say, irritated.

"No Jo, that guy has the hots for you! I see the way he looks at you!" He snaps.

"You couldn't be further from the truth," I sigh, bored with this rehashed conversation.

"Are you sure nothing has ever happened between you two?" He asks. I swallow hard and lie.

"No, nothing has ever happened, I told you." My skin begins to burn again at the memory of Davis and our shared kiss.

"Ok, I'm sorry, it's been a long day," he relaxes and I try to do the same. We speak for a little while longer, and I can't help but feel differently. Things between us have changed lately, Jake seems more possessive and we hardly have fun anymore. When I hang up, I shower and climb into my large comfortable bed.

Davis leans against the door frame of the small office space. The smell of the warehouse, the taste of metal and dust, along with the sounds of the dock workers and the vision of him dishevelled and sexy all combined, invade my senses, transporting me back here.

"Kicked out?" His voice is husky, as he mocks me. I roll my eyes, crossing my arms, protecting myself from the energy that pulsates between us. He looks good, his crumpled shirt and messy hair only adding to his appeal.

"No, I'm giving them some space to talk, they have been through a lot," I retort, angrily. I'm angry with him for putting us all in this position.

"Yes, but they are together now and Bree is safe," he bites back, his green eyes glaring at me with a heady mixture of anger and attraction. I ignore this realization and stick with my annoyance.

"Ha, no thanks to you," I remind him and he steps forward, crowding me, matching my fury with his own despising stare. His eyes are emerald green, but this close, I can see some brown flecks.

"I did what I thought was right Joanna," he growls, towering over me. His nearness sends my pulse racing, but I hold strong in my resentments.

"You wouldn't know the right thing, if it hit you in the face!" I begin to scold him but instead, feel my body lift from the ground in one swoop, as he grabs the collar of my red blazer and pulls me flush against his hard body. My eyes are almost level with his and I'm forced to lean against him, only my toes remain tipping the ground.

"You have a lot to say Joanna, maybe we should put that mouth to work in another way." I see his head dip and have no time to react before his lips meet mine, his hands leaving my collars and entangling in my curls. I push at his chest, to break free from his demanding kiss but instead, he moves me against the door, imprisoning me with his body. I gasp trying to breathe and he takes full advantage, his tongue dips in slowly, massaging mine and eliciting a new fire within me. I stop fighting and instead wrap my arms tight around his neck, tasting and returning each stroke with the same passion. I feel his hands come beneath my ass, lifting my legs from the ground and wrapping them around his back, as he grinds his powerful erection against me. I gasp hoarsely when he finds my neck with his lips, before capturing my mouth again. My mind is completely frazzled and I'm left breathless...

My alarm clock cries out, waking me from my dream. I jump up, hitting the snooze button, before falling back on the pillow. My breathing is shallow, as my dream comes back to me. I squeeze my legs together, cringing at how turned on I am. I have rarely thought of me and Davis' shared kiss and when I do, I usually cringe because of the rejection, not because I enjoyed it. I jump from bed, refusing to indulge in any erotic fantasies of Davis, but they follow me to the shower and I eventually crumble, allowing myself to find release.

****

"Lunch?" Eric pops his head into my office, just as I'm leaving.

"Sorry, I have to go shopping. I'm starting self-defence classes tonight," I widen my eyes in horror and Eric laughs, knowing full well how much I despise getting sweaty.

"It will do you good," he teases.

"I really feel like pulling out already," I pout, before laughing at my lazy attitude. The truth is a little more complex. My head is all over the place at the minute. Things with Davis last night felt weird and along with my dream, I'm feeling really on edge about going to the classes. I don't think being around Davis with this newfound attraction or rediscovered attraction, is a very good idea. I haven't told Jake yet either and he will definitely lose his cool. I walk towards a small shopping mall, not far from my office and try to concentrate on Jake instead of Davis. We are great together, both our schedules are busy and we have a mutual respect for each other's career, but... I stop myself short. There should be no doubts; nothing has ever felt wrong, until the last few weeks and I'm ashamed to admit it, but the spark has fizzled out for me. My mind wanders back to Davis and a rush of butterflies whirl inside my tummy. I bite down hard on my lip, to counteract the sizzling sensation that travels all over my body. It has been awhile since I felt anything close to this tingling excitement for Jake and even in the early stages, it was never this intense. Frustrated with how I'm suddenly questioning my relationship with Jake, I stroll into a sports shop and take out my phone to call Bree.

"I swear, I could afford to just have liposuction and be done with it, with these prices," I moan down the line a few minutes later, putting the $150.00 trainers back on the shelf.

"It will be worth it in the end and you just need the basics Jo, it's not a fashion show," she laughs and I roll my eyes, it's easy for her, she looks amazing in anything she wears. Davis' face pops into my head and the idea of him seeing me in anything less than the best, is unsettling.

"Hello Jo, you there?" Bree's laughing voice brings me back to my shopping disaster.

"Sorry, yeah, I'm here, I was just trying to figure out if the friggin things come in my size," I lie. "Ok, well I better make a decision here, I'll see you tonight at seven."

"Ok, can't wait and do not pay $150.00 for sneakers," she warns me, before ending the call. I quickly look at my watch and curse my big ass, before pulling out my credit card and getting the over-priced footwear.

Razor

It's only been three days and already, I'm bored shitless watching this boring fucker. The only interesting part of my evening, is watching his pretty girlfriend arrive night after night. My job is to keep a close eye, but hands off, so I'll stay away from the little bitch. I lean forward, twisting the steering wheel in frustration.

"How much longer are they going to stay in there?" I mutter aloud, not that anyone can hear me. I walked in yesterday and the pig showed me around his fancy gym, I can't believe he has the neck to show his face around here. His day will come, I'll take my notes and get paid, like the good dog I am and have my fun somewhere else. I reach for my pen and paper when a red sports car, pulls into the parking lot and I jot down the registration, in case I'll need it later. I look up from my ledger, as a blonde woman steps out of her car, the overhead spotlight illuminating her for me to see. I lean forward again, taking her in and my cock twitches with want. My eyes travel up and over her curvy hips, coming in at her slim waist and out again at her large breasts. Her long neck is exposed, her wild hair tamed high in a bun. Her creamy skin, from where I sit four spaces over, is too tempting. I swallow hard, trying to control my urges to take her. *Not here, it's too close to home.* I sit back, smiling, into my seat, maybe this gig won't be too bad after all.

CHAPTER 4

Jo

The gym is not at all what I expected. To my shame, I haven't had free time to come down and look it over before now. The large open room is a concrete jungle. I expected fancy machines and mirrors but instead, I'm met with bare floors and walls, a small grass area, a weights area with bench equipment and a large boxing ring, in the centre of the room. I smile, taking in the motivational posters on the wall. It's so easy to spot Bree's, *you will get far when you do your best,* from Michael's, *your only option is to fight harder and succeed.* It's nice that he is including both their personalities in the place, even though he is the one putting in all the hard work.

"Hey Jo Jo," Michael calls when he spots me. He was busy with a client when I first came in so I didn't want to interrupt him. The floor beneath me shakes, as his large, muscular body, jogs across the grass area to meet me. His large blue eyes stand out more than usual, against his electric blue vest. He normally only ever wears black, so it's a nice change. He fixes his baseball cap on backwards and hugs me, just as a bunch of twelve year old boys arrive.

"Hey Michael," they all holler and he pats a few on the head, as they pass us.

"Go get changed boys and be out here in five minutes," he orders and they rush to the locker room.

"The place is great Michael, I'm so proud of you," I turn around, taking it all in again and beam with pride. He has come a long way.

"Yeah, it's still a work in progress but it's only been two months so you know, I just gotta give it some time and put in the hours," he blushes.

"I can already tell it will be a great success."

"Thanks Jo Jo, oh here's Davis now," he says, looking over my shoulder. I turn my body sideways, opening up our circle to invite him in. He strolls through the large double doors with ease, his red gym bag hanging loosely from his shoulder. My eyes scan his body, from his broad shoulders down to his large feet. I feel myself blushing and try to discreetly look away, but his eyes catch mine and that same look from the night before, remains.

"Hey man," Michael nods.

"Hey," he nods back, "Joanna," he turns to me with a tight smile.

"Hey Davis," I chirp, trying to sound unaffected. The door bangs again and I look up to see Bree arriving; perfect timing.

"Hey guys," she smiles. "Davis, I was calling after you, didn't you hear?" She laughs, walking over to join us, panting slightly.

"Sorry Bree, I must have been in a world of my own," he says flatly, his face unmoving. I normally ignore Davis' moodiness, but he seems distracted or on edge and I find myself wanting to know more. *Shush!* I stop my mind from focusing on Davis, *I have a boyfriend, I have a boyfriend, I have a boyfriend*, I repeat over and over.

"No worries, Jo is here too, so I can give you both these," Bree reaches into her bag and pulls out two white envelopes. "It's your invites." She beams with pride and I giggle, watching her dance on the spot with excitement. I hurriedly open the envelope to reveal a tri-fold invitation. I smile at the *M* and *A* initials that are linked in fancy text and covering the front of the elegant invite. I open either side of the soft blush stationary and read the details;

Michael Ryan & Aubrey Richards,
Request the company of
Joanna Carmody and Jake Matthews,
To celebrate our marriage at
The Makena Coast Hotel, Maui, Hawaii,
On September 16th

Bree and I gush over the beautiful handmade invitations.

"Great job Bree," I hug her, before carefully placing it into my gym bag. I will put it away in a safe place when I get home. Bree and Michael have come so far over the past few years and looking at them now, both clinging to the other's hip as they chat with Davis and me, fills me with pride.

"Davis, are you bringing a date or not?" Bree calls to Davis, who is looking down at his invitation. He looks up but he seems distracted.

"No, I'm flying solo," he announces proudly, before stuffing the invitation into his bag without care.

"Ok, can we quit the friendly chit chat and get some work done?" Davis demands, the distant look in his eyes returning.

"Yeah, the kids are waiting for me," Michael kisses Bree before he scarpers to the kids, who are messing around in the boxing ring. I watch Davis walk to a nearby bench to put his bag down.

"What the hell is that?" Bree looks at me with wide, incredulous eyes.

"What?" I say nervously looking behind me. I turn back, confused. "What are you talking about?" I ask again and Bree laughs.

"I'm talking about you, staring all gooey eyed at Davis," she whispers and I look over her shoulder to make sure he isn't close enough to hear her.

"Don't be silly Bree, I was thinking about the wedding," I lie, mortified to have been so obvious.

"Sure," she shakes her head in disbelief. I don't have time to convince her before Davis returns.

We line up on the grass after our warm up and already, I'm sweating and out of breath. Davis directs us to stretch our bodies and I can't help but look him over, as he bends forward, touching his toes. I have never seen him in workout gear, he is normally sporting his jeans and leather jacket or a suit, but tonight, he is wearing a black tank top and sweat pants. A pang of guilt shakes me from my perusal of his broad shoulders, what the hell is wrong with me? He pulls one arm over his shoulder and using his other hand, pushes it down and begins talking, as he continues to stretch his body.

"Ok, so I'm going to show you some basic moves today, but this class isn't to make you think that you're untouchable. The best defence is prevention," his stormy eyes pin us and hold our attention, while he changes arms. "Always take personal security precautions, make sure that you are aware of your surroundings and never walk alone late at night." Davis drops his hand and joins us in the centre of the grass area. Sweat, mingled with a soft spicy smell, floats around us as he walks back and forth and I try to concentrate on what he is saying.

"So, an attacker will always prey on the vulnerable and will go for someone who won't cause trouble, so that's your first lesson, fight back initially, with all your might, and don't let anyone control you easily. Bree stand here," he says, pointing to the grass area next to him. Bree does as directed and I watch, as he turns with his back to her, my eyes once again roaming too freely over his body.

"Ok, JOANNA! PAY ATTENTION," my eyes dart up and meet his. He looks pissed off and I swallow hard, nodding at him, I think he just caught me ogling him.

"Ok Bree, I want you to come behind and try to attack me," he looks forward again, when he is satisfied that I'm behaving.

Bree steps forward quickly, but before she reaches Davis, he whips around and yells.

"STAY BACK," causing me and Bree to both yelp. We begin giggling and pat our chest, my heart racing from the fright of Davis' assertive tone.

"This is a serious matter girls," he says sternly. I stop laughing and roll my eyes, he is taking this way too seriously.

"Jeez Davis, lighten up, you gave us a fright. We didn't expect you to shout at us," I snap.

"Good, because you want to have that same effect on your attacker. They don't want trouble and screaming at them, immediately makes you trouble! In most cases, this will be enough to run them away and it alerts people in the area too."

I bite my tongue to prevent myself from moaning any further. I know it's not a joke, but I refuse to defend laughing any further, Davis is being over the top. I force a smile, keeping my lips tight; I can't believe, I thought I could be attracted to this grouchy bear.

Davis

I squeeze my eyes shut in frustration, when Joanna's tongue peeps out between her lips to moisten them. The sheen of her saliva, glistens against the soft pink of her lips and I look away, trying to refocus. I've had a rough day in work and this is the last place I wanted to come when I finally finished, but I'd promised Bree. The image of Joanna in sexy yoga pants was pretty much as I expected, but I hadn't factored in the skimpy pink tank top, that hugs her bust perfectly. I also never considered how enticing, tiny droplets of sweat could be, especially when they roll slowly between the offending breasts, daring you to taste. I shake my head and try concentrate on the job at hand.

"Ok Joanna, I'll come up behind you," I direct and wait for her to stand ahead of me. I sneak a quick peek at her ass, *did I catch her checking mine out earlier or did I imagine that?* I wonder. I move quickly behind her and grab her in a choke hold before she even has a chance to turn around.

"Joanna, you need to be more aware of what's happening around you, go again," I move back to my place and start over. The second time, she is better but still not quick enough.

"Don't wait for me to get too close, if you are suspicious of someone behind you, you would be more hyper aware, so trust your gut. If you feel them move quickly behind you, turn on your heel and scream loudly," I remind her.

"But what if it's just an innocent bystander?"

"Either way, you won't be attacked so why risk it? In case you offend a complete stranger?" Her brow furrows, as she contemplates what I'm saying.

"That makes sense, I suppose. Ok, let's try once more

before you move onto Bree," she says, with a determined glint in her eye. I repeat my movements but this time, she spins around before I reach her and yells.

"STAY BACK."

"Good job," I smile firmly at her, "ok Bree, your turn."

Bree swaps places with Joanna and gets it right first time round, I high five her, delighted;

"Great work Bree," I say proudly.

"Ok, practice with each other for a minute, I need to get something from the car," I say, jogging towards my bag to grab my car keys. When I return, they are both screaming, stay back, at each other and laughing. I roll my eyes but leave them to it, before moving on to the next part of training. These are basic self-defence moves, but it's important they know them.

"Ok, move in. If your attacker is undeterred by you yelling, you need to look at how quickly you can flee. I will show you one or two moves that will disable your attacker, allowing you to run." I pull at the head of the male shaped self-defence dummy that I have just taken from my car. "This dummy is used to help show you weak points on the human body, you can practice how and where to aim your kicks, punches etc," I tug up my sweat pants, preparing to kick. "Ok, so if the attacker is still far enough away that you can kick them, then aim low and connect with the groin. This will put a male attacker on the ground for at least thirty seconds, giving you ample time to run for help." I clench my fists and go up on one leg, kicking downwards, my foot connecting with the dummy lightly, to demonstrate where they should be aiming. Both ladies take turns and manage to follow my instructions well.

"Ok, from the top, pretend the dummy is an attacker, coming up behind you Joanna. Show me the first two modes of defence you can use." I have them do both techniques, one after the other. When I am satisfied with their progress, we move on.

"Ok, so imagine you scream, stay back, but he is already on top of you and you have no way to kick the attacker, you need a back-up plan." I lift my right hand, palm facing them and tilt it towards the ceiling, running my fingers along the base. "Using the palm of your hand and shooting it upwards, aim for his nose. If you use enough force, you could not only break it, but water their eyes and again, giving you a chance to escape." I walk to the dummy and bend my knees slightly, facing it before bending my fingers and use the flat of my hand to connect with the dummies nose. The force causes the rubber head to snap backwards.

"Ok, one at a time, try it," I step away. Joanna is scarily strong and a bit too good at this part but Bree holds back, afraid to break the dummy. I show her the move again and she improves slightly.

"You can practice that Bree," I laugh.

"So, staying with the face, you could go for the eyes by poking and scratching or you can pull at their ears, the key to remember is, put up a fight." I look between them both as I deliver my speech and stop when I catch Joanna yawning.

"Am I boring you?" I enquire softly. Her eyes widen and her hand flies up, covering her gaping mouth, as she tries to hide her boredom.

"Sorry, I'm just exhausted from work," she fumbles, looking embarrassed. I have been working since 6.00 a.m. and still came here to help them, so I expect their full attention.

"Remember, the basic rules are simple, no phone in hand or head down when walking alone, especially at night. If you must walk alone at night, wear your hair down."

"Why?" Bree asks gently.

"Because if you have your hair in a ponytail," I walk towards her and grab the brown mass of hair on her head, held up by a small band, "it's easier to grab hold of." I tug gently on her hair to demonstrate my point.

"Wow, I never thought about that before, that's scary," Bree can be so naive, even now after everything she has been through, she sees the good in people.

"If you think someone is following you, start to move quickly, change directions, cross the street and head to the nearest shop or lighted area. If you are driving and know you won't be back to your car until after dark, make sure you park your car in a place with good visibility. Never leave your car open and always, no matter what, do everything in your power to avoid getting dragged or forced into a vehicle with your attacker, your chances of survival greatly diminish from that point. Don't take out cash or carry anything expensive in your hands and always make sure your keys are ready, as you approach your car and house. You don't want to be caught off guard rummaging through your bag."

"Jeez, there is a lot to learn," Joanna blows out a bewildered breath.

"It is a lot to take in so I will show you one more move, how to escape the clutches of an attacker who grabs you from behind. Just watch me first and then we will practice." I stand sideways and begin to explain each movement, showing them with my body, step by step.

"If someone grabs your shoulder, instead of pulling out of the attacker's grasp, turn into it, ball your fist at your chest, bend your elbow and swing low with force, you're going to power punch them...,"

Jo

"...in the groin if they are taller," Davis moves to the side. Bending his knees, he drops down low and balls his fist, punching the imaginary attacker. My mouth waters as his arms flex, highlighting his toned arms and shoulders.

"Or if they are smaller, elbow them here in their solar plexus." Davis points just below his rib cage and I wonder, briefly, how toned the rest of his body is. He swings around again at his ghostly assailant. This time, he grabs his fist and throws his weight into his elbow jab, stamping down heavy on one foot. His face contorts with rage; I'd hate to be at the end of that elbow. I could imagine how bad it would be if someone actually attacked him.

"If they are a similar height, then you can elbow them in the face. You will hopefully startle them and create an opportunity to run. To finish up, we will go over everything from this evening," he stands and calls Bree out with a wave of his index finger. I watch as Bree goes over each move, starting with prevention, then kicking low, before moving to the dummy, demonstrating an upper-cut and then finally, Davis comes behind her and she practices the new movement, swinging low at his groin but stopping just before her fist connects with his penis. I think I'll try elbowing his solar plexus, my hand anywhere near that area, for any reason, is a bad idea. I take my position and repeat the steps but when it's time for the final technique, Davis' hand grabs my bare shoulder and I freeze. His rough hand against my damp skin, sends delicious shivers all over my body and I turn pink, as desire pools in my groin.

"Joanna," he nudges me, his hand still in place and I shake my head, clearing my mind of all thoughts of Davis.

"Sssorry, go again," my voice is deep and husky and I clear my throat quickly, shocked at my behaviour. I'm more prepared this time for my reaction and when his calloused thumb grazes against my neck, his four fingers cradling my shoulder blade, I turn into his heated gaze and swing low.

"FUUUCK!!"

I jump back as Davis falls to the ground, his body crumpled over in pain. He rolls onto his back, clutching his nether regions. I react almost immediately and fall on my knees beside him.

"Oh shit, I'm sorry, I'm sorry, are you ok?" Without thinking, I pull at his hands to inspect his injured member.

"Jesus woman, leave me be," he growls deeply through clenched teeth. I realize my actions and apologise profusely, but he is still in pain. His face is red and scrunched together. I stand up to move away from him. I think my close proximity might be increasing his level of discomfort. I bite my lip and look at Bree who is covering her mouth, her eyes watery and alight with humour, as she holds back her laughter. I lose it completely and like Bree, I clamp down hard on my lips before spluttering loudly. Davis pulls himself from the ground, his eyes displaying a completely different emotion. I would describe it as anger, except the look he gives me is a raw, unrestrained look of disgust, which catches me unaware. My laughter stops abruptly.

"Davis, I'm truly sorry..." I try to apologise again before he cuts me off.

"Forget it, I'm done for tonight. I'm working tomorrow so we can pick this up on Thursday, goodnight Bree." He turns his back on us both and walks straight to the locker room. I'm left standing, gobsmacked and licking my wounds.

"Bree, he is really mad at me, I think he hates me," I gasp in horror.

A cold chill runs down my spine, a complete contrast to the warm buzz his touch left on me, only seconds before I floored him. I decide to skip showering at the gym in favour of the privacy of my own bathroom. I decide to wait outside for Davis. Bree is going to hang around and travel home with Michael, but I didn't want to leave without apologising, again. I wait in my car for him and jump out when he leaves, twenty minutes later.

"Davis," I call to him as he approaches his SUV and I jog over, just as he unlocks it. He turns in my direction, his icy glare still in place.

"Um, I didn't want to go home without apologising again." It's hard for me to admit when I'm wrong but this is different. I hurt him, caused him actual physical pain and then to top it all off, I laughed in his face. I feel like a shithead.

"Let's just forget it," he shrugs, turning away and I pull his elbow, stopping his retreat. He looks down at my hand still touching him and I pull back, catching both hands behind my back where they can't do anymore damage.

"I just want to be sure that you know it was an accident, but I should never have laughed," I flush a deep shade of red; it's a struggle to be around him again. I feel like a crazy person, all of a sudden Davis is everywhere, in my thoughts, my dreams, the shower, last night, tonight and my reaction to it, is not good. These feelings will only get me into trouble. He gives me a firm nod and I return it, stepping back and allowing him to leave. I get about two feet away when he calls to me.

"Joanna, get your attacker like that and you should be ok," he flashes me a brief smile.

"Yes Sir," I salute him, before jogging back to my car, happy at least that he isn't as angry as before.

CHAPTER
5

Jo

Jake is waiting, with a bunch of flowers, at my apartment when I arrive home. I lean up, kissing his lips gently before taking the offered flowers.

"Where were you?" He asks when I push open my hall door, allowing him to follow me inside.

"I was at the gym, working out," I hold my hands up and twirl, pointing out my workout clothes.

"Since when did you start working out?" He asks, taking a seat at my kitchen island. I move around it, taking out two glasses and pouring some white wine from the fridge.

"Since tonight," I shrug, "oh, Bree gave me the invitation for the wedding." I say excitedly, taking out the invitation and handing it to him.

"Looks great," he smiles, briefly looking it over and handing it back to me.

"So, was it just you and Bree working out?" He takes a sip of his wine, looking over the rim of his glass. I consider brushing him off again and decide against it, I haven't done anything wrong and even though I have found Davis attractive over the past few days, I would never cheat on anyone.

"Michael was there, he has set up a free evening class for kids in the local community," I smile, thinking of how good Michael is with the boys.

"Well it's the least he could do, I suppose," I look up, disgusted.

"What the hell is that supposed to mean?" I snap. I know Michael made mistakes in his past, but I'm not having anyone who hasn't even bothered to get to know my friends properly, talk down about them.

"I just mean that he mentioned before about giving back to the community, sorry it came out wrong," he says, sheepishly and I narrow my eyes, not convinced. "So what did you and Bree do?" He continues and I know what information he is really looking for, so I bite the bullet and tell him.

"Davis taught us some self-defence moves," I shrug

unapologetic, he has annoyed me now.

"I knew it!" He smirks triumphantly, as if he solved some complicated mathematical equation.

"Knew what?" I frown.

"That guy is like a bad rash in this relationship Jo, he needs to go! I'm not having my girlfriend being friends with someone who wants to get into her knickers," he stands, pulling his tie loose. His face is red, his body tense, as he prepares himself for an argument.

"Jake, you need to calm down, Davis is a friend and a close friend of Michael's. He is a small part of my life, but I won't risk my friendship with Michael or Bree by demanding he not be there when I am," I say firmly.

"You are purposefully putting yourself around him, Jo! It's weird, the whole fucking set up," he barks.

"Explain what you mean, Jake!"

"I mean your best friend is shacking up with the guy who kidnapped her and he is best friends with an FBI Agent and you're a Junior District Attorney, hanging out with a criminal," he blusters.

"So, when you asked me about my friends, all you heard was the negative stuff. I don't have time for this, see yourself out," I walk past him and he grabs my upper arm.

"Let go of me."

"You like him, don't you," he squeezes my arm tighter and I try to pull from his grip.

"Let go Jake, NOW!" I say louder and he glares down at me, his eyes bulging with anger.

"Fine, fuck you both," he pushes me slightly, before grabbing the bunch of flowers and storming out of my apartment. I quickly lock my door and secure the latch, before phoning Bree.

When she picks up, I tell her about the fight with Jake. She is still in the city, so she and Michael decide to come by mine before heading home. I jump in to have a quick shower and change into my pj's, just in time for their arrival.

"You didn't have to come by," I hug Bree as they both

come into the apartment.

"Did he hurt you?" Michael asks, his nose flaring and I shake my head, no.

"It wasn't like that," I hug Michael too and lead them to the kitchen. I pour Bree a glass of wine and make Michael a coffee, before sitting at the table with them.

"He has been jealous of the time I spend with you guys for a while now," I confess, leaving out the real reason behind his jealousy.

"That's no excuse to grab you like that," Michael grinds his teeth again.

"I know, it's over now between us. I can't spend my life tip toeing around him," I shrug; the saddest part of it all, is that I'm relieved. Looking back over the past year with Jake, he has always tried to spend time alone with me, away from my friends. I've never even met his friends or family, he always preferred nights in, rather than nights out and I'm the opposite. We have been invited to Michael and Bree's on countless occasions and most of the time, I would show up alone or I just wouldn't go. He has only ever been in Davis' company once before. He took an instant dislike to him and he made little or no effort to get to know Michael and Bree properly.

"Are you ok?" Bree leans forward, clutching my hand and I smile broadly.

"Yes," I answer her honestly.

*****

I hate you! I repeat the words over in my head, hoping that Davis will telepathically pick up the message. My legs hurt, my arms are tired and he wants us to wrap up tonight's class by planking, for one minute. I'm only twenty seconds in and already I can feel myself beginning to shake.

"Come on ladies, keep it going," his annoying voice growls at Bree and I, "good job Bree, Joanna, lower your ass," he barks. *I'm going to kill him*, I scream loudly to myself and the anger helps me to keep going. The last thing I want now is to fall and have to look at him treating me like I'm a failure.

"Times up, well done," he announces and I drop to the ground, rolling onto my back, unable to stand yet. I look to the side and Bree is in the exact same position, opposite to me.

"Good job," Davis stands over me, looking down at me with a huge grin on his face. He has a look in his eyes; I wouldn't describe it as evil, but it's close. He loves torturing us.

"I hate you," I finally say the words that I had contained during the workout.

"No you don't," he winks, before leaving me, to pull Bree from the floor.

"Come on Bree, you need to stretch," he smiles warmly at her, but Bree pushes his helping hand away.

"No, please, I feel sick," she moans and I sit up straight. Her voice is shaky and looking at her now, she is far too pale.

"You ok?" I ask concerned, but she simply shakes her head, no.

"Michael," I call to Michael who is putting away equipment and his head immediately snaps in our direction before making his way over.

"Sorry, I pushed too hard," Davis bends down, this time, easing her from the ground and both he and Michael, lift her to her feet.

"I'm sorry, I feel light headed, I think I'm going to be sick," Bree pushes them away weakly and we all share a concerned expression, before her knees buckle and Michael catches her.

"Whoa, whoa, baby, I got you," he says, lifting her in his arms and sitting on a wooden bench close by, holding her on his lap. I rush to the small kitchen area and find the wash bucket. I quickly spill the dirty water down the sink and rinse it, before bringing it to Bree.

"I'll grab some water," Davis moves quickly to the small

water fountain.

"Bree, are you in pain?" I try asking her and she shakes her head, no, pushing weakly at Michael's chest.

"I'm going to throw up," she snaps forward with new found strength, before spewing into the bucket.

"Shit," Davis curses, arriving back at the scene just in time to watch it unfold.

"Sorry guys," Bree moans, her eyes welling with confusion and embarrassment. I know Bree will be mortified about this and I narrow my eyes at Davis for pushing us so hard.

"Babe, I'm going to take you to the hospital," Michael stands but Bree shakes her head.

"Don't be silly, I just over exerted myself," she insists and I can see Michael is frustrated.

"But you almost fainted and just vomited, we need to get you checked out," he pleads.

"I think she will be fine Michael, if you're still sick tomorrow, you should go the doctor then, but spending hours in the emergency room tonight, won't help," I side with Bree.

"I'm sorry guys; I thought you could handle a big finish," Davis rests his hand on my shoulder and I look up into his green eyes.

"You ok Joanna?" He asks.

"Yeah, it was pretty tough but I'm fine," I step away from his touch. It has been a week since Jake and I broke up, but along with that relationship, I have shelfed any infatuations I had for Davis. We are friends, we can't mess around, there is too much at stake.

"I'm sorry guys, I wasn't feeling well earlier and haven't eaten much today, it's my fault more than anyone else's," Bree confesses.

"You didn't say," Michael pulls back looking at her face, "why didn't you tell me?" His voice is still laced with concern. I move away to give them some privacy and to grab some tissue paper for Bree.

"You guys head off, I'll clean up here and take Bree home," Michael stands, taking the tissue paper from me and placing Bree on the bench. We hug goodbye before Davis and I leave for the evening. I have been enjoying the self-defence classes, but this week Davis is like an army sergeant. We have been lifting weights and doing drills to build on our core strength, *whatever the hell that means.* Even though it's tough, I am making healthier food choices, not wanting to undo my hard work in the gym. It has only been a week, but I feel better and I can see a small improvement.

"I hope Bree is ok." Davis's chews his bottom lip as we walk to our cars and I can tell he is feeling guilty.

"I could say it's your fault, maybe then, you will go easy on us next week, but that would be mean. It's only half your fault," I nudge him playfully with my hip. He loses his footing only slightly before smiling and I'm happy to see him cheering up.

"I'll take it easy... for a day or two," he winks and I roll my eyes. It's hard to not find him insanely attractive, especially when he looks so boyish and handsome. His damp hair is flopping over his eyes and I lick my lips as I imagine how good it would feel to run my fingers through it.

"It's working though," he smiles as I step towards my car.

"What is?" I arch my brows together, not sure what he is talking about.

His eyes roam up and down my body, purposefully and cause me to tingle all over.

"You're toning up already and you're getting fitter," he smiles walking backwards to his own car.

"Is that a compliment from Agent Davis?" I lift the back of my hand to my forehead jokingly and he laughs before turning and walking away.

He lifts his hand. "Goodnight Joanna" and waves without looking back.

Bree
I hear Michael moving about the bedroom looking for

me, I know he will worry when he sees me, but I can't drag myself from the bathroom floor. After spending the day in college, vomiting; my energy is completely zapped. Initially, I thought I had a stomach flu, but two days later and no sign of it passing, another diagnosis came to mind.

"Bree, you in there?" Michael calls from behind the locked door.

"Just a minute," I groan, trying my best to sound upbeat, but failing miserably.

"What's wrong?" He instantly picks up on my distress. Sometimes it's not so good when someone knows you, as well as Michael knows me. I turn from my sitting position against the back of the bathtub onto my knees and using the tub, I pull myself from the floor.

"Bree, what's wrong?" He demands urgently.

"Nothing Michael, just a minute," I beg, moving to the wash basin and splashing some cold water onto my pale skin. My reflection in the mirror matches how I feel, dyer. There is a series of raps on the door again so I pull it open, before Michael has a hissy fit. I want to smile at him, he looks so concerned, but the impending gloom of what his reaction to my news might be, prevents my lips from lifting upwards. His long fingers run over the top of his favourite, red baseball cap that he is wearing backwards, before dropping into the pockets of his black shorts. Michael is the complete opposite of the man I thought I would fall in love with and yet, here he is, tall and muscly with tattoos and soon he will be my husband, and I couldn't ask for more.

"Babe, what the hell?" He sighs, his tone frustrated. He has tried to convince me to go to the doctors for the past two days and I'm thankful now, that I put him off.

"Michael I...," my eyes well up, before I can get three words out of my mouth and I shake my head, unable to utter the words I know could cause him to resent me.

"Bree, you're scaring me, what's going on? Is it the wedding?" He frowns, grabbing my hand and pulling me from the en-suite towards our bed. I reach into my back pocket and pull out the white stick, cowardly avoiding his eyes.

"What's that?" He takes it from my hand. "Are you...?"

I nod my head, my eyes still avoiding his. I can't bear to see the disappointment. I promised him we would wait, I would be careful and when the time was right, we would discuss it. His biggest fear is bringing a child into this world, having spent years convincing himself that he wouldn't be a good role model.

"Bree, please say this isn't true," hearing the shock in his voice, I finally look up and into his stormy blue eyes. The look of fear and anger there; causes me to lose it again and tears spring from my eyes.

"I'm sorry Michael," I shake my head, before reading the results of the pregnancy test one last time, to be sure, "I'm pregnant," I gulp. I watch as his face contorts in anger, his nose flares and his lips jut out.

"How could this happen?" He snaps, I haven't seen him this angry in a long time. "Talk to me," he growls again and I flinch.

"I don't know Michael, I'm on the pill," I cry.

"Bree, tell me the truth, did you plan this?"

I wipe my eyes quickly, removing my blurred vision and look incredulously at him.

"How can you ask me that?" I whisper, shocked that he could think that I would ever deceive him.

"I'm sorry," he pulls off his hat, running his hands through his hair, "I need some air," he announces and moves to leave the room.

"Michael, we need to talk," I jump up after him.

"Bree, I need space," he whips around, angry again and I stop in my tracks, while he continues down the stairs.

"Michael, please don't leave me," I call out, begging him to stay. The front door slams behind him and I sit down on the stairs, crying. Michael has never left me while I've been upset, he never leaves me, full stop.

Davis

"Michael, you need to get home and apologise to Bree and sort this shit out," I duck, as Michael's fist comes at my face. The power and force behind his punch, matches the steely determination in his eyes to connect with the target, me!

"She promised we would wait," he snaps, his balled fist coming towards me again and I dodge his hand.

"Jesus Christ, calm the fuck down before you take my head off," I roar, out of breath.

"You have no idea what kind of shitty childhood I had, I'm going to fuck it up," he growls, dancing on his toes, giving me chance to steady myself.

"Grow a set and get over it," I taunt him and he lunges forward. He manages to land one punch, before I clip his ankles, putting him on his back.

"ARE YOU DONE?" I stand over him shouting. "Now, you asked that girl to marry you, knowing that she wants a family, so don't blame her if shit got serious before either of you expected! If you don't want to be a father, let her go!" I finish, pulling off my gloves and leaning against the blue ropes.

"I'm going to ruin the baby's life," he chest rises and falls as he lies, catching his breath.

"No Michael, you are going to show this kid that you fight for what you love, for what is right and there is always a way back! Stop being a shithead, this is right where you want to be, you're just terrified of messing it up, but guess what?" He sits up, in the middle of the ring and stares nervously at me.

"What?"

"So is every other man who is about to become a Dad!" I roll my eyes.

I left her crying," he looks away, ashamed now.

"Well then, you better get home and make it right!"

"Can you give me a ride?" He jumps up, like someone lit a fire under his ass.

"Where is your car?"

"I needed to clear my head so I went for a run before taking the metro."

"You're a pain in my fucking ass!" I dip low and catch him with a blow to the stomach "...that's for almost breaking my jaw" I smile as he coughs.

Bree

"I worked out my dates and my last period was eight weeks ago Jo, what am I going to do?" I lean forward on the kitchen table, throwing my head into my hands. I have tried calling Michael at least twenty times since he left, but his phone is off. Thankfully, Jo was free to come over.

"You have seven months to prepare. Michael will come around Bree, he loves you, so he will love the baby you both created," Jo reaches over the table and squeezes my hand, trying to reassure me. If she hadn't been here to calm me down, I think I would have gone insane with worry. I feel so disappointed in Michael; no matter what his feelings are, he should have stayed and talked to me.

"I don't know Jo, he ran out at the first sign of trouble and even asked if I had planned it," my eyes well up again, Michael has really hurt me. It's heart breaking to think that he could ever doubt me.

"Bree, he was in shock, you need to try understand his concerns; this is a big deal to him," she shrugs gently.

"BREE?" Michael's voice booms throughout the house and the front door slams. I look over at Jo, who is smiling triumphantly.

"See, I told you," she squeezes my hand again, happily. I hear Michael go into the living room first, still calling out for me. I stand up from my seat as Davis walks in.

"In here Michael," he leans against the door frame and calls over his shoulder. Michael comes storming in a second later.

"Bree, I'm sorry babe, can we talk?" His eyes are wide with fear as he reaches for me, but I hold up my hand before he grabs me. He stops his advances.

"You left Michael," I sniffle, my angry resolve already

crumbling, just knowing that he came back to me.

"I know, I'm scared shitless Bree, but I was selfish. I should have checked that you were ok before I worried about myself," he reaches forward to cup my face and I stand back, not ready yet to forgive him.

"You accused me of deceiving you," my voice breaks, and I gulp back tears. Davis tilts his head to Jo, indicating that they should leave and she nods back to me before following Davis out. I allow them both to go, without seeing them out or even saying goodbye.

"I never really thought that, I was angry and wanted to blame someone," he shrugs guiltily.

"I'm terrified Michael, I needed you! I just started college after all these years, we are getting married in ten days and I'm pregnant for a man who doesn't want the baby," I gulp. His arms come around me, hugging me against his strong body. He always knows how to make me feel safe, just his embrace is enough to make me feel that everything will be ok and I take comfort in his smell.

"I love you, I love every part of you and I will love our child Bree, I promise," he whispers softly into my ear. "I'm afraid that I'm going to mess it up, I need you to help me be good at this," he pleads and I pull away, looking up into his blue eyes. He looks like a child, lost and afraid and I remember that things haven't been easy for him. The only childhood he has known, was filled with fear and beatings, he doesn't know how to do this, but I can show him

"Michael, you're an amazing man, we will help each other," I promise. He leans down, kissing my swollen lips softly.

"I'm sorry Bree," he whispers against my mouth, before deepening the kiss.

"Bree, I'm going to be a Dad," he says, allowing himself to get use to the idea.

"No Michael, you're going to be a great Dad," I smile.

CHAPTER
6

Jo

From the sky, I look down on the island of Maui, in awe of its beauty. The coastline is marked with white sandy beaches, the bright blue ocean, ebbing at its feet before moving inland. There, it comes alive with colour, as lush green forests triumph, creating a truly exotic getaway. Michael and Bree flew in yesterday, so it's up to me to make the forty minute journey from Kahului Airport to Makena beach. I'm excited to drive around the island and hopefully find some hidden treasures. I move promptly through departures and then on to the security gates before collecting the keys to my rental car. I picked a white Audi Cabriolet to drive while I'm on the island, mainly because it's a convertible and small, but also because it looked so cute in their online brochure.

I'm taken aback when I'm handed a map of roads that I'm unauthorized to travel during my stay, but as they are not anywhere near my destination, I pop it into the glove box and get on my way. The past few weeks have been a nightmare in work and this week away, is long overdue. Jake and I had booked to stay on after the wedding so without him here, I will be alone. Initially, I was nervous about travelling by myself, but after my hectic work schedule, being away from it all is more important. With the top down and music blaring, I take highway 311 toward Makena beach. I feel alive as my hair whips around my face, the sun heats my bare shoulders, the warm breeze a welcome change from the cool summer we experienced in Boston. My body is in desperate need of some vitamin D. My pale skin almost transparent at this point, could do with some color. I sing along loudly, despite my voice being drowned out by the cars that pass me at speed; I continue to belt out one of my favourite power ballads with glee. My behaviour is similar to that of a prisoner on day release, the freedom going to my head. I laugh at my comparison, turn up the volume and put my foot down; I'm thirsty for a cocktail.

"Jo Jo," I turn to see Michael and Bree, walking

hand in hand, across the hotel lobby. Bree looks adorable in a white strapless summer dress and straw hat, while Michael becomes accustomed to the islands flare for fashion and flaunts a colourful Hawaiian shirt and white shorts. I squeal with delight and leave the stunning receptionist, to run over and hug them. Michael lifts me in the air and I squeal again, before hugging Bree.

"Only two more days!!" I remind them of their impending nuptials.

"That soon, I'm off so..." Michael pretends to leave but is caught by the hem of his shirt.

"You're going nowhere," Bree laughs and I watch as Michael bends his head kissing her deeply.

"Never," he pulls back, wiggling his nose against hers.

"Hello! Bridesmaid present," I clear my throat and they walk me back to reception before we all head to my room.

The hotel so far, is the height of luxury, every hallway lined with cream marble floors. The staff are impeccably dressed and all wearing colourful leis around their neck, the same one that they draped around me when I arrived at reception. We take the elevator to the third floor and turn towards room 3109 and I'm bursting with excitement to throw down my bags and explore this amazing resort further.

"Oh, we stayed on this floor last time we came, the rooms are fabulous," Bree claps her hands excitedly.

"Here it is," I turn back, smiling at them both before inserting the wine colored key card into the slot. The green light beeps and I push down the gold handle, stepping into a wide open space. Walking further into the room, I turn full circle, taking it all in. A wide patio door is open, leading out onto my own private balcony, overlooking the ocean. Soft white curtains drape on either side, blowing gently in the breeze and matching the canopy that surrounds a huge bed, which happens to be scattered with pink petals. A bouquet of exotic flowers, pour over a gold vase sitting in the centre of a small coffee table, donned on either side by pale grey couches. There is a small but efficient kitchen area for storing food and drinks, along with a small table to dine at. I run to the balcony. looking down onto the resort, watching the people below sunbathe or take a dip in the pool.

"This place is out of this world," I gasp, overwhelmed by its beauty and luxury. I walk into the en-suite bathroom, the marble floors are a deeper shade of cream and continue off the floor, up steps and into a hot tub. The walls hold a huge floor length mirror and above the tub, I see a built in, plasma TV.

"Holy cow Bree, you never said it was this fabulous," I cover my mouth, feeling guilty that I have all this to myself for a full week.

"I know, right?" Bree laughs and we both jump up and down like giddy school girls.

"Hey, calm down Bree, don't exert yourself," Michael grabs Bree around the waist, settling her against his hip.

"Michael, its ok for me to be happy and excited two days before my wedding," Bree chuckles, "the baby is fine," she reassures him.

"Ok Jo, get settled in and meet us downstairs in an hour for dinner," Bree moves forward hugging me.

"Actually, when does Davis arrive?" She swings back to Michael.

"I think he got in on the earlier flight, I'll call him in a bit," Michael shrugs.

"Ok, well let's meet in the hotel bar in an hour for dinner and we can discuss the plans for the wedding, if that's ok?" Bree finishes.

"Sounds great, I'm dying for a cocktail," I nod, walking them to the door. When I am alone, I take a deep breath, allowing the experience so far, to wash over me. *This trip is going to be just what the doctor ordered*; I smile to myself, flopping down onto the bed.

The hotel bar is busy when I arrive down 10 minutes early, after deciding that, I couldn't wait any longer for my first official holiday drink. I step cautiously into the bar, now feeling self-conscious on my own. My eyes move about, taking in the groups of holiday makers laughing loudly before searching the bar for a free stool. I smile happily when I see Davis standing alone, ordering a drink and I move towards him, without further hesitation. My stomach twirls at the sight of him and I bite my lip to stop the grin that begs to cross my face. He is wearing jeans and a casual shirt, his favourite leather jacket hanging on the back of his stool... *you can take the man out of Boston, but you can't take Boston out of the man.* As I approach to sit next to him, a tall brunette slides onto the seat beside his, kissing his cheek. I stand behind them shocked to have found him with a companion. My heart thuds faster, heat creeping up my neck as I stand, dumbly, behind them, not sure if I should retreat to the other end of the bar or interrupt.

"There's Jo," I hear Bree call from behind me. I close my eyes, mortified and when I open them, Davis is staring at me. I feel like a grade *A* loser standing all by myself. My skin turns a deep shade of red and I cringe as his green eyes sweep over my body.

"Hi," I croak, looking away and turning to Bree and Michael.

"Who's your friend?" Bree asks Davis, smiling to his date.

"This is Ruby; she is going to join us for dinner if that's ok?" Davis steps aside to introduce his female friend. My hand trembles slightly as I reach out to greet her.

"It is so great to meet you all, Davis has told me so much about you," she jumps up, ignoring my hand and hugging us all instead. Bree looks over her head as she hugs Michael a bit too enthusiastically, her eyes questioning me and I shrug. Davis leans back on his heels.

"Ok, shall we make our way to the dining hall?" Seeming baffled at his date's flighty behaviour.

"I'm going to order a drink here, I'll follow you guys," I smile and move to the bar.

"Don't be too long," Bree furrows her brows, looking suspiciously at me. I am relieved when they leave, happy to have some time to settle my nerves. My breathing is off and my hands are still trembling. Davis is seeing someone and I think my heart just took a major blow.

Davis

How the hell did I manage to get myself into this situation? I cringe, while the energetic Ruby, powders her nose. I only wanted to sit by the pool, enjoy my beer, check out the beautiful women in bikinis and relax before dinner. That's were Ruby found me. The woman is persistent; I'll give her that, if only she wasn't a little cuckoo. At the sound of Bree's voice, I eagerly turn around, happy that my friends are arriving; hopefully they can help me shake off Ruby. It is however, Joanna's face that I see first, her eyes cast downward, her chest lifting as she takes a deep breath, before looking up to meet my stare.

"Hi," she smiles weakly before breaking eye contact to turn in search of Bree and Michael. *How long has she been standing there?* I wonder, taking her in. Her simple yellow dress; clings to her curves and I'm finding it hard to look away. She looks so tiny standing next to me and I can't help but spot the lost look in her eyes. Her hair is swept up into a lively knot, with a pink flower tucked between the waves of curls. Joanna is breath taking. It takes a few moments for me to realise that she is alone and I wonder, silently, where Jake is. *Maybe he's following her out in a day or two*, I surmise. The guy is a proper dickhead and having spent little time in his company, I'd be content to never being subjected to his boring drawl about hospital life, ever again. I get that he is a good looking guy, but with the personality of a wet rag, I have no idea what Joanna sees in him, unless it's his money.

"Ok, shall we make our way to the dining room," I quickly suggest while peeling Ruby off of Michael before a cat fight breaks out. Bree has already thrown me a dirty look and I'm mortified. Joanna stays behind to get a drink and a wave of guilt assails me, I only agreed to Ruby tagging along so I wouldn't be a fifth wheel tonight and ultimately, that's where it has left Joanna.

We are seated at a round table close to the patio, overlooking the beach. The sun is beginning to set on the horizon and I can see why Michael and Bree have chosen this location to get married. It is magical. I pull out the seat next to Bree for Ruby to sit down in, keeping her away from Michael, but also keeping the seat to my right free for Joanna. My pants tighten just thinking about the curve of her hips in her yellow dress and I shift uncomfortably in my seat, to hide my arousal. The waiter arrives with the menus and we sit patiently waiting for her to return. When ten minutes' tick by, I decide to go in search for her and find her still at the bar, just about to order another drink.

"Hey, why are you drinking alone at the bar?" My eyebrows pull together in surprise to see her looking so down. I can usually rely on her to tease me and make me laugh, but tonight she seems out of sorts and not really herself.

"I'm just avoiding the couples table for a few more minutes," she glances up, with a mischievous glint in her eyes. With the intention of keeping her spirits up and the mood light I suggest more alcohol.

"Want to do a shot?"

Her cheeks flush, as she shakes her head, giggling, and I can't help my body's reaction to her. My fingers itch to pull her close and taste her luscious pink lips. I control my basec instincts and instead I order two tequilas. We both down them before scrunching up our faces at the bitter after taste.

"Holy crap, that's strong," Joanna fans her face before quickly sipping from the orange coloured cocktail glass in front of her.

"I guess we better join the others," she pulls back her shoulders and we walk to the table together.

"You look beautiful tonight Joanna," I blurt out as we turn into the restaurant. I watch her eye lashes flutter in shock before a satisfied grin crosses her face.

"What took so long?" Bree calls, pulling our attention to the table.

"I was just waiting to be served," Joanna answers, before placing her cocktail on the table and picking up her menu and quickly covering her face.

CHAPTER 7

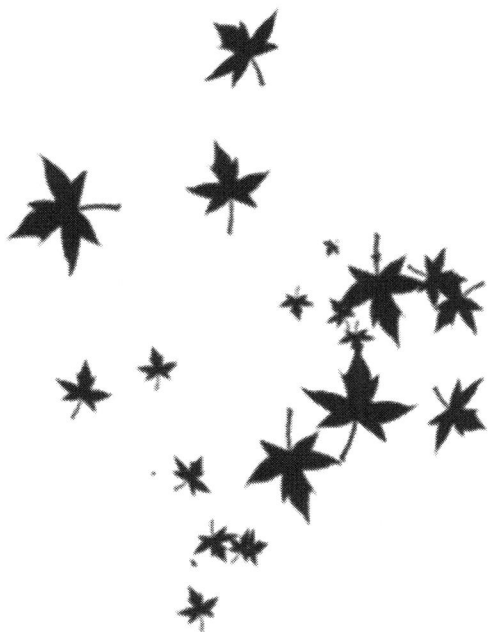

Jo

Four cocktails and an hour later, my patience for Ruby's cackling is wearing thin. Poor Bree has been interrupted a dozen times, trying to fill us in on the wedding arrangements. Even Davis seems a little irritated with his guest.

"As I was saying, it's a small number attending," Bree clears her throat, cutting across Ruby's overtly affectionate mumblings in Davis' ear.

"Only you both, my Dad's two sisters will arrive tomorrow with their husbands and my five cousins, along with my Mom's sister Zoe..." Bree calls out the guest list.

"Oh, so Zoe can make it? That's brilliant news," I interrupt, thrilled for her. Zoe is a photo journalist and despite keeping in contact over the phone, they rarely get to spend any time together. Growing up, Bree's Dad was too busy with work to spend any real quality time with his sisters, or sister in-law, so Bree's relationships with them all is minimal.

"I know, she is giving me away," Bree gushes and Michael leans over, kissing her cheek.

"So the ceremony will take place at 6.00 p.m. on the beach where Michael proposed and then we will come back here for cocktail hour, before moving into the *kipona aloha suite*, just down the hall for dinner."

"Bree is sounds magical," I gush.

"Won't Ruby be there?" I ask, only realizing that Bree has left her out of the head count for tomorrow. When Davis looks around for the waiter and Bree looks nervously to Michael, I suspect that I might have touched a sore spot.

"I wish I could, but I go home tomorrow," Ruby finally answers with a pout. I can't help my confused expression and again I look to my friends for an explanation. *Didn't she and Davis arrive together?*

"Davis met Ruby today," Bree coughs up the missing piece of the puzzle.

I want to break out into a huge grin but I stop myself, everything is suddenly making sense. I think over the dinner and cover my mouth with my napkin, my eyes watering to the point of blurred vision, as I hold in my laughter. Davis had looked in pain as Ruby fondled him, whispering in his ear and giggling like a hyena at every joke he cracked. The whole time, I thought he was enjoying her attentions but in hindsight, he was merely keeping her amused. I take a sip of my drink and the memory of Ruby calling Davis, 'boo,' as he poured her wine returns, and I splutter out laughing, my drink going everywhere. I avoid meeting Davis' eyes and apologise, quickly wiping myself and the table. My body rocks as I continue to laugh, which is only made worse, when Bree and Michael join in. Davis too, is trying to hide his laughter when I look up, but poor Ruby is like a dear in headlights. Feeling guilty, I reign in my amusement.

"Do you have a date, Jo?" She asks me, narrowing her eyes when she figures out that she is the butt of my joke. I know it was unforgivably rude, but the whole scenario is ridiculous.

"Yes she does...," Davis answers.

"Actually, I don't," I smile brightly to them both, hopefully seeming laid back.

"Oh sorry, I thought Jake was coming," Davis blushes and everyone at the table goes quiet, again.

"We broke up," I announce openly, I think the cocktails are starting to go to my head.

"Oh," Davis shifts in his seat, his lips lifting upwards at the corners.

"Don't worry Jo, my cousin Peter will dance the second dance with you," Bree waves her hand, trying to swipe away the painfully embarrassing topic of my failed relationship.

"That's Davis' job," Michael butts in and Ruby harrumphs, sitting back with her arms crossed. Before anyone can respond, I stand.

"It's time for bed," I pretend to yawn.

"I'll walk you," Michael moves to stand, but I put my hand up to stop him. "No, I'm fine, please finish your drinks, I will see you at breakfast," I insist and he nods, sitting back down. I say my goodbyes and head back to my room, falling asleep as soon as my head hits the pillow.

Davis

The sleeve of my leather jacket drags along the marble floor as I walk, deep in thought, back to my suite. Tonight has to have been one of my most embarrassing yet, but somehow I'm feeling in top form. Joanna Carmody is single. It's an unsettling thought; in a way, it makes me nervous. So many times I've wanted to kiss Joanna again, but I held back. She was out of bounds, untouchable and I'm not sure that with nothing stopping me, I will be able to stop myself. I hook my finger through the loop in my jacket and throw it over my shoulder to stop it from ruining and saunter, casually, to my room. The look on Joanna's face when I turned to see her standing behind me in the bar, is the last thought on my mind before I fall asleep.

Jo

I spent all morning sunbathing by the pool, turning over every thirty minutes in an attempt to get an even tan all over. I was very careful to select a strapless bikini; heaven forbid I would have tan lines in Bree's wedding album. I chose to skip lunch, in favour of reading my book in delightful tranquillity. Moments of still and quiet are rare in my life; I take full advantage; I just know that the next two days are going to be so hectic. My stomach begins growling at me as I apply the finishing touches to my makeup for the pre wedding dinner. Standing back, I take one last look in the floor length mirror. My outfit is simple, made up of a long, floating coral skirt that sits high on my waist. On top, I kept it light, tucking in a cream silk vest and adding a small, gold leaf necklace and gold belt to finish it off. My hair is as wild as ever, but I'm already running late so I decide to leave it down and quickly grab my blue clutch bag, before heading to dinner.

Everyone is already seated when I arrive, so I grab the only seat available, next to Bree's cousin Peter.

"Jo," he exclaims cheerfully before pulling me into an awkward hug. Peter is the only cousin of Bree's that I've met more than once. He stayed with Bree and her Dad during summer break when we were teenagers; he was one of the first boys I kissed. I smile warmly at him and blush at the memory.

"Peter, you look wonderful," I exaggerate slightly, pulling out of his embrace. He was once tall and lanky, but had boyish good looks and charm to go with it. He wore shades everywhere he went and could skateboard circles around the other guys we hung out with. His face hasn't changed much over the years, but he definitely stopped growing and is now small, compared to every other man at the table. I can't help but notice his extra weight and receding hairline and scold myself for being so judgemental.

"You too Joanna. Wow, you sure turned out looking fine," he winks.

I wave my hand in the air, dismissing the compliment playfully before looking around the table and finding Bree. She looks up from talking with her Aunt Zoe and waves. Michael sits at her side, as ever, chatting away to Davis and I feel left out at this end of the table, I'm a little disappointed that no-one thought to keep me a seat beside them. Both men have made an effort tonight and left their jeans at home in favour of dress shirts and slacks. I wait to catch their eye, but they are too engrossed in their conversation to look up.

"So, are you still kissing boys behind the bushes," Peter laughs hysterically, nudging me. I offer a tight smile, ignoring his question and offering one of my own.

"How have you been?"

"Great, still single but things are looking up," he jiggles his eyebrows suggestively, before nudging me again and laughing.

"Oh stop," I laugh uncomfortably, not sure if he is joking or not.

"Are you still living in California?" I try again to make small talk.

"You know me Jo, I'd never walk away from all the hot women in Cali," he slurs, cracking himself up again. I would have preferred to have had at least one drink in me, before I had to listen to a half sloshed buffoon, rant. I could use the help to numb me against his sleazy remarks.

"Oh, have you met someone?" I say dumbly, trying not to encourage him.

"I have my eye on one or two," he nudges me again and I give up being polite, he is not getting any mixed signals from me, the last thing I need is Peter Richards tormenting me for the weekend.

"Good luck with that," I turn away quickly and introduce myself to the lady next to me.

The dinner gets quickly underway and Bree's female cousin Janet and I hit it off. She is funny, down to earth and not very fond of her step-brother, Peter.

"My Mom died when I was seven and unfortunately, Peter came with Cynthia, that's his new wife," she points to a pretty woman sitting next to Bree's Uncle Eric.

"Cynthia is lovely but I think Peter must take after his Dad, he's a real sleaze ball," she screws up her face in disgust.

"Oh I never knew that he wasn't Eric's son," I'm surprised that Bree never mentioned it before. "He stayed with Bree for the summer when we were teenagers," I inform Janet.

"My Dad always treated him like his own, so we don't make a big deal out of it in the family," she shrugs, explaining. "He embarrasses me a lot by hitting on every woman with a pulse, so I make a point of mentioning it with my female friends," she laughs.

"I kissed him when we were kids," I confess, covering my mouth with my napkin and Janet's eyes widen in shock.

"He will be so all over you like a rash," she teases and

we both laugh out loud.

"It's a pity he hasn't met someone, maybe he is just lonely," I suggest, feeling guilty now for making fun of him.

"He met plenty of nice women and cheated on every one of them," she rolls her eyes. It's pretty obvious that Peter's step sister doesn't make any excuses for his behaviour and I like that about her.

"He was funny and charming when we met as teenagers," I say, surprised that he has turned into a sloppy Casanova wannabe.

"Oh, he was wild back then, my Dad and Cynthia almost broke up because of him. Uncle Geoff agreeing to take him down to Boston for that summer, saved Dad's marriage," Janet shrugs and I smile fondly, thinking about Mr. Richards. He was a lovely man and poor Bree doesn't get to have him here to walk her down the aisle or dance with, on her wedding day.

"What are you two whispering about?" Peter pokes my sides and I move uncomfortably away and closer again to Janet.

"Never you mind Peter," Janet dismisses him quickly and I feel bad when he blushes profusely.

"Just girl stuff," I smile, to soften the blow. There is a clinking of glasses and I look up to see Michael standing. If I wasn't looking at it, I would never believe it. Michael is about to do a speech.

"This won't take long," he announces, clearing his throat, visibly uncomfortable and my heart swells with pride. He looks around the table at everyone present before resting his eyes on Bree. She looks up at him with an expression of shock, wonder and love.

"Bree, tomorrow you have agreed to marry me, you have chosen me, despite my flaws, despite my past and despite what others might think and I still can't believe how lucky I am. You have changed my life in so many ways and continue to make it better every day. You are the other half of me and you make me complete and I want us to be partners in life, friends and soulmates forever. When we say "I do," and you become Mrs. Aubrey Richards Ryan, I will become Mr. Michael Richards Ryan and take your name to honour my love and respect for you, your family and your father. To my future wife, Bree."

Everyone raises their glass, cheering, before sipping the sparkling champagne and clapping, as Michael takes his seat next to Bree who engulfs him with hugs and kisses. I hear Davis wolf whistle and everyone laughs.

"What a dick," Peter hisses into my ear. I stop clapping and turn from Michael and Bree.

"Who?" I wonder aloud.

"That guy next to Michael, some hotshot FBI Agent," he shrugs. Initially, I'm surprised that he would address me about Davis, considering he knows I'm Bree's best friend and therefore, I would know Davis but then, I am sitting away from them all.

"Davis? He's a good guy, why don't you like him?" I enquire further, curious about what Davis did to annoy Peter.

"I tried to sit next to him earlier, but he told me the seat was taken," he harrumphs. "My cousins took the seat while he went to the bar, the look on his face when he came back was priceless," he lets off an evil laugh. My stomach tightens, was Davis saving the seat for me? I ponder, allowing the warm buzz that it stirs inside, to consume me.

Ignoring Peter's continuing ramblings, I look down the table towards him. Michael and Bree are cosily chatting away, oblivious to everyone else around them and radiating love. Davis is busy entertaining another one of Bree's female cousins, who I haven't met before and I'm jealous of her. She gets to sit next to him and enjoy his company, amongst other things, like his scent, he smells so good. It's hard to explain, a mixture of warm and fresh, spicy and clean and completely intoxicating. It's the kind of aroma that makes you want to grab your man's shirt and pull him in, just so you can sniff his neck. I'm so deep in my fantasies that I don't realise I'm staring at him, until he waves and I jump from my thoughts. Smiling sheepishly, I wave before turning back to Peter; unfortunately, Janet is deep in conversation with her other neighbour.

Peter immerses himself in the moment, taking the opportunity to relay to me how amazing he is for the rest of his dinner. By the time the waiters have removed the last empty plate from the table, I have heard all about how he refuses to pay child support to his ex-wife because she cheated on him and not the other way around. He has "walked out" on numerous jobs because the employers couldn't appreciate his abilities to push their businesses further. I tried arguing that the child shouldn't go without because of how he felt towards the mother, but his reaction made me want to punch him.

"Her new boyfriend has money," he shrugged and I just stared in horror. I have never met anyone so blatantly irresponsible and immature and to actually brag about not paying child support, was the last straw. I excused myself and went straight to the bar to grab a drink and escape his roaming hands for a few minutes. I was seconds away from calling him out on his "accidental" brushes against my chest.

"Who's the slug with his hands all over you," I hear and smell him before I look up to see him smiling down at me. His hand caresses my lower back as he slides in beside me at the bar, causing my heart to accelerate as I stare up, mesmerised by Davis' deep green eyes. His recent effect on my pulse rate, has me a nervous wreck around him. I can't think of one witty rebuttal about how his hand is on me now and instead, nervously stumble over my words.

"Bree's cousin Peter! I was about to chop those hands off," I joke.

He looks away and catches the bartender's attention as he passes and quickly orders two beers and me a cocktail. I don't tell him that I wanted wine; instead, I skip giddily in my head at the fact that he bought me a drink.

"You're not the only one," he turns back while we wait

for the drinks, his eyes gleaming with intent.

"Great, you hold him down, I'll get the axe," I splutter, while mentally trying to fan away the thick fog of lust that his stare is creating. The tension between us is palpable; has it always been there, lurking in the background, waiting for an opportunity to arise?

"$21.00," we both break eye contact and look to the bartender, who hands Davis a tray with his drinks.

"Didn't you order before me?" He looks at my empty glass on the bar and it dawns on me that he hadn't actually ordered me a drink. I say a silent prayer that the ground would just swallow me up, not that he knew I thought that he bought me a drink, but because I knew.

"White wine please," I turn crimson, ignoring his question and addressing the bartender.

"Shit sorry Joanna, let me get that," he flusters to get another bill from his wallet.

"Don't be silly, go enjoy your drinks," I insist, pushing his outstretched hand away from the bartender and handing over my own bill. An awkward silence falls before he gingerly puts away his money and looks towards the table.

"Are you coming to sit with us?" He asks and I look to Michael and Bree, still enamoured with each other and the eager blonde, who is staring at us, desperate for his return.

"No thanks," I laugh, tilting my wine glass at him before, reluctantly, taking my seat next to Peter. An hour later, Bree's family begin to retire for the evening and I jump on Zoe's vacated seat. Peter looks disheartened at my sudden departure, but he is a too drunk to entertain any further.

"Jo," Bree exclaims, "sorry we have neglected you tonight," she pouts.

"I think you neglected everyone after that speech, you haven't taken your eyes off each other," I roll my eyes, winding them both up and Michael rewards me by turning pale.

"Really? Are we that bad?" Bree covers her mouth, laughing giddily.

"Yes!" Davis turns from his conversation joining ours.

"Don't mind her, she was getting cosy with Peter again," Bree winks at Michael.

"Again?" Davis jumps in, never missing an opportunity.

"You and Peter?" Davis' companion joins in.

"Jo, this is my cousin Britany," Bree introduces us and she reaches across to shake my hand before continuing.

"I wondered if you were his date for the wedding," she finishes and Bree dissolves into laughter.

"No, we haven't seen each other in years," I hold up my hands to stop any rumours getting back to Peter.

"I don't see him that way," I drive home.

"Anymore," Davis smarts and I narrow my eyes in his direction.

"Jeez, we kissed as kids, nothing more."

"You fancied the ass off him Jo," Bree continues to bate me and I throw my hands up in the air in defeat. They are going to continue, no matter how much I deny it.

"We're going to call it a night," another young woman, who I assume is Britany's sister, interrupts everyone, standing with who I assume is her husband.

"Britany, are you walking with us," she asks, before hugging Bree goodnight. Britany looks awkwardly at Davis before agreeing to leave.

"Nice to meet you Will," she smiles warmly at him, resting her hand on his arm as she passes him to bid farewell to Michael and Bree.

I try to control my expression, fight for my inner calm and yet I still feel my face scorch and steam burst out of my ears. How does she know Davis' first name before me? He never introduces himself to anyone as anything other than Davis and yet he tells her! I've often wondered about his first name, but he never shared it, so I never asked and now she knows before me! I should be shocked more at my level of anger, but I'm too offended to care if it's irrational. I can't look at him and strain to concentrate on the conversation between myself and Bree as she apologises again for neglecting me.

"Ok, I'm taking you to bed," Michael announces, thirty minutes later.

"It's early yet," Bree sulks and he ignores her, standing and putting out his hand for her to take.

"It's after midnight, you're pregnant and have a big day ahead of you," he reminds her sternly and she sighs in agreeance.

"You are supposed to stay with me tonight," I remind her.

"No way!" Michael huffs and I laugh at his instant refusal.

"Its tradition, you can't tell her no."

"This is our last night together as girlfriend and boyfriend, we are not spending it apart," he folds his arms across his chest, defying tradition.

"Yeah, I want to spend it with Michael," Bree jumps up by his side, stuffing her hand under his and holding onto his large bicep.

"Suit yourself but its bad luck!" I warn but they both ignore me, hurriedly saying their goodbyes before walking hand in hand, out of the dining hall. I look from their retreating figures and directly at Davis. His eyes lock with mine in one intense passing gaze. I can't tell if he is drunk or if the glazed look is one of admiration.

"I guess we better call it a night," I mumble, looking away and rustling my fingers through my tangled hair, moving it to the other side of my head.

"OR!" He leans back in his chair. "Now bear-with me on this Joanna," he drawls, "we could finish our drinks and enjoy each-others company without chaperons," he proposes, lazily.

"What makes you think I would enjoy your company," I retort, leaning back in my seat, taking my wine with me.

"Well, your glass is half full," he looks at my wine, "so you could give me to the end of your drink to show you," he winks. "Right, now I would say its half empty," I grin.

"Only an alcoholic would think like that," he counters and I burst out laughing. "See, you're already enjoying yourself."

CHAPTER
8

The waiters interrupt us sometime later, requesting we move so they can remove the table cloths and I look around the empty dining hall. All the other guests have left, both of us oblivious to their departure as we poked fun and teased each other.

"I'll walk you to your room," Davis offers and I hesitate, before nodding at him.

"So you and Peter...really?" Davis wrinkles his nose as he saunters beside me towards the elevators.

"It was a teenage kiss! I'm sure you have some skeletons in your own kissing closet," I roll my eyes, laughing at his level of disgust.

"Nope, I only ever kiss the pretty girls," he grins wickedly.

"We WILL see," I purse my lips and he picks up on my use of his first name.

"Ah, you heard that," he looks down at his feet, stuffing his hands into his pockets.

"Oh I heard it and I'm offended," I don't betray myself by revealing my actual annoyance at it, instead, keep my tone light and non-chalant.

"Why?" He laughs. "Oh let me think, we have known each other for over two years and you never mentioned it before."

"You never asked! Bree and Michael know because they asked and so did the lovely Britany."

"You should have walked her to her room if she was so lovely," I narrow my eyes at him, stabbing the button for the third floor on the elevator.

"I'm happy right where I am, but if you preferred Peter as a chaperon, you should have said," he stands over me, looking down at me, as I relax against the gold handrail of the elevator. His eyes are burning with delight at my jealousy, begging me to embarrass myself further by revealing my attraction. The elevator chimes and we snap out of our heady stand-off.

"Saved by the bell," he smiles, before stepping back and allowing me to pass.

"Bell or no bell, I wasn't going to entertain the Peter thing again," I throw over my shoulder, trying to wipe the satisfied grin off his face.

"That's not what I meant when I said that," he announces as we arrive at my door. I turn around confused by what he meant. I'm about to ask when his hand cradles my neck, pulling me to his mouth. His lips find mine, softly applying pressure before his tongue dances along its crease, teasing my lips apart and diving deeper. My limp hands come up holding his elbows, as both his hands cup my face, his body pressing me against my door. His kiss is soft and seductive, pulling my stomach and causing desire to pool there. I am drowning in his smell, his touch as his body encompasses mine, his tongue torturing me to a state of dizziness. I move my hands to his shirt, gripping it and pulling him closer to my body. I inhale his scent again and groan, deepening the kiss and nipping his bottom lip with my teeth. He growls, dropping his hands to my ass and pulling me tight against his erection, our tongues dancing fiercely, rhythmically and in perfect sync.

"Goodnight Joanna," he pulls back, resting his forehead against mine briefly. I lift my heavy lids and pant for air; I've never been kissed with such care and attention before.

"Goodnight," I finally gasp out but remain still, afraid my legs will go from under me. He chuckles at my dazed response and takes my room key from my hand before inserting it in the door.

"Go, before I do something you might regret when you're sober," he grinds out, pushing the door open for me. I nod dumbly, wanting him to make me regret whatever promise lies behind those passionate eyes. I lick my swollen lips, still tasting him there and he groans out, pulling me into his arms again and kissing me with much more force, moving my body backwards as he goes.

"Goodnight," his gravelled tones plead with me to release him from the death grip I have him in and I laugh, mortified, letting my hands fall from his neck.

"You have no idea how hard this is for me right now," he

moans and I drop my hand.

"I have some idea," I purr and he steps back, running his hands through his hair.

"You're drunk, let's see if you still feel this way sober," he sighs, moving away from me, his foot still holding my door open.

"I'm sober enough to know what I want," I say, frustrated.

"Say that to me in the morning and tomorrow night, drunk or sober, I won't be stopping," he dares.

Bree squeals in delight when I open my door to her the next morning.

"Here comes the bride, here comes the bride," she sings, skipping into my room and jumping onto my bed. I run over, hopping on top of her, careful not to go near her tummy, instead pulling her shoulders back until we are both laughing and staring up at the white ceiling.

"Are you nervous?" I turn my head looking at her and she shakes her head no, as tears well up in her eyes. I sit up. "Hey, why are you upset?" I hug her.

"I'm so happy," she laughs, causing me to cry along with her. We sit together, reminiscing on our old crushes, laughing and crying and laughing again for over an hour before we order room service. Our plan is to avoid Michael all day until the ceremony, so we are having a spa day. Bree will be plucked and pampered before she's hauled up to my room for hair and make-up and of course, the maid of honour will receive the same treatment. We start with the steam rooms, before moving on to get a hot stone massage. When our muscles are loose and relaxed, we walk in our fluffy white robes to the beauty salon for facials, manicures and pedicures.

"Do you need to be waxed for tonight?" I tease, as we sit soaking our feet and Bree gawffs, pretending to be coy.

"Jo," she nods towards the young Hawaiian girls who are tending to us and I laugh.

"Bree, we are all women here, now answer, are you fully prepared for your wedding night or not?" I burst out laughing at her stunned expression.

"Jeepers, yes if you must know, I had it done last week, worry about your own fairy," she cracks and begins to join in on the laughter, even one of the girl's splutters at her use of the word fairy.

"I take great care of my fairy, she is very happy."

We almost bump into Michael and Davis as we walk towards the elevators and I pull Bree behind a large plant pot, allowing them to get on before us and avoiding eye contact.

"That was close," Bree giggles, "Michael looked nervous."

"It's his wedding day," I roll my eyes, "besides, he's only worried that you won't show up so stop acting like a baby, you know he will be there."

"I know," she scrunches her shoulders and squeezes her eyes in happiness.

"So guess what?" I say pressing the button for the elevator.

"You and Davis kissed last night?" Bree blurts out without hesitation and my mouth drops open, devastated not to be dropping what I thought was a bombshell.

"How the hell do you know that?"

"Michael and I made a bet, he said it wouldn't happen yet and I said Davis was definitely going to go in for the kill last night, I could see it in his eyes," she claps her hands together, delighted with herself.

"You made a bet!" I exclaim. "What the hell, did you win?" I laugh.

"I get to pick the babies name," she bounces off the elevator.

"I still don't understand how you knew we were going to kiss before I did," I pout. Bree pushes me playfully into the room.

"Oh Jo, it is so obvious that you two have chemistry, you have been fighting it for two years! How do you feel now that you finally kissed?" She asks and I grin, delighted to drop a new bomb.

"We kissed in the warehouse two years ago," I announce,

a bit too haughtily.

"You never told me!" It's her turn to act shocked and I smile triumphantly, ain't nobody stealing my thunder!

"It was a long time ago, besides, last night's kiss was different," the tingling in my tummy returning, spreading bursts of electricity around my body as I remember the kiss.

"Oh Jo, you have that look in your eye," Bree chirps. "Imagine you two got married, we could double date and our kids could be best friends," she looks dreamily into the air.

"Calm down, little miss pressure pot, we shared two kisses in two years, it's hardly the foundations for a marriage," I snap my fingers to drag her back to reality.

"You should dance the second dance with Davis, I put him with Britany when I thought Jake was here, but I'll switch it around," I can see the cogs turning in her head as she works out ways to push us together.

"No Bree don't, let's see how he acts today, he might regret the whole thing and then you're forcing us into an uncomfortable position," I sigh, beginning to regret telling her.

"I hate the politics, just get together already, so we can share the school run," she plops down onto the couch and I shake my head laughing. She is hilarious.

Davis

The priest stands between Joanna and Michael, all eyes looking towards Bree, as she walks towards her soon to be husband. I stand to Michaels left and sneak a peek in Joanna's direction. She looks breath taking in her pale blue dress, its lightweight material, catching in the gentle breeze and flowing towards the ocean. Her wild hair is pulled to one side; the mass is tamed into soft curls and falls down her chest. I can't help but fantasize about how easy it will be to access her amazing breasts later, the dress is held up by them. I look up and her eyes sparkle with awareness, she caught me ogling her and I wink before turning back to Bree as she arrives, takes Michaels hand and beams up at him. She too looks radiant, her simple white dress wraps around her neck before hugging her body, perfectly. When she turns sideways, I notice her dress is backless but also that her bump has begun to show, causing me to smile broadly. They couldn't have chosen a more beautiful setting for their ceremony. Tall wooden torches are spread around the beach, the fire flickering in the wind, lighting up the dusk, as the sun sets on the horizon. The crashing waves singing, as they repeat their vows, encased in their own bubble of love. They would make anyone want a small slice of what they share and my heart swells with joy for them and this amazing love that they have for each other. The small crowd claps when the priest announces that they are husband and wife. Michael wastes no time lifting her up and holding her in the air as he kisses her deeply, apologising to no one when the priest clears his throat to separate them. Joanna takes my arm and we follow behind the happy couple, back towards the hotel.

"You look beautiful Joanna," I admit and my stomach lurches when I notice the spray of freckles that have appeared across her cheeks and over her nose.

"You look very handsome yourself Davis," she smiles, embarrassed by my compliment. I like this shy side of Joanna, I've never seen her off kilter before and I puff my chest with a surge of male pride.

Jo

We return from the beach after the photographer gets all the outdoor snaps he needs and both Bree and I make a beeline for the bathroom, while Michael and Davis head straight to the bar. My stomach was cramping all morning. Initially I thought it was nerves and excitement but unfortunately, Mother Nature decided to stop by for a visit. I curse my body, the universe and myself, for forgetting I was due my period. So much for having a wild night with Davis, my shoulders drop in disappointment, as we make our way back to the party. When we arrive back, they are surrounded by the guests, everyone shaking Michael's hand, while Davis chats easily to Britany. I try to bite back the pang of jealousy but fail, when her hand caresses his chest while she lets out a goofy giggle. Davis seems comfortable enough to have her maul him so I stand aside, refusing to fight for his attention. I spot Peter in the corner of my eye preparing to approach me and turn smiling at him, welcoming the distraction. Michael and Bree are too busy circulating the room to worry about keeping me entertained right now and I'd rather be talking to Peter, than standing alone like a spare part, despite his overly friendly approach. I laugh at Peter's terrible jokes and even play along, making up my own, in an attempt to let Davis know I don't care, even though I do care, a lot. I can see him from the corner of my eye, throwing daggers in our direction from time to time but I ignore him, refusing to look at him. We move towards the reception suite a little while later, the small room is perfect for the number of guests. It has its own bar and a sizeable dance floor for us to enjoy later this evening. I am seated to Bree's right and Davis is seated to Michael's left at the top table, while the rest of Bree's family sit around a large oval table. I sip champagne and laugh with Bree during dinner service, Michael joining into our conversation from time to time and Bree joining into his and Davis' also. I don't allow him to bother me, I'm going to enjoy this day, no matter who he flirts with. He stands as the meal ends, to deliver his best man's speech.

"I want to start by saying how beautiful Bree looks today, Michael you are one lucky man," he begins, slapping Michael on the shoulder and digging his hands into his pockets. "I'm not very good at the soppy romantic stuff so I won't try, instead, I'll just speak truthfully, from my heart. So on that note, honestly Michael, how the hell did you manage to bag such a babe?" Everyone laughs, rooting him on. "No seriously, you two are perfect for each other. Michael asked me to be his best man today, but there is no better man in the room, than Michael. He loves Bree and trust me, that is one tough job," everyone laughs again and I join in, despite myself. "Love is tough work in the easiest of circumstances but you two have defied all odds, you fought for what was good and right and the universe has rewarded you kindly. There is no better example of true love than the two people sitting in this room today, so please raise your glasses, to Bree and her best man."

Everyone claps and cheers and Davis takes his seat again, giving the floor to me. I nervously take a sip of my champagne before clearing my throat.

"Bree's Mom and Dad would have been so proud of their little girl today," my eyes instantly well up and I begin to choke, before I even finish my first sentence. I take a moment to contain myself before continuing. "Because he can't be here, I wanted to say a few things on your Dads behalf, if that's ok?" I look to Bree, who nods, her eyes also overflowing with silent tears.

"I remember when I was thirteen or fourteen coming by your house after school. You were out sick that day and I was worried, but when I got there, you ran to the door full of excitement. Your Dad had been away and when he got back, instead of sending you to school, he took you to the movies and then bowling. I was so jealous that you had such a cool Dad," I laugh. "Anyway, you dragged me into the living room where Mr. Richards was waiting for you to come back. The furniture was pushed back and the wooden floors, bare; he was teaching you to dance." My voice breaks again and I drop my head to hide the deep emotions that this memory is causing me, "I'm sorry," I gulp back tears, trying to apologise to everyone. Davis leans forward, handing me a tissue and I take a deep breath. "He was teaching you to dance and I watched on as he twirled you in and out of his arms, you both laughed loudly and before I knew it, he had me on my feet too. I know how much he would want to have the father/daughter dance today and how much you wish he could be here too. But I want you to remember that he did get to dance with his little girl and more than once. He loved you so much and so did your Mom and they are both here today, in spirit and Michael," I look square into Michaels eyes, addressing him directly. "Mr. Richards only ever wanted Bree to be safe and happy. Today you granted him his dying wish," I turn back to the other guests. "I would like you to raise your glass in memory of Bree's parents and to Bree and Michael," Bree jumps up, hugging me and we both shed a few more tears, before sitting down, as everyone cheers and claps.

.

CHAPTER 9

Michael leads Bree onto the dancefloor hand in hand, as the male guitarist begins to gently strum his guitar. I rest my chin on my hand and watch on as his deep voice fills the room in a husky melody and Michael pulls Bree against him. They gaze into each other's eyes, their bodies hardly moving from the spot, instead, they sway romantically in each other's arms. As the music picks up a little pace, Michael twirls Bree out and quickly pulls her back in to him, to the sounds of cheering around the room, before kissing her deeply. I can't help the smile that crosses my face, as she rests her head against his chest, her arms gripping his broad shoulders. Michael dips her low when the song finishes before kissing her again, both of them laughing and happy. Bree quickly comes over to usher me towards the dancefloor, Davis is already with his partner Britany and Peter is waiting in the wings for my arrival. I take his hand and shoulder as he leads me around the dancefloor and I'm impressed, he has moves on the dancefloor at least. The band is in full swing now, the female singer taking her place as they all collaborate, creating a fun, upbeat atmosphere. I look across at Davis, who is really taking the role of best man in his stride as he entertains Britany with stellar hip movements, rotating her with ease around the dancefloor. I swallow the lump of jealousy, as her head falls back in laughter, he whispers in her ear and I return my attention to Peter.

"Ok, switch dance partner's folks," the female singer comes over the mic during a musical interlude and I watch as Michael takes Britany from Davis and Peter moves to Bree, leaving Davis and I standing idle in the middle of the dancefloor. His face slides into a side grin and he puts out his hand

"Shall we?" He smiles and I take his hand, dipping my head to hide my own smile. Pulling my body quickly against his, he drops his hand and I inhale a mouthful of air as his fingers graze my hip, entwining his free hand with mine, holding them both against his chest. I have no choice, but to look up at him or to rest my head against his chest, I choose the latter.

"You feel good in my arms," Davis sounds hoarse, as he whispers against my hair, his hand on my hip pulling me closer against his hard body. I look up into serious dark eyes.

"I don't understand you," I say honestly, unashamed to admit that he confuses me.

"I think I made myself pretty clear last night," he smiles down wickedly.

"Yet today you are all over Britany," I remind him. I'm aware I sound like a jealous girlfriend, but I don't like being made a fool of.

"Britany mentioned that you looked a little jealous," I narrow my eyes at him and try to pull from his hold. He tightens his grip, holding me in place.

"Have you been making fun of me?" I growl.

"Joanna, I told Britany at the bar that I planned on asking you out on a date," he lifts my chin, his expression serious. The song ends and everyone begins clapping, breaking us from our trance. We step gingerly apart and look to Bree and Michael, while joining in on the claps and cheers. My cheeks are flush, my heart racing, as Davis' words sink in. The band quickly begins playing a faster number, encouraging all the guests to join in. I make my way off the dancefloor but Davis has other plans, he snags my wrist, twirling me into his arms. Catching my face, he cups my chin and plants a hard kiss on my lips. My lips part, my arms coming around his neck as his tongue slips into my mouth, finding mine and dancing with that too. I begin laughing at the idea of our tongues dancing and he smiles against my mouth.

"Sorry, I've been dying to do that all day."

Michael and Bree begin cheering loudly, alerting everyone to our public display and we both turn crimson. We try to ignore the round of applause and continue to dance and laugh, it's hard to not kiss him when he is being so playful and fun, but we somehow manage.

In the early hours and long after Bree and Michael have retired, we are still sitting at the top table. We haven't kissed again since earlier on the dancefloor and I'm itching to run my fingers through his hair, before dragging his handsome face towards mine. When Peter is escorted by his step father to his room, leaving us alone, I seize the moment. I stand looking down at him. Reading my body language, his eyes turn serious. I run my fingers through his silky brown hair, tugging it at the back before bending and catching his lips with mine. A gruff moan escapes his mouth before he pulls me onto his lap, wrapping his arms around my waist. His kisses are the best I've ever had, sending random spasms of electricity around my body.

"Jesus Joanna," Davis pants breathless before standing up, taking me with him. He holds me against his body and begins walking towards the door. I burst out laughing and push away from his mouth.

"What are you doing?" I giggle hysterically.

"I'm taking you to my bed," he says, in a low carnal drawl.

"My purse and shoes are under the table, your jacket is on the back of the chair," I laugh again and he looks back at our now vacated seats before dropping me onto my bare feet. We both grab our belongings before Davis tucks me under his arm, escorting me to his room. My stomach cramps and with it, my eyes widen in horror.

"SHIT," I curse out loud, dipping out of his embrace. My hands are busy holding my shoes to express my true level of disappointment, it's moments like these that a good ole face-palm or head slap expression is really called for.

"What?" Davis asks confused and I cringe. I don't know if there is anything more embarrassing for a woman to have to explain to man who is expecting sex. We have all been there.

"Davis, I can't sleep with you," I bite my lower lip, but keep my eyes trained on his. I watch on, as the realisation of my words begin to settle in before he turns away, his lips pursed in what I think is anger but could very likely be sexual frustration.

"Are you playing some kind of game with me?" He finally

asks. I move closer to him, pulling on his shirt hoping he will look back towards me and it works.

"I would rip this shirt off you here and now if I could, but unfortunately I can't, because I'm a woman and..."

"If you think having sex with me is disrespecting yourself then you shouldn't, but it's not ok to tease me all night," he growls out, not allowing me to finish. I start laughing but quickly stop, noticing his angry glare.

"Davis don't be so dramatic, I want to and I don't think I would be disrespecting myself, I want to spend the night with you but my body had other plans," I roll my eyes, hoping he will pick up on what I'm saying.

"Oh," he blushes, making me feel embarrassed all over again.

"I'm sorry if you think I was teasing you, I was having fun and I wasn't thinking past that," I shrug. We step onto the elevator and Davis presses the button for the third floor.

"How long are you staying in Hawaii?"

"Five more days, why?" I'm surprised by the sudden change in direction.

"I'm not going to lie Joanna, right now I want to pull off that dress and bury myself inside you, but I'm willing to wait and maybe spend the next few days together having fun."

I narrow my eyes suspiciously, waiting for the "but" or the "however." Instead, he dips his head, kissing my lips again, causing me to sigh. Grabbing my hand, we stroll lazily towards my room, our hands swinging.

"I feel like I'm sixteen again," he laughs, "holding hands was a big deal back then."

I lean back against my door, unsure whether to invite him in or not.

"What about kissing?" I grin.

"Kissing wasn't such a big deal, but holding hands was a huge commitment."

I begin laughing, "So, does this mean we are going steady," I joke and enjoy watching him pale.

"It means that I'm happy to explore things," he leans

back on his heel and I begin laughing.

"Slow down Davis, jeez, no need to get all hot and heavy on our first hand holding session," I tease and he finally realises that I'm winding him up. He purse's his lips to stop the smile from spreading across his face.

"Bree and Michael leave for their honeymoon first thing, so after that, I'm going to take you exploring this lovely island," he tips my chin up, looking into his eyes again.

"Can't we just lay on the beach?" I wrinkle my nose, surprised when he bends and kisses it.

"You look so cute with these freckles," his sweet attention catches my breath, weakening my knees. I grab his elbows for support, as fear grabs hold, these feelings are dangerous. I can feel the power slip through my fingers like water, Davis is stirring something deep within me, something that I'm not ready to face.

"Wear comfortable shoes, Joanna, I think we will have fun exploring things." His mouth finds mine again for a brief parting before he firmly stuffs his hands in his pockets, says goodnight and quickly walks away.

My phone shrills causing me to stir in my sleep. I roll over and pull it out from under my fluffy pillow and it rings louder, causing me to wince. I squint at the bright flashing light and just make out Eric's name. Groaning, I sit up, pushing back the light sheets to try cool myself in the warm bed.

"Eric, its 8.00 a.m. this better be good," I yawn.

"It's bad, actually, bad is an understatement for what I'm about to tell you, I hope you're sitting down," his tone is serious and although we work in a high stress environment, Eric never normally allows himself to become overwhelmed.

"What is it?" I furrow my brows, trying to think of the cases I left behind. Everything was in order and I have no idea what could be wrong.

"Seamus Lynch appealed to the Federal Appeals yesterday morning to have his case thrown out," he blurts out.

"Jesus Christ, under what grounds?" I jump from my bed and begin pacing, instantly nauseated, as the sinking feeling of dread and confusion erupts in my tummy.

"Under selective prosecution, claiming that your close relationship with Bree and Michael, greatly impacted the DA's decision to prosecute, he is claiming that the DA's office was biased."

"Holy shit, when is the appeals date?" I swallow hard, unable to believe what I'm hearing.

"It won't be for months yet, probably a year, but we have seventy days to file a brief responding to his application and notify any victims involved."

"That slime ball," I grind out. "He did it on Bree and Michaels wedding day, he must have known about the wedding!" My stomach turns again, wondering if it is a coincidence.

"Look, that doesn't matter right now Jo, if he is granted the appeal, we are in for a media shit storm! You should tell Bree and Michael as soon as you can."

"No, they are going away to Mexico for two weeks; it can wait until they get back. I'll fly home tomorrow to make a start on the brief."

"No Jo, you enjoy your trip, we have it under control."

"No, I'll be home in the..."

"JO," Eric talks over me, "boss man said you are to have no involvement with this from here on out, just stay there and let the dust settle for a week," he pleads.

I sit down on the edge of the bed, rubbing my sleepy eyes, this is not good.

"Ok, will you keep me informed if anything else happens?"

"I will and try not to worry," Eric soothes, but it's a little too late for that now.

When I hang up the phone, it's almost thirty minutes later and I rush about getting dressed. Bree and Michael are leaving for the airport in ten minutes so I quickly throw on some brown cargo shorts and white vest top, with my white trainers. Pulling my hair into a high pony, I throw a few essentials into my over the shoulder, brown purse, before quickly spraying on some deodorant and running towards the main entrance.

"I'm here, I'm here," I call to them as Bree and Michael load their luggage into the trunk of their taxi.

"Jo," Bree turns from the taxi, "we were starting to think you slept it out," she smiles warmly.

"I know I'm sorry, I got a call from the office," I pant, exhausted from my run.

"Everything ok?" I turn to the sound of Davis' voice to find him looking suspiciously at me. My expression must be revealing more than I want it to. I force a wide open smile.

"Yep, just one or two small blips," I lie. I can see he isn't convinced, but I'm happy when he lets it drop.

"Davis, take care of Jo Jo," Michael turns serious and both Davis and I laugh. Michael is such a worrier, but it's endearing. I know it drives Bree mad at times but she loves feeling secure and protected. My stomach turns again thinking about the idea that Seamus Lynch could have his appeal heard and the possible outcomes, if it is found that he was illegally tried. Davis wraps his arms around by shoulder, tucking me against his side.

"I've got this," he says proudly and Bree gushes.

"Ok, have fun you two," Bree comes over, hugging us both goodbye.

"Aren't we supposed to say that to you?" I laugh, embracing her before passing her back to Michael.

"We will see you back in Boston," Bree yells from the window, waving goodbye as the taxi pulls off. I blow them a kiss and turn back towards the hotel, with Davis at my side.

"Are you ready to go?" His eyes travel down my body, unashamedly stopping to admire my breasts and legs. I push him playfully, surprised by how at ease I feel with him in this new role of aggressor.

"I need to eat something," I say, my stomach rumbling, as if on cue.

After breakfast, Davis leads me outside towards his

rental car.

"So will you tell me now where we are going?" I roll my eyes as he opens the passenger door to the black SUV.

"No, it's a surprise but trust me, you will like it," he insists, pulling on his seatbelt.

"I can't believe you chose an SUV Davis, you could have chosen any car and you pick exactly what you drive at home," I forget about where we are going and concentrate on how we are getting there instead.

"I don't know these roads but I know this car, you chose a car you never drove before, in a place you have never driven, kind of a dumb move if you ask me," he shrugs unapologetically. I remain silent, considering his point of view and when I'm unable to find fault in it, I go back to trying to figure out where we are going. He refuses to tell me anything except to say that we will be driving for almost two hours. I shift in my seat, my body arched towards his, chatting and before I know it, we are pulling into the car park of the Haleakala National Park. I can hear the Pacific Ocean as it crashes against rocks nearby and look out towards the vast blue to my right, before turning to the thriving park to my left.

"Wow," I breathe in a gulp of clean air, Davis stands next to me doing the same. The beauty of this spot excites me and we are still in the car park.

"Let's go to the visitor centre and get a map," Davis grabs my hand, entwining his fingers with mine and the butterflies in my tummy high five each other.

"What is this place?" I ask, still in awe.

"This is the Northeast coast of Maui; this entire coastal area is inhibited by native people," Davis looks so geeky as he plays tourist guide and I am amused to know that if I looked at his google search history, I would find all this information. I say nothing, instead, I smile like a love struck teenager as he continues to educate me.

"This part of Maui is steeped in culture and there is no running water or electricity here. There is so much to discover on these trails," he looks down at me. "What?"

He asks.

"What do you mean, what?" I laugh.

"Why are you looking so amused?" He stops outside the visitor centre, standing aside so as not to block the entrance.

"I just think it's cute that you know all this," I shrug.

"Cute my ass," he splutters, completely offended. "This is proper manly stuff here, hiking, climbing and exploring," he puffs out his chest to drive home his point.

"Ok, Bear Grylls, let's go get you your map," I tease. His eyes widen in shock before he grabs me quickly, punishing me with his lips. I don't complain when he pulls back.

"I won't have my woman question me when I'm in the wilderness," he slaps my ass and I burst out laughing.

I've never seen Davis so playful and childlike and I can't help but get immersed in his good humour. We decide to take the Pipiwai Trail because despite all his research, Davis forgot to tell me to pack sun-cream, rain gear, hiking boots, sun hat, mosquito repellent, basically everything you need for an eight hundred elevation trail in one of the hottest, most humid parts of the world. It is still a four mile round-trip but the visitor centre supplied me with sun cream, water and rental hiking boots. Unfortunately, they don't supply food which means that after two to three hours of hiking, we will be famished. We opted to travel alone so the tour guide warns us not to swim due to falling rocks and flash floods; we are warned to stay on the trail laid out before us and not to get too close to the ocean on the coastal part of the journey, due to rip currents and rough surf. I listen carefully to the advice; Mother Nature is not a force to be messed with. Having respect for her could save your life. After our pep talk, Davis returns to his car, pulling a back pack out of his trunk.

CHAPTER 10

"What's in there?" I wonder.

"It's a surprise," he winks.

I suspect he has brought a picnic, but decide not to ruin his surprise. My heart leaps when he grabs my hand again, following the trail along the coast line.

"I've never seen anything more beautiful," I gasp as we walk along the cliffs, listening as the blue waves break against the shore. The sun is beaming over-head, causing the ocean to sparkle and the lush vegetation of the forest ahead to flourish. Davis stops suddenly as we begin walking down the cliff, the landscape opening out onto a beach area. Pulling his phone from his pocket he points it towards a large rock.

"How amazing is this?" His eyes light up as he begins snapping. I look towards the rock, not sure of what I'm missing, when it moves. Bending down, I notice a head pop out and then some legs and become animated with pleasure.

"That is the biggest turtle I've ever seen," I squeal in delight, pulling out my own phone and taking some photos. I look up and catch Davis happily snapping away in my direction and I try to grab his phone.

"Hey," I pout.

"You look too damn sexy bent over that turtle," he holds his phone over his head and I jump up and down trying to grab it. Davis laughs hysterically, before wrapping one arm around my waist to stop my unsuccessful attempts.

"I'll make a deal with you," he announces rather haughtily and I peer up at him with warning, "let me get one of you kneeling beside him and I'll delete the other ones, deal?"

I consider his suggestion and happily agree; I would like a picture with the beautiful sea creature so it's win, win for me. We take a few more snaps before moving along on our trail, which bends inland through a bamboo forest. We keep a good pace, deciding not to saunter too long which will allow us more time at the bigger attractions, like the waterfalls and lakes. I look up through the thick forest at the bright blue sky and sun, as it breaks through the small gaps in vegetation. I feel like I have stepped into the Amazon rainforest and marvel at my beautiful and peaceful surroundings.

After about two hours of listening to birds chirping and the crunching sounds of the bark, leaves and branches that line the forest floor, the faint but nearing sound of rushing water can be heard. We pick up pace, excited to discover the hidden gem and when it comes into view, we both stand, awe-struck and open mouthed, at the four hundred foot Waimoku Falls. My feet itch to climb the moss covered cliffs and nose dive, side by side with the white foamy water before splashing into the transparent, glassy pool below it. We walk off the path and onto the small picnic area that has been clearly marked.

"Thank you," I turn to Davis, feeling a huge sense of gratitude towards him for bringing me here. I couldn't imagine that there are many things in the world that could top this. It has made me forget about my small life in Boston and appreciate nature, even if it is only for one day.

"You're welcome." We both sit on the grass area and, as I suspected, Davis pulls out some lunch. I had imagined a picnic blanket, maybe some champagne, fresh fruit and deliciously prepared salad but instead, he whips out mashed up sandwiches, in cellophane. I can't help but laugh, it is the biggest anti-climax but I wouldn't change it for the world. We sit in companionable silence, eating the awful sandwiches and watch the water cascade down the rocks. This will be one hell of a first date for any other man to top, I note to myself and the idea of dating any other man, feels wrong. Davis is reeling me in and I am falling hook, line and sinker.

We stand, packing our rubbish away when the heavens suddenly open up and a heavy downpour, unlike any I've ever seen, unleashes itself on our date. Within seconds, I am soaked through and Davis grabs my hand, pulling me towards the nearest tree to take cover. I run my hands over my face and hair, pushing the warm water from my eyes, laughing and panting from our quick dash. I look up, expecting Davis to be equally amused but instead, his eyes are closed and his face is wrought in a dangerous expression. We are surrounded by a mist of steam, which only thickens when his long lashes lift, revealing his dark, lustful eyes, as the rain bangs against the hot ground. I blink away the rain water that continues to pelt against my skin, despite the shade of the large tree, unsure what to do or say. His eyes run along my body and I follow them down, noticing for the first time, that my white camisole is now see through. My white lace bra beneath it, doing nothing to hide my pink, perky nipples and I gasp in horror, pulling it from my body. Davis takes a deep breath, jutting out his chin and looking to the skies.

"Give me strength," he groans out before dropping his bag and lifting me in one foul swoop. I feel the tree at my back and Davis' hands on my ass and legs, as he wraps them around his waist. His mouth devours mine, unrelenting and full of possession and I relish every flick of his tongue, returning the kiss with unmasked fever. I feel my body slip and he adjusts me in his arms again, this time I feel the power of his attraction between my legs, as he grinds his hardness against my tender bud. His hands are all over me, in my hair, pulling at my camisole and bra, releasing my breasts. His mouth drops from mine as he sucks in my nipple, causing my body to rock, as he unleashes a maddening volt of electricity throughout my body. The slide of his tongue against my nipple, mingled with the rain falling against my aroused skin, drives me wild with need and I cry out in frustration. Davis catches the tail end of my moan in his mouth, his tongue crashing against mine in desperation. We are like wild animals, demanding our primal needs be met and just as quickly as the rain started, it stops. We continue our ministrations for a few minutes, until eventually, Davis steps back, his eyes wild with unmet desire and I squirm in his arms.

"Holy fuck, that was," he pants, dropping me to the

ground and stepping away to gather himself. "That was hot," he finishes, turning towards me as I pull myself together. I nod, trying to catch my breath and remain standing on my jelly legs. I have never felt so deprived in my life and feel like a tease for denying our needs. Once again, I curse my blasted body.

"Joanna," Davis is still panting as he lifts my chin, "you are so beautiful," he smiles. He closes his eyes again, taking another deep breath and when he opens them, they are full of colour and composed. We finish the trail before getting on the road back to the hotel.

*****

Today is our last day in Maui and tonight, Davis and I are having dinner. We haven't kissed since our trip to Haleakala National Park and despite spending time with each other every day, I am beginning to wonder if Davis is still interested. He hasn't held my hand, his eyes haven't roamed my body and he has kept flirting to a minimal. I'm never usually insecure or emotional, although I was having my period this week, but I'm checking myself in every mirror or fretting about what clothes to wear on our day trips. I keep reasoning that he couldn't go from a mind blowing kiss, to being indifferent but people can be strange and weird at times and really, I have no idea what is going on in his head. I decide to have a spa day, I want to primp and prepare myself for a possible night of passion, but also because Davis is working from his suite today. Roche was calling so much yesterday that I thought he might have to leave sooner. I relax into the hotel Jacuzzi and hope that Bree and Michael are enjoying their honeymoon; this will probably be their last romantic getaway for a long time, once the baby arrives. The familiar feeling of despair returns when I think about breaking the news to them that Seamus Lynch is appealing for a mistrial. I try to wipe it from my mind again, I had decided earlier in the week, that I wasn't going to waste my trip worrying and talking about Seamus Lynch, Boston is only a day away and Seamus Lynch is safely tucked behind bars, for the time being. I remove myself from the water when I am sufficiently wrinkled and wrap myself in the warm robe, before returning to my room to get ready for my last night in Maui. The anticipation of what the night might hold, sends a shiver of delight down my spine and I hurriedly prepare myself to meet Davis in the lobby.

Davis

I can hardly think straight. All afternoon I worked over the phone with Roche, as he filled me in on a case we have worked hard on over the past six months. The fruits of our labour are beginning to pay off, as the drug cartel that we have been tracking between Miami and Boston, are finally beginning to show some cracks. Roche has a lead on a possible informant, which will break our investigation wide open, but he is not prepared to meet with us until the end of the month when the current shipment they are working on, clears customs. With umpteen calls back and forth over the past few days, we decide to call a halt on it until I get back to Boston early tomorrow. I close down my laptop and get ready to meet Joanna for dinner. The woman has me in knots all week and I've used every fibre of my being, to not touch or taste her again; cold showers, proving only to be a myth, in dampening the flames of my attraction towards her. I can't hold back any longer, her leg could be hanging off later and I plan on ending this torturous week for us both. I know she feels it too, her eyes revealing her every desire to me in one glance. I take a hot shower, the warm water reminding me of our time under the tree, my urge to rip off her clothes, had been so overpowering that I have forbidden myself from looking or touching, until I know we can take it to the next level and tonight, will be that night.

I walk to her room, deciding to pick her up at her

door instead of meeting in the lobby. She brings out the gentleman in me, I muse to myself as she opens the door. My hand comes up to my chest before rubbing my stubbled jaw, in astonishment. Just when I thought I was civilised again, she dances all over my ideals by taking my breath away, as a surge of carnal need freezes me to the spot. Her hair is groomed in a sleek, up-do, displaying her creamy shoulders and long neck. Her eyes sparkle the same colour as her deep blue navy dress that clings to her chest and drops to her feet, her toes peeking out beneath it.

"Oh, I thought we were meeting down stairs," she says, surprised. I look beyond her to her open patio doors and the pink sky beyond it, speechless. Even with such a beautiful back drop, she outshines it.

"I thought it would be nice to come get you," I clear my throat as I follow her inside.

"I just need to grab one or two things and lock up," she smiles, moving into her bathroom. I walk further into her room and smile at how neat and tidy she keeps it. My own is strewn with clothes and paperwork and not suitable for bringing home a date. I close her patio doors, locking them just as she arrives back into the room. I shove my hands into the pockets of my grey slacks and try to find somewhere to look, before all my resolve disappears.

Jo

"Do we have reservations?" I ask, trying to pull his eyes back to mine. I can't stand this static atmosphere between us, it's unbearable. He rocks back on his heels, keeping his eyes averted, as he pretends to admire a painting.

"Yep, we should go actually," he flicks his wrist, tugging on his white shirt to reveal his watch. I press my lips together to hide my smile, he is just as nervous as I am.

"You could try looking at me, I'm not going to bite," I challenge him, he hates to lose against me and like putty in my hands, his eyes dart to mine.

"I seem to remember you nipping my lip a few times

Joanna," his husky voice betrays him and he looks away again. He begins to move towards the door and I get there ahead of him, turning the latch. His breath is on my neck; his body close to mine as he encases me against the door.

"What are you doing," he whispers in a low sensual tone. I turn slowly to face him.

"I'm not hungry," I swallow hard, shocked at my daring seduction, but he doesn't keep me waiting.

Taking my hand, he leads me towards my bed, turning me at the foot. I can tell that his mood is different now, controlled, as he runs his fingers down my arms creating goose pimples in its path. My chest rises and falls, as sharp, short gasps of air leave my lungs while his finger dips beneath the rim of my strapless dress, grazing against my hardened nipples. His eyes burn as he watches my reaction, before he pulls down the material exposing my naked chest. I expect him to go wild but he surprises me by stepping forward, wrapping one arm around my back, the other entangling in my hair as he kisses me soft and deep. My nipples strain against his shirt begging for attention, my damp folds, scream to be touched and as if reading my body to perfection, he pulls my dress down further allowing it to pool at my feet, before bending to lather attention on my breasts. A low whimper reverberates around us as my head falls back in pleasure and his hand finds my slickened centre. Walking me backwards, he lays me down on the bed before falling to his knees and pulling me to the edge. I lay open and bare for him as he begins to lap up my arousal, my hips jerk and my knees tremble, as he pushes my body higher. I feel my stomach tighten, my pulse quickens and body tingles, as I burst into flames, exploding like never before. I hear the shrill of a phone and for a moment, confuse it with my own purrs of pleasure. Davis moves on top of me, finding my mouth and quieting my sobs. Through the sexual haze, I feel a vibration against my leg, as Davis' phone begins to ring again.

"Fuck," he grinds out, taking it from his trouser pockets

and hanging it up. I reach down, caressing his large erection, pleasantly surprised by his size and excited to mount it. He begins to ravish my chest again, when his phone begins to ring once more.

"Fuck, fuck, fuck," he curses, picking up the phone, this time answering.

"Davis," he snaps harshly and I feel sorry for whoever has interrupted him.

"Roche, it better be fucking good," I reach up, kissing his sweaty brow as he continues to talk. "When?" He grinds out. "FUCK!" He says a little louder and I lean back to look at his face. His expression is no longer filled with lust, replaced only by rage. He hangs up the phone and rolls onto his back.

"I'm sorry Joanna, I can't turn it off and he would have kept calling," he rubs his face in frustration.

"Is everything ok?" I ask tentatively, not sure if he can discuss it or not.

"I don't know how to tell you this Joanna, but Seamus Lynch has filed an appeal against the DA's office," he sits up again, his eyes assessing mine and I debate whether I should tell him, but my hesitation tells him everything he needs to know. I watch as his eyes widen in horror.

"You knew?" His nose flares, before he sits up looking down on me. Suddenly self-conscious, I rise with him, reaching for my robe and covering my chest.

"Yes, only a few days," I croak. I can tell he is angry with me, but I'm not sure it's deserved.

"ONLY A FEW FUCKING DAYS!" He yells and I jump with fright. My reaction is enough to calm him, but he moves away from me, pacing the end of my bed.

"Seamus Lynch, the man that nearly destroyed all of our lives, will be appealing to the Federal Court for dismissal of his case and you thought that you should keep that from me," his tone is low and menacing and I think I prefer him to shout.

"I didn't want to ruin my trip; it wasn't about keeping it from you!" I shrug, my own voice meek.

"Are you crazy, I could have been back in Boston trying to prevent this, instead I'm here," he looks at me again, shaking his head in disgust.

"Don't you dare look at me like that," my own temper flares. "There is nothing you or I or anyone can do, it's with the Federal Court, so don't try make out like I somehow aided his appeal," I jump from the bed, tying the robe on securely.

"What about your best friends, don't they deserve to know that the man who wants them dead, might be getting out!" He barks again, his body radiating a different kind of heat towards me.

"They are on honeymoon; would you have me ruin it?"

"Don't act like you care about their trip, you just admitted you were only worried about ruining your own fictional, romantic trip," his words are like a slap across the face.

"Get the hell out," I push him towards the door.

"Don't worry, I'm going, back to Boston to sort this mess out! What you should have done the second you heard that animal was trying to get out," he shakes his head one last time before storming out.

CHAPTER 11

There is a stale stench hanging in the air of the packed courtroom. The heavens opened as I landed in Boston, ten days ago and there is still no sign of it letting up. It is a far cry from the blistering heat and blue skies of Maui and I long to be back there. Like the dull and dreary weather, my mood has been miserable since that awful last night. Made worse by the fact that Davis told Michael and Bree when they returned home two days ago before I had the chance to see them, once again making me feel like a bad friend. I wanted to tell Bree, I wanted to support her and reassure her but it was left to them to visit with me, because of my hectic work schedule. They both arrived on my door step after checking in on the gym last night and I was relieved to see that they seemed to be handling the news well. I, however, feel more distracted and on edge than I did before my holiday, it was supposed to ease my stress, not add to it. The tension in the overcrowded courtroom is palpable, as people wait, eager to find out the fate of their loved ones or themselves. I pull out my stack of case files, each one representing the defendant being brought forward for their arraignment today and I let out an exhausted sigh.

"Docket number 554673, the people versus Ronald Humes," the court officer calls out the next defendant, snapping me out of my daydream. I watch as a tall, skinny kid is carted out in handcuffs, his head down as he makes his way to stand beside his attorney.

"How do you plead?" The Judge keeps his head down, reading over his documents.

"Not guilty, your honour," his muted tones are barely audible in the overcrowded court. It saddens me to see someone so young, just out of high school and here he is, facing charges for aggravated assault. His victim, who he beat with a baseball bat, had owed him $50.00.

"Do you have any notices Ms. Carmody," Judge Klein asks, looking up from under his reading spectacles in my direction. I call out my notice number, "190.50 your honour," which means that we are pushing forward with a felony charge.

"I would ask the court to set bail at $20,000, due to the serious nature of the crime, your honour," I request.

"Your honour, my client has no previous brushes with the law and Ms. Carmody is aware that his family can't afford such a huge amount of bail, I ask that you release him on ROR," Peter Levitt, the defendant's attorney, pretends to be surprised at the bail request, trying to persuade the Judge to release him, solely on a promise of return.

"Your honour, this crime was a serious assault," I push harder for the bail.

"I know how serious the crime is Ms. Carmody, I am setting bail at $5,000," the Judge cuts me off, slamming his gavel down hard to move proceedings along. I purse my lips, looking down at the next case. I am happy with the results, but I would have felt happier with a bigger bail amount.

"Case number 554674, people versus Henry Vincent," the court officer's distinctive deep voice bellows throughout the courtroom once again and effectively, shushing the rumble of voices behind the wooden pews. I wait for Henry Vincent to appear and, unlike the last defendant, he walks out with his head held high and a smug grin on his face.

The preppy, well turned out defendant, hides his true identity well and my stomach turns in disgust.

"Not guilty," I hear him say to the Judge; no surprise there. This asshole knows that proving our case will be tough; at least he should, considering he just finished law school.

"Do you have any notices, Ms. Carmody?" The Judge calls to me again and once more, I call out "190.50." The judge looks up in shock, surprised that I am pushing forward with a felony charge, but I want to rattle this guy. I want him to spend the next four weeks worrying about the lengthy prison sentence he will receive, if he is found guilty. At the pre-trial hearing, I will give him a plea deal if he confesses, if not, I will convince the Judge or jury of his guilt. Without very much physical evidence and only the victim's testimony to go on, I know proving criminal harassment in this case will be challenging, but I didn't sign up for this job to shrink away when something got tough. I interviewed his victim, seen the fear in her eyes after months of being tormented by her ex-boyfriend. The final straw was when he was arrested on her property, dressed all in black, in the middle of the night.

"Your honour, I request bail to be set at $100,000," I pull my shoulders back and face the three men, Judge, attorney and defendant, head on.

"The prosecution has very little evidence your honour, my client has only just finished college and is an asset to society. I request ROR," his attorney feigns disinterest. I roll my eyes at his laid back approach, trying to make light of these charges.

"Bail is set at $20,000," the Judge rules, once again slamming down his gavel and moving onto the next case. I see the sly smirk on his face as he passes me, his family have money to burn and I'm confident no matter how much money the Judge ordered, he would be walking free today. I have a bad feeling about him being on the streets, thankfully the Boston P.D agree and will keep an eye on him.

By the end of the day, my feet ache, my head pounds and my stomach is rumbling. All I want is to strip out of my blue shirt and pencil skirt, before soaking in a long, hot bath and climbing into bed. If I could fall into bed and just sleep for the winter, I would gladly hibernate. It's dark when I eventually leave the office and make my way towards my car. I parked down a small side street, just one block from my office and I search through my oversized bag for my keys when I finally arrive. I'm too exhausted to notice my surroundings, too deep in thought about everything that happened in Maui. Maybe I should have told Davis, I muse, as light drizzles of rain caress my face and I close my eyes for just a moment, remembering my time with Davis in Haleakala National Park.

"Do you have a light?" The strange male voice startles me and I turn quickly to find a very tall and very broad man behind me. His presence immediately scares me; he is too close, peering down on me with ominous eyes. Small and black, they are trained on me, wide and unwavering in their assessment. My instinct is to back away, but with only my car behind me, I won't get far. Alarm bells ring loud in my head, but I remain calm and try to remember what Davis taught me; rule number one is prevention, Davis' voice pops into my head, giving me strength.

"NO," I say loudly, pulling back my shoulders and asserting myself before moving sideways along my car, in an attempt to put some distance between us. He stalks me, step for step.

"Where are you going, Joanna?" His caustic laugh and knowledge of my name, confirms my worst fears, this is not an innocent interaction. I rack my brains for step two and remember it is flight. He is too close to kick, so I drop my bag, knee him in the groin and run for my life. I make it two steps.

"You're going to pay for that," he sneers and I'm violently pulled back by the hair. I scream out but to my own ears, it's not loud enough, I try again, crying as my head comes down hard against the bonnet of my car. I twist and turn out of his grasp, but the power behind his grip is unyielding. With one hand, he slams me down hard against my car again and I taste blood in my mouth.

"Shut the fuck up," his menacing tones are low and controlled, unlike my cries for help which are muffled, as I choke on my own blood. I feel powerless, as he twists my wrist behind my back, pushing it up to control my body before dragging me down a side alley. It is only a few feet from where I parked my car, I hadn't even noticed it. I continue to struggle in his arms, but my mind is blank and the self-defence moves, vanish from my memory. Helplessness and fear rip through my body when he pulls open the back door to a parked white van. Using the other unopened door as leverage, I lift my legs and push backwards.

"You, stupid bitch," he growls low in my ear before

dropping my body to the ground and kicking me hard in the ribs. I crawl along the dirty wet floor, only to be rewarded with the heel of his shoe slamming into my side and toppling me over. I can feel the adrenaline beginning to wane and my fight beginning to falter, until he pulls me by the hair again, dragging me along the ground. My heels scrape as my shoes come off in the struggle. I reach up and pull at my hair trying to stop him from ripping it from my scalp, but it is no good. I am alone down a dark alleyway, my screams for help have gone unanswered and despite my very best attempt to escape, I am now in his van.

"FUCK," he growls, angry and out of breath from the struggle. Taking the opportunity, I move as fast as I can and try to climb over into the front seat. With one simple tug of my feet he pulls me back in and I wallop onto the metal floor. He is standing over me; his huge body crouched down so he can fit. There is a strange moment between us, his dark eyes find mine and I see the pleasure my terrified reactions have given him. Through the fear and the confusion, there is an instance of clarity, an acceptance of fate. I have no idea what his ultimate plan for me is, but I know that my distress and my pleas for leniency, will only make it all the more pleasurable for him. I can't stop the tear that rolls down my cheek or the trembling in my body from the unrelenting trepidation, but I can control every other reaction from here on out.

"You're a coward," I bare my teeth and look him square in the eyes, without hesitation, noting the scar above his left brow and his crooked teeth. He says nothing, his eyes reveal nothing apart from the pure evil soul which lies behind them. Dropping to his knees, he reaches forward and pulls down a rope, already tied to the metal pole along the back of the front seats and ties my hands to it. I close my eyes.

"Open your eyes," he demands. I keep them closed. "Open your fucking eyes or I am going to stab you," his voice is shaky, his earlier composure beginning to slip and I open my eyes. He dangles a large knife over me, playing with the tip to further terrorise me, I keep my face blank. It takes everything in me not to scream or cry again, but I have no way out and the only thing that might save me now, is power play. Without another word, he easily slices through my skirt and shirt, nipping my stomach. He moans in pleasure, his fingers running slowly down my stomach and I squirm away from his ugly touch.

"I'm going to make you pay for teasing me for so long," he licks his lips before lowering his head. I lie, allowing silent tears to fall down my face, as he savagely bites my bare chest before ripping away my panties. I close my eyes, not wanting to see his naked body, but I can hear the rattle of his belt buckle and the unmistakeable slow sound of his zipper, sliding down. He plunges inside me with painful force and my shoulders rock, my body trembling, as I hold in my despair.

"NOOOOO," I cry out before his hand covers my mouth. I squeeze my eye lids, wishing I could be back on that date with Davis and I go there in my mind, trying to escape reality.

"Open your eyes," he roars load and this time, I shake my head no, remembering Davis' awful sandwiches and how he looked at me that day. I need to remember something good.

"Open your eyes," his fist comes across my face, but I continue to shake my head.

"NO," I cry out in agony from his ferocious assault. His hands close around my neck squeezing it and I struggle for air, gasping and wriggling beneath him. I welcome death now, I even hope it comes soon and on my last breath, before succumbing to unconsciousness, I refused to open my eyes.

CHAPTER 12

"Joanna," the pretty blonde nurse softly calls to me, standing up from her internal examination. Her eyes are full of pity and concern, "you can wash up now," she presses her lips together, removing her latex gloves before disposing of them.

I sit up, staring at the cream walls of the hospital room.

"Thank you," my hoarse voice whispers, feeling like I'm being stabbed by a thousand blades. I glance down at the white bandages covering my sprained wrist. The pain became unbearable not long after I arrived at the hospital but they gave me some painkillers, which must have numbed everything. There is a strange emptiness that I feel, it's like I'm not really present in this moment. I know what has happened, I remember everything but the impact of those memories, is minimal. I feel nothing, not joy or relief to be alive and not fear or pain, at what has happened. My bare feet dangle from the edge of the bed, dirty and bruised, so I lift my head and look out the window. The rain is still beating down. Its faithful companion, grey clouds, hang above, watching as it falls against my window pane. Each drop spreads as it lands against the glass, rolling around in every direction, creating a watery design only for me. I watch from the safety of this warm bed as the clouds flash blue and lightening streaks across the sky, threatening to strike.

"There are some police officers here to see you," the nurse places her hand on my shoulder, gently nudging me from my trancelike state. I turn slowly, hating that I will miss the electricity as it dances with the clouds, creating terror on us mere mortals. I wonder if I am like the rain, just falling aimlessly, in the hopes of creating something beautiful, or if I'm a cloud carrying the weight of the rain, waiting to be struck down. I've met lightening, I'm not lightening, my mind continues to wander.

"Joanna, I am Detective Hazel Reed and this is Gail Jones, a crisis counsellor, she is going to sit in while I ask you some questions, is that ok?"

The new, unfamiliar voice breaks through my muddled

thoughts and I blink twice at the two female figures that have appeared from nowhere. My heart leaps and I gasp with fright.

"Sorry Joanna, I didn't mean to startle you," the dark skinned officer steps back, holding up her hands to reassure me. Pull yourself together! My own voice scolds me now and I massage my temples confused.

"Joanna, my name is Gail Jones, would you like to speak with me privately first?" Another soothing tone comes at me. Joanna wake up, they're talking to you! I scream at myself.

"NO," I yell and this time, it is my own croaked tones in the room. I look up, covering my mouth with my bandaged hands, "I'm sorry," I yelp, shocked that I was so rude. They both stare kindly at me and I gulp for air, as a wave of fear and dread crashes over me, plunging me into the depths of despair.

"Nooooo," I cry out again. The flood banks open and my chest vibrates, as gasps of air mingled with trembling sobs, rake my body. I feel arms come around me, holding me.

"You're safe now," she shushes me.

I squeeze at the sheets with all my might, fighting for composure but her warmth and the realisation that this is all happening, succumbs me and I let go, releasing the heaviness in my heart. When I finally manage to stop the emotional outburst, exhaustion settles in. I stay awake long enough to give my description of the events to the female officer, who makes notes in her brown leather notepad, before leaving me alone with Gail. We talk a little longer before she is called away, promising to return later this afternoon. I fall back against the feather pillow, my eyes weary and allow myself to sleep.

Davis

I arrive at the crime scene within minutes, having raced through traffic with my lights screaming all the way. My hands shake nervously, as I park the car, taking a moment to breathe. I know Joanna has been moved to the hospital, but I'm not ready to see and hear it all just yet. I swallow bile as I imagine the possibilities, before stepping out into the murky alleyway.

"FBI," I flash my badge at the officer, who lifts the yellow tape around the crime scene, allowing me to enter. The streets are empty at this hour of the morning, but it hasn't stopped the local media vultures picking up on the story.

"Agent, Agent, its Chloe Greco from Morning News, can you tell us what happened? How is the victim? Why is the FBI involved?" One of them calls to me as I pass.

"No comment," I growl, ignoring her as she continues firing questions to my back. I move into the alleyway, my eyes scanning the perimeter at the same time. The lead detective is Victor Breen and I see him up ahead, speaking with the forensic photographer.

"Vic, what have we got?" I ask him, wasting no time with fancy greetings, Joanna is one of us and the clock is ticking. Every second this scumbag spends on the street, will be a second too long.

"Looks like he grabbed her at her car, it's parked on the side street, before dragging her down here. The rain washed away a lot of the physical evidence, but we can make out one set of tyre tracks here," he leans under a small roof, pointing to the ground and I can see the tyre indent in the ground.

"That's fresh, a witness in the apartments across the street said a white van was parked here last night and pulled out this morning, no plates though," he sighs. I clench my sweaty palms into fists at my side, trying to calm the sudden rage that assails me.

"Is it random? Has she said anything?" I ask, again swallowing past a thick lump in my throat, not sure that I am ready to hear it all.

"Hazel Reed is interviewing her now."

"How is she?" I look down, ashamed that I haven't got

the courage to see her just yet. How do I look her in the eyes after everything I've done?

"I can't tell you, the paramedics said she was disorientated and mumbling," he shrugs, looking away in distress too. Joanna is known by all the detective's; this case is close to home for everyone.

"What do you need me to do?" I turn back, desperate to do something, anything I can do to help.

"Forensics is collecting evidence as we speak; my men will be canvasing the area for witnesses. I'm hoping that the traffic cameras picked up a white van heading away from this direction."

"What about convicted rapists in the area? Anyone she may have put away that has been released?" I jump in, reminding him of other avenues to explore.

"We are looking into all of that, I will keep you posted," he promises, but it's not enough.

"Vic, I need to help on this, I will stay out of your hair, but Joanna is a friend."

"We all love Jo, we are gonna get this prick, but I can't have you messing around in my case Davis. I will give you all the information I have, but this is not FBI jurisdiction."

"Jesus Vic, I know, I'm asking you to give me something to do," I plead, desperately.

"There is nothing you can do right now Davis; I will keep you posted. I gotta get back to work," he finishes, before walking over to his partner, Greg Bishop.

Both men are decent detectives and have years of experience, I completely trust their ability to catch the scumbag, but it doesn't lessen my need to help. I walk the scene myself and images of Joanna lying, dumped, on the cold, wet ground, haunt me. There is nothing more I can gather from here, I take some photos on my phone and a few notes, before heading to the hospital. I have no idea if she will even see me, but I'm done being afraid to face her, she needs me and I need to be there more than I need to breathe right now.

CHAPTER 13

The air in her room is cold and a chill runs up my back, as I stand at the foot of her bed. I can't help the tears that fill my eyes, as I watch her sleep. Her face is black and blue on one side, her cut lip, still covered in dried blood, opens slightly, as she exhales a long, shaky breath. I move to her side and take her bandaged wrist in my hand, running my thumb along her palm. I lean closer to her and for the first time, I notice his handprints on her neck. Images of him squeezing her delicate neck as he tried to take her last breath, haunt me. She looks so broken and I hate myself for not being there when she needed me. I lay her hand back down and rush from the room, holding in my distress until I make it to the stairwell. Without restraint, I ram my fist into the wall and let out a howl of pure, unadulterated rage. I want to hunt him down and kill him. I want to torture him, I want to inflict the same pain he caused her, and more. Tears blur my vision and I sniff them back. I should be out there finding this fucker, instead, I'm crying like a baby, hiding away like a coward. I pull myself together and move to the bathroom, splashing cold water on my face before returning to her side. She has shifted in her sleep and is now lying on her side; her face is unrecognisable, now that only her bruises are showing. I reach forward and pick up a small white feather that rests on her swollen cheekbone. I want to take away her pain, rewind the past twenty four hours. Yesterday, she had been on my mind all day, I had wanted to come to her to apologise for my behaviour, in the hope that we could be at least friends but I was too stubborn and because of it, she almost died. Until this fucker is caught, I won't let her out of my sight.

Jo

The room is dark when I open my eyes and I jump up, my heart racing.

"Joanna," I turn to the sound of Davis' voice and find him sitting in a chair next to my bed. I look away, tears immediately brimming. I don't want him here; I don't want him to see me like this.

"Why are you here?" My broken voice is weak and I despise myself for being so fragile. I don't want to face him, so I keep my eyes averted towards the window. I feel the weight of my bed shift and can see him sitting down next to me through the corner of my eye, why won't he leave me, just leave! Silently, I scream for him to be gone, for this to all just go away.

"Joanna, please look at me," his voice is a whisper and I shake my head no, without looking at him. My emotions betray me, as two tears spill over and roam freely down my swollen face. I hold the blanket to my chest, refusing to wipe them away, refusing to look at him and let him see my pain.

"Joanna, I want to help, please, I need to help," the sincerity in his tone, the rasp of his own voice startles me into turning towards him and I'm not prepared to see a dishevelled and distraught Davis. I shake my head no again, closing my eyes to hold the treacherous tears at bay.

"Please just let me hold you," he begs me, our faces only inches apart, our sides almost touching. I remain frozen, unable to speak for fear of losing my false composure. I feel one hand come around my shoulder and gently, I fall into the crook of his arm, my undamaged cheek resting against his chest and he holds me. His body is stiff and the awkward embrace pushes me over the edge, as fresh sobs rake my body. His body relaxes, as I cry loudly against him, freeing myself once again from the pain. I feel his lips against my head, his thumb softly wiping away the tears from my bruised cheek, before he lies back on the bed, holding me. The sense of security soothes my fears and when I can cry no more, he continues to hold me tight against his body. It suddenly occurs to me that I haven't washed yet, that I am in Davis' arms while that animal's smell is still on me. I become frantic and jump up and off the bed, I want to go home.

"I need to go home now," I step away from the bed and look around for my clothes.

"Where are my clothes?" I say a little breathless, terrified he might try to stop me if I don't move faster.

"They took them as evidence but I have your handbag, do you want me to go to yours and get you some bits?" He asks attentively.

"No, I need to go home," I run my hands through my hair, feeling overwhelmed by the desperation coursing through my body to be at home, in my own bed, in my own shower, with my doors locked and the world with all its evil, on the other side.

"The nurse told me earlier that you could stay the night or leave if you wanted, you don't have to be here," he walks over, holding his jacket. "Put this on and we can check out," he takes my hand from my hair and tucks it into his sleeve, before moving around and putting the other in.

"Do you want me to call Bree?" He asks and I pull on his wrist, making him turn to face me.

"No, I don't want anyone to know, please promise me Davis, I can't handle it right now," I beg him. I love Bree but I can't have her worrying about me, not now while she is pregnant. Davis runs his hand along his forehead, conflicted by my request.

"Joanna, this is too big to keep from her," he begins to argue with me.

"I don't want anyone to know until I'm ready," I say, adamant that he keeps my shameful secret. He nods his head before leading me to the nurse's station to check out. My nurse from this morning, who is wearing a tag with the name Juliette, pulls me to one side.

"Joanna, this is a phone number for a rape crisis centre, if you need to talk to someone, Gail Jones works there voluntarily twice a week, her number is on the back," she places the business card into my hand and sure enough, on the back is a cell phone number. I nod, before thanking her and making my way to the exit with Davis. He looks down at my bare feet.

"I don't want to leave you here while I get the car," he looks around the quiet lobby before picking me up in his arms and walking out the doors.

"What are you doing?" I say shocked, too embarrassed to put up a fight in case my hospital gown comes away.

"I'm not letting you out of my sight and you can't walk in your bare feet," he walks swiftly to his SUV and buckles me in. I'm surprised at how tired I feel again and close my eyes for just a moment.

****

I snuggle against his chest, not fighting him when he lifts me from the car and carries me into my apartment complex. I stir from my sleep, as he struggles to get my keys from my handbag and feel guilty as he holds me at the same time.

"Put me down," I say groggily and he looks a little relieved that I have woken up.

"Sorry, but what the hell do you have in here?" He jokes, putting me on my feet but continuing to hold me against his side.

"They are in the small zip pocket," I rub the sleep from my eyes, preparing myself to take over but he finds them and follows me inside. My home feels empty and cold somehow. I walk towards the kitchen and pour myself a glass of cold water to ease my sore throat before moving into my bedroom. Davis follows silently behind me.

"I can run you a bath?" He asks from the doorway, fiddling with my keys and looking nervous.

"You don't have to stay Davis, you can leave," I turn, taking some fresh clothes from my wardrobe.

"I can turn on the light," he offers.

"Noooo," I say, a bit too sharply. I don't want to see myself; I don't want him seeing me. "I'm sorry, I just have a headache, the light will irritate it," I half lie because I do have a headache.

"I'll get you some painkillers," he moves towards the kitchen and I sink onto my bed. He returns with more water and two tablets and I happily swallow them.

"Are you hungry, I could order some food?"

"No Davis, maybe you should go," I sigh. I don't want him to feel responsible for me out of some warped sense of guilt.

"I'm not leaving you," he says, adamantly and I look up into serious eyes.

"I want you to go," I snap.

"No," he refuses, shaking his head and putting his hands on his hips. I bite back my anger; I don't want him to witness me like this anymore than he already has.

"I want you to leave Davis, please," I stand up and move towards the bathroom.

"I'll order some food," he says from behind me and I ball my fists letting out a deep sigh.

"I asked you to go, just go," I yell at him meanly, before storming into the bathroom and slamming the door.

I turn on the shower and untie the hospital gown at the back and let it fall to the floor, revealing my naked body in the mirror.

For the first time, I see myself and I'm horrified by how ugly I look. I lift my trembling fingers, gently examining the tender skin of my face. My black eye and cut lip are mild, compared to the rest of my body. I move my hand to my neck and measure my small hand against the large handprint he left behind and images of him standing over me, flash to the forefront of my mind. I look down and shake them from my thoughts before facing myself again, forcing myself to look at his creation. I unravel the bandages on my wrists, revealing the deep grooves he left behind after he bound me. My body aches all over, my shoulders feel tight and my back hurts. My arms are marked and a sob escapes my lips as I count the bite marks he left on my breasts, one, two, three, four, five. I stop counting and splash cold water from the faucet onto my face. I don't want to see anymore. I pull open my shower door and step under the scalding hot water, it pains me at first but I'd have boiling water if I could. Anything to eternally wash away his scent, to scrub away his touch and to erase the damage he left behind. I watch the suds roll down my body, revealing my pink skin and a rage burns deep inside me. I grab the loofah and begin the process again, scrubbing harder until it hurts, before crumbling on the basin. An unmerciful aching scream, leaves my body and I cry hard, sobbing loudly. I just can't believe this has happened to me.

I pull myself up from the wet tiles and step out, drying myself with a soft towel. Gently, I dab my swollen cheek, careful not to press too hard. As I lift my face from the fluffy towel, I catch sight of myself again in the mirror. A surge of fury at my unrecognisable face, rises within me and I quickly wrap the towel around my body, trying to hide the bite marks. When I can still see his teeth marks peeping out and staring up at me, my rage becomes uncontrollable. I reach for the first thing I can find on my countertop, which happens to be a stone toothbrush holder and throw it with all my might against the mirror, screaming with indignation.

Davis

I rush to the bathroom door, ready to burst in, when I hear the sounds of glass shattering and Joanna screaming.

"Joanna," I call to her.

"Don't come in," she cries back and I stop squeezing the door handle, but not pushing inwards.

"Joanna, please," I rest my forehead against the door as I listen to her muffled sobs.

"Please just go Davis, JUST GO!" Her tears and anger mingled, pulls at my heart and I ignore her protests and push open the door. Quickly, I come to her side as she sits crying, her back against her shower door, surrounded by fragments of mirrored glass. I pick her up and carry her out and straight to her room.

"Just go, please I don't want you to see me like this,"

she continues to gulp back tears, her breathing shallow. I kiss her lips gently.

"I'm not going anywhere," I whisper, before placing her under her duvet.

"He bit me," she moans into her pillow, "I just want to die." Her heart breaking pleas, scare me.

"Joanna, you're going to get through this, I'm going to help you and then I'm going to hunt him down and kill him," I promise, wholeheartedly.

"I'm afraid Davis," her lip trembles and I climb in next to her, staying outside the covers.

"I promise Joanna, I will never let anything like this happen to you again, I'm going to find this fucker," I wrap my arms around the blanket and pull her body against mine.

"He was so strong, I tried to use the moves you showed me but he was so quick, I promise I tried," her frail tones stir an instinct within me, I need to protect her. All of my training, all of my experience has led to this moment and I am going to use it to catch him. Then I'm going to kill him.

CHAPTER 14

Bree

Boston PD have not yet released the name of the victim in yesterday evenings brutal attack in downtown Boston. It is believed that the female victim was attacked while walking to her car and dragged into this nearby alleyway....

I look up from the pastry I am rolling out, towards the news report, pointing the remote to raise the volume.

...where she was beaten, raped and left for dead. While we have not yet established if the victim knew her attacker, early reports have suggested that the victim worked for the nearby DA's office. This morning we spotted an FBI Agent arriving at the scene, but he refused to comment.

I drop the remote from my hand and call out.

"MICHAEL!" I yell and he runs in.

"What's wrong?" His eyes are wide with fear and I stare at the TV, my hands covering my mouth.

"Davis is on the TV," I mumble, please tell me that's not Davis.

"It's Davis, why are you crying?"

"Jo, I need to go see Jo," I rush about, turning off the oven and grabbing my jacket.

"Bree, what the hell is going on?" Michael snaps angrily.

"A woman was raped last night leaving work."

"Davis is working the case, so?"

"So?! They said she worked for the DA's office and Jo didn't answer her phone all night and Davis never showed up at the gym this morning," I rattle my hands in front of me.

"Jesus," he finally musters before grabbing the car keys. I fret all the way, Jo's phone is still off and Davis' is ringing out. I was compelled to listen to the TV and without any proof or certainty, I know Jo is in trouble, I know she needs me.

Jo

There is a loud thud on my front door and I turn

quickly towards Davis who rolls off the bed and moves with stealth, out of the room. I sit up watching him, my heart pounding. He turns back; fully dressed except for shoes, he puts his finger to his lips, signalling for me to be quiet. I nod, terrified.

"Jo, its Bree, are you in there?" We both sigh in unison. Davis looks to me for direction and I step out of the bed, still in my towel, grabbing my white robe.

"What will I tell them?" Davis asks, when they thud on the door again.

"DAVIS, I know you're in there, I saw your car outside! You better open this door now!" Bree seems frantic and I shrug, unsure what to do. I don't want them to see me differently.

"What if every time they look at me all they think is, she was raped?" My eyes well up again and I can't stand crying again. I want to feel strong; but I feel broken.

"Joanna, she is your best friend, you need to trust her," he tucks my hair behind my ears and I nod for him to tell them.

"Just warn her before I come out what I look like, the baby," I sniff.

"I will," he promises, before closing the door behind him. A few seconds later, I here muffled voices.

"What the hell are you playing at? Where is she?"

"Bree wait, stop please, Bree, come back, don't go in there," I stand up from the edge of the bed when my door pushes open and Bree walks in, her eyes red, her face wrought with concern. She freezes halfway through and stares at me.

"Jesus Jo," she cries out before walking straight over and hugging me.

"Who did this to you?" She continues to question me, but I can barely manage to breath let alone talk. She pulls back and I see Michael in the doorway.

"Jo Jo," he whispers, I can tell Davis has filled him in.

"Michael, I need to talk with Jo, alone," Bree walks over and touches his chest, calming him. His nostrils are flared, his fists balled at his sides. He stands rigid, I think if he moves, he might destroy something in his path. Bree's soothing hand on his chest, settles him.

"Michael, come outside, I'll explain what we know so far," Davis suggests and I look down and away from Michael's stare, ashamed.

"Jo Jo," he ignores everyone and I turn back to look at him. "Don't look away from me, I'm your friend and we all love you, we are going to be here, do you hear me?" He pins me with his loving stare. Using the heel of my hand, I wipe away fresh tears and walk over, hugging him, he had said everything that I needed to hear. He holds me in his big arms and when I pull away, everyone is teary eyed and I begin to laugh.

"What are we all like?" I laugh, which leads to a new wave of tears.

"Joanna, we will be outside, I'll leave you and Bree to talk," Davis pulls Michael from the room, closing the door behind him. I walk over and take a seat back on the edge of my bed, keeping my head down to hide my injuries. They look worse than they feel but then again, I have taken pain medication. Fiddling with my bathrobe belt, I keep my hands busy until Bree's small hand, folds over one of mine.

"Jo, you can look at me," she sniffles, taking a seat next to me on the bed and I scoot over giving her more room. I feel exhausted from the emotional rollercoaster of the past twenty four hours and her steadying hand seems to calm me.

"I feel stupid," I admit.

"You have no reason to feel that way, you have been assaulted Jo. You are not to blame."

"I think of all the women who I worked with, raped, beaten, stalked," I look towards her with a watery smile, "some of the worst things imaginable and I never once thought it could happen to me, how stupid to think I was invincible."

"You helped those women Jo, you put away their

attackers, and you listened and fought for them. This time, you are fighting for yourself, you're a survivor! He doesn't get to destroy you, he won't win." She growls out her final few words, choking back tears.

"Every time I look in the mirror, he's there, every time I close my eyes, he is there! I have to wait on test results to make sure he wasn't diseased, I feel dirty." I lift my hands, covering my face. I haven't told Davis or anyone about the test results. I had to swallow a pill to prevent pregnancy and even that, has a five percent chance of not working.

"Jo, this is scary, but you need to keep your head high and anything that comes along, we will tackle it, together, one step at a time."

"Bree, I'm not sure I can get through this," I sob again and she wraps her arms around me, pulling me to her shoulder.

"Jo, I'm going to help you and so will Michael and Davis, we all love you and we are all here! Davis will catch him and you will feel safe again," she hesitates for a moment, "can you tell me everything that happened?" My rational mind knows that everything she is saying, is achievable but there is a hollow ache in my chest that disagrees. My stomach recoils when I think about going over it all again, my palms become sweaty and my breathing shortens.

"Bree, I can't," I stutter nervously, my throat suddenly dry.

"Jo, yes you can," she grabs my shoulders, addressing me with determined eyes, "he doesn't get to take my best friend away from me, we are going to face this monster together, starting with you sharing some of your pain."

"Ok," I whisper through trembling lips.

ONE WEEK LATER

Davis

I readjust my black tie before pulling my elasticated shoulder holster over my white shirt and securing my Glock 22. Bree and Michael are on their way over to stay with Joanna while I'm at work again today. I have stayed here with her every night since it happened, held her every night until she slept and lay awake, listening to her nightmares. I feel useless, like a failure. I can't make this better and instead of improving, her mood seems only to be darkening. Bree told me yesterday that she has been sleeping all day, barely eating and when she does come out from her room, she seems distant. I can feel her barriers coming up and despite my best efforts to get her to open up, she refuses point blank to talk any further about it. The lead detective, Vic Breen, called by two days ago and updated Joanna on their investigation; which was pointless, they know nothing. I have been in the field all week and this is my first day back at my desk, where my own investigation will start. I have already obtained some information over the phone with regards to forensics, the lab has agreed to push Joanna's evidence to the top of the pile. Attacking a DA in Boston, won't be tolerated, attacking Joanna, won't go unpunished. This was a sloppy attack, he left behind DNA and Joanna saw his face. She didn't recognise him as someone she had put away, but he knew her. He called her name before he attacked her; it was personal on some level. My mind has been whirling with possibilities ever since she admitted to Bree that he had called her name, she had forgotten about it in the initial interview. It tells me that her attacker was either a serial rapist who stalked Joanna and therefore, will do it again, or that he had a personal vendetta, for some other reason. He had tried to kill her, which means that until he is caught, he could come back to finish the job. Over my dead body, I ball my fists in fury.

I finish up in the bathroom, not bothering to shave again. It has been three days now and the dark shadow my stubble is creating, suits my mood just fine. I walk in to check on Joanna before leaving her again, I can't stand to leave her. She is still sleeping; her body snuggled beneath a heavy layer of blankets to keep her warm. She keeps complaining that she is cold, despite the thermostat being at the highest. She hasn't looked me in the eyes since the night after the attack and it kills me, I can feel her slipping away. When I think about the attack, which is often, my heart stops for just a second, the fear it creates is like a bolt of lightning every time. I have to remind myself that it's real, that she survived and that there is nothing I can do to take it back. I fantasize about finding him, torturing him and slowly killing him, but then fight with myself because it goes against everything I have ever believed in. My entire career has been about fighting the good fight, about serving and protecting and upholding the law. Its right to just kill him, stop him from hurting anyone ever again, making me a murderer. Can I live with that? Yes, I whisper into the quiet room. I can live with it, if it means that Joanna feels safe again, if it means that she will get better and move on from this. I would do whatever it takes to make this better. I move closer and bend, leaving a feather light kiss on her forehead before going to let Bree and Michael in.

CHAPTER 15

Roche

It's not easy to work with Davis on a good day; the past week has been like walking through a minefield. I have quickly learned that his feelings for Joanna Carmody, run deeper than even he knew and I have never seen him so despondent. I came into the office early this morning to try to help him solve this case, despite it being out of our jurisdiction. I can tell he hasn't slept properly in days, his usual clean cut appearance, has gone downhill and I haven't seen food or drink touch his mouth once. I'm not good with emotions, I don't do deep, meaningful conversations but I am good at catching criminals. I power up my computer and shove some earphones into my ear, music helps to clear my mind before I hone in on the matter at hand. There are always breadcrumbs, clues that these fuckers leave behind, I just need to find the trail and then follow it. I close my eyes, leaning back into my chair and run through some questions in my mind.

He knew her name, how? He was strong, does he work out? Does he go to Michael's gym? Did he come across her there? I sit forward in my chair and make note to follow that line of enquiry. Joanna said that she had never met him before, but they may have crossed paths without her knowing. I lean back again, taking my yellow stress ball with me and squeezing it as I return to my thinking.

He drove a white van, why a van? Is it for work?

I sit up again quickly, as an idea strikes me. Davis had mentioned that all of Joanna's clothing had been sent to forensics. I pick up my phone and dial the number and listen patiently for someone to answer. It's not even 9.00 a.m. yet, but there is always someone eager to make an early start, like me.

"FBI Laboratory Services," a sprightly female voice answers the phone, jeez, someone likes their job, I acknowledge before addressing her.

"Hi, this is Agent Roche, from the Boston Bureau; can you connect me with your Scientific Analysis Department please?"

"One moment please," she puts me on hold and I pull the receiver away from my ear, preferring not to listen to the crap music playing down the line.

"Agent, this is Derek Grace, head of this department, how can I help you?" A male voice comes over the line, sounding stressed, before I even give him my query.

"I was wondering if the trace analysis for reference 8809 has come back yet," I roll my lips together, hoping he will look up the file without questioning my involvement. I can hear him typing away on a computer before he comes back on the phone.

"It seems there was a special request for this to be dealt with sooner," he tells me what I already know. "There was analysis run on three different materials found on the skirt and two on the blouse sent to us. I can fax you over the results."

I punch the air happily, before calling out the fax number quickly. A few minutes later, my eyes scan the document, Bingo! I punch the air when my suspicions are confirmed just as Davis walks off the elevator.

"I got the trace analysis back from the lab this morning," I inform him as he sits at his desk next to me and watch as his brows furrow in confusion.

"For which case?"

"Joanna Carmody, it looks...," Davis reaches forward, snatching it out of my hand before I finish my sentence. I leave him looking over it, knowing full well that he will come to the same conclusion as me.

"Mother fucker works in construction," he finally mutters, when he gets to the information regarding the white cement, found on Joanna's skirt. I nod, it is a small lead but it is the first we have had.

"Let's look through the database to see which stores stock this kind of cement," Davis stands, eager to hunt him down.

"Slow down a minute, this is a generic brand sold all over the country, but white cement is usually only used for prestigious developments, so we need to look at high class development projects that are in the final stages."

"Why the final stages?"

"This stuff is used indoors for panelling or for decorative purposes, so we have to assume it is the final stages of development," I shrug.

"We also have to consider that he may not have cleaned his van for a long time, so let's go back a year." I nod and we both pull up Google.

"You take the North, I'll take the South," I say, as I type 'South Boston prestigious developments' into the search bar.

An hour later, Davis throws his pen across his desk, slamming down his phone. "I thought we were in a fucking recession," he growls, running his fingers threw his hair. "That's a total of six developments that have used white cement in the last year. Only two hired the same construction company, which means we are dealing with a total of five construction companies on just the North side," he pinches his eyes. "The good news is that I have zero companies on the South end, so we are looking at workers from five construction sites. The bad news is that they probably outsource some of this to contractors," I shrug. "I'm not happy to call these guys, let's hit the ground and get some answers," Davis stands and I follow his lead.

Jo

The sun seeps in through a small crack in my dark, drawn curtains, arousing me from my sleep. I squint against the bright light and turn away to face the wall. I can hear Michael and Bree talking throughout my apartment and guilt courses through me, I have no energy. I want to drag myself from this dull and dark place, I want to get up and go for a run, but I wouldn't dare be seen looking the way I do. The swelling on my face has gone down and the once deep purple bruising, has now begun to turn yellow and red. I try to convince myself that when the bruising is gone, then everything else will fade away too, the memories will no longer haunt me and I will be able to face the world again. There is a nagging part of my brain that keeps calling bullshit on my theory, calling me a coward and telling me that I am wallowing in self-pity. Joanna Carmody, District Attorney, is kicking my ass to get out of bed and look fear in the eyes, her voice is getting louder as each day passes and today, the volume is full blast. My mind turns to Davis and tears brim in the corner of my eyes, he has been here by my side since it happened and I can't even look him in the eyes.

Joanna, it's time, my sub conscious gently urges me again to reach deeper and find the strength that I so want to feel. I sit up and look around, nothing has changed and yet, everything is different. I am different and I don't like the new me, I don't want to lie down and take it. I want to help get this monster off the streets, I want to continue to get monsters like him off the streets, but more than anything, I want to be myself again and I know what my first step needs to be. I pull back my covers, feeling warmer than I have in days and move to my wardrobe. I want to be comfortable, so I pull some indigo jeans from the top shelf and a cosy mustard coloured, knitted jumper out. I pull open my underwear drawer and look into the array of silk and sexy lingerie, pushing them aside for my Bridget Jones pants. They aren't exactly that big, but they are soft and anything but sexy, I don't want to be sexy.

I gather everything and move towards the bathroom, bumping into Michael on my way.

"Jo Jo, you're up," he smiles broadly.

I look at the tray he is carrying. "Is that for me?" I ask, looking at the warm soup and soft bread, resting on the metal tray. The smell alone warms me and my tummy rumbles. I haven't eaten properly in days, my appetite completely non-existent and although I still feel nauseated, I'm going to force myself to eat.

"I'm going to shower and get dressed, I'll heat it up when

I come out," I smile back. I ignore his shocked expression and make my way to the bathroom.

I walk barefooted from my bedroom, after managing to contain my wild hair into a braid. I didn't bother to blow dry it, wanting to save time. I am barely across the threshold when Bree envelopes me in a huge bear hug;

"You got dressed, oh Jo, I'm so happy to see you up and about," she pulls back, smiling from ear to ear and I take in her bump.

"Oh my God Bree, your bump," I point at the huge mound that was once her flat tummy.

"I know, I'm only four months, the doctor is bringing me in for a scan this week to check everything is ok," she smiles, rubbing her hand across her stomach, lovingly.

"Wow, you just grew over night," my eyes are still wide with shock; I can't believe how pregnant she looks.

"Enough about me," she looks over her shoulder, "Michael, did you reheat the soup?" she calls and I listen as my microwave pings.

"Just done now," he calls back. Bree takes my hand and leads me to my dining table, pulling me down onto the chair, as Michael places the food in front of me. They both sit across from one another and stare at me as I take my first sip.

"Ok, you can stop staring at me in wonder," I roll my eyes and laugh.

"We missed you Jo Jo," Michael reaches over and squeezes my hand and again, I want to cry.

"I miss me too, I'm a little bit lost right now you guys, but I'm going to find myself again," I promise them both and they nod in unison.

"Ok, well enough blubbering, what do you want to do today? I can run out and get us a movie?" Bree suggests, standing from the table.

"I have plans," I announce and they both pause, I think they are in shock. I laugh again and begin to explain the phone call I made before coming out of my cave.

I have walked these floors before, with my brief case in hand and my interview questions rolling around my mind. I have met with the young lady behind the reception area and she has directed me to whatever room I would be conducting my interview in. I move closer to her now and wonder if she recognises me with all my bruising and day time attire. I pull off my baseball cap and sunglasses as I approach her desk.

CHAPTER 16

"Ms. Carmody," her eyes widen in horror and my question is answered. I smile to ease her discomfort at the situation.

"Hi," I falter a little, I don't know her name, "I have an appointment with Gail Jones," I whisper, feeling ashamed again. She nods firmly and moves out from behind her desk.

"Follow me," she ushers me out of the waiting room.

"Gail will be with you shortly," she walks into a warm office space and directs me to sit down on the cream coloured sofa. Her smile is laced with pity, before she pulls the door behind her, leaving me alone. I look around at Gail's office, its cosy and inviting. Across from me, is a single armchair, matching the one that I am sitting on. Beyond the chairs, there is a large desk where I assume she works and behind that, rows of books. I stand up and move towards them, running my fingers along the spines with curiosity. There are all kinds of psychology books, legal aid books and mixed in with them, I find a small romance novel. I smile, pulling it out and turning it over in my hand;

"I read that when my mind gets bogged down with legal jargon and the ramblings of Freud, it helps me escape for a little while," I turn to see Gail walking into her office.

"I'm sorry for snooping," I blush, before quickly returning her book and move back to my seat.

"Don't be silly," she brushes her hand through the air, "this is an open space, feel free to nose about," she winks.

I smile and sit back nervously, into the soft chair. She takes a seat across from me, resting a soft, brown leather briefcase, against the leg of her chair and pulling out a writing pad. I watch as she clicks the top of her ball point pen and makes some notes. I wonder if she is recording my snooping incident, when she looks up from under her red rimmed, reading specs, before pulling them down her nose.

"Sorry," she smiles and shifts to get more comfortable, "I'm delighted that you reached out this morning Joanna." I press my lips together and nod, now that I am here, I have no idea why I came. You came to get help, I remind myself.

"I would like to start this morning Joanna, by letting you know that this was not your fault. Many victims of sexual assault will go through many emotions, ranging from numbness to depression. Blaming yourself for this, is taking the burden of responsibility away from your attacker. They are the only person to blame for this and I want you leaving here today knowing that." I feel my shoulders relax, as my body settles into its surroundings. I am not sure what to say yet so I listen and wait for her to question me.

"This is not something that will go away over-night; it may take time to rebuild your trust in other people, to feel in control of your life again and to open up about your experience. I can't tell you how this will play out emotionally for you because everyone will deal with their own experience differently, but coming here today, will help you to move through each emotion as it develops. This is not something that you can just get over and sweep under the carpet, so when you feel like you should have moved further along, pull yourself back, reign in those negative thoughts and remind yourself to take care of you," her tones are soft and encouraging and for the first time, I want to open up.

"Today is the first day that I have left my bed since it happened, I feel tired all the time. Is that normal?" I chew my lip.

"Joanna, everything that you feel, is normal, there is no right or wrong in how you deal with this. Your body was attacked, not just physically, but emotionally and mentally and it is healing." I nod in understanding and I'm happy I came.

An hour later, I leave Gail's office, promising to return in two days to meet with her again and climb into the back of Michael's SUV. Both of them insisted on driving me here and waiting outside until I was done and to be honest, I was ok with that. I am still a bit nervous about being outside but having talked with Gail, I'm ready to start taking back control of my life. I don't want to live in fear and I don't want to have a twenty four hour babysitter.

"How did it go?" Bree twists around in her seat, as I buckle myself in.

"I'm glad I came, I'm coming back on Thursday again," I shrug and look out my window at the building, as Michael pulls away.

"I'm so proud of you," Bree smiles happily and I remember how I worried about her after her kidnapping and after Michael had faked his own death. I was so worried that I would lose my best friend, but she came back to me and I want to rise from the ashes too.

"I need to ask you guys for a favour," I bite the inside of my cheek; I know I will have a fight on my hands.

"Anything," Michael chimes in.

"I need you to not come by tomorrow, I'm going to ring Eric this evening and start catching up on my caseloads and when the bruising is gone, I'm going back to work." I watch as they both eye each other, looking for the other to respond.

"I don't think Davis will be happy about that," Bree finally mumbles, before shrugging her shoulders at Michael.

"I'll take care of Davis, but I need this, I need to feel normal again," I plead. The atmosphere between us all is thick with fear; I can see them struggling to accept my wishes.

"Jo, I don't know how not to worry about you and I can't promise I won't call every ten minutes, but I know what it feels like to need your life back, so I will respect your request, as long as you promise to keep in touch throughout the day with us, at least until they catch him," Bree finally breaks the silence, pressing down on her lips to stop them wobbling.

"I promise."

"No way!" Davis pulls off his black jacket and runs his fingers through his soft brown hair. "Michael, how could you agree to this?" He growls loudly and I step in to defend them.

"They have no choice Davis; I want to get back to normal. I don't want a babysitter," I stamp my foot down, determined to make him hear me out.

"Today is the first day that you have dressed Joanna, you're not ready for all these changes so soon," he throws his hands in the air.

"I am not a child," I grind out angrily, "you are not my boyfriend, I don't want you here anymore," I lash out unfairly, still unable to meet his intense gaze. I cross my arms at my chest and clamp my mouth closed, to prevent anymore anger spilling out. The room becomes uncomfortably quiet.

"I think we should go and give you some space to talk," Michael suggests and I look up as Davis nods in agreement, his cheeks tinged with embarrassment. My stomach drops; I didn't mean to be so curt. Bree and Michael both hug me and not another word is spoken, until I hear the door close behind them. "Joanna, I know that I hurt you in Hawaii, I'm not trying to be your boyfriend. I want to be your friend and I can't leave you while he is still out there," his voice gets closer and I keep my eyes to the floor until his feet come into focus, forcing me to look up. Our eyes meet briefly, before I shift mine to a photograph of Bree and I, sitting on a shelf on the other side of my small living room. I mull over his words, I don't want to be your boyfriend and my skin heats with anger. I can't say I blame him, who would want to be with me after some monster violated me? Who would want to lie next to me and listen, as I relive it night after night in my dreams? I know that he doesn't want to be my boyfriend, shit I knew that in Hawaii, but I don't need to hear him say it. I don't want to hear it out loud.

"I don't care about Hawaii Davis; I have bigger fish to fry than how you treated me in Hawaii!" I can't help the new anger bubbling up to the surface, I can't help that I am directing it all at him. I've cried, I've felt numb, I've felt depressed and right now, I feel so fucking angry that I want to tear him down and make him feel an ounce of my pain. I know it's not fair, I know it's irrational and displaced, but I'm so tired of being considerate and rational. I want to blame the world and be damned with whoever doesn't like it.

"I'm sorry I brought that up, it was stupid. I am only trying to explain that I can't leave you while you're like this, while he is out there. I won't do it Joanna, I won't leave," his tone goes from soft and apologetic, to sharp and determined and I reach forward, pushing at his chest.

"You get out now, get out of my apartment," I scream, pushing him with all my might. He doesn't try to restrain me; he doesn't move aside. He allows me to push and shove him.

"Joanna, stop this," his tone is soft again and it is my undoing. I step away and look him dead in the eye.

"Are you hanging around, hoping to finish what we started in Hawaii, you're sick!" I spit, venomously and watch as he pales. He moves away from me, reaching for his jacket and walks towards the door.

Pulling it open, he speaks, "I'll be close by, call me if you need me," his head is down, his voice defeated, as he closes the door behind him. "Joanna, please put the dead bolt on," I hear him from the other side and I move forwards and reach with shaking hands for the dead bolt, securing it.

"Typical," I say to nobody a few hours later. For the past week, I have fell straight asleep as soon as my head hit the pillow and tonight, I'm restless. I don't feel the better of my argument with Davis and really regret being so mean to him, he didn't deserve to be made to feel like a pervert. I directed all my rage towards him and instead of feeling better, I feel ashamed. I close my eyes again and attempt to sleep'

"Open your fucking eyes or I am going to stab you," his voice is shaky, his earlier composure beginning to slip and I open my eyes. He dangles a large knife over me, playing with the tip to further terrorise me, I keep my face blank. It takes everything in me not to scream or cry again but I have no way out and the only thing that might save me now, is power play. Without another word, he easily slices through my skirt and shirt, nipping my stomach. He moans in pleasure, his fingers running slowly down my stomach and I squirm away from his ugly touch.

"I'm going to make you pay for teasing me for so long," he licks his lips before lowering his head.

My eyes pop open and I am shrouded in darkness. I feel pinned to my bed, my body paralysed. I can't scream out, I can't move and I will my leg to kick. I am terrified and close my eyes again, afraid that someone is in my room, before my leg finally moves. Power returns to my entire body and I quickly jump up and switch on my bedroom light, panting and sweating in the cold air. The clock on my dresser reads 3.30 a.m. and I lean forward, grabbing my knees, trying to control my breathing again. My wardrobe is open a crack and I stand staring at it, was it open before I went to sleep? My heart beats hard against my chest and once again, fear pins me to the spot. My phone buzzes on my locker and I move to it, keeping my eyes on the wardrobe.

CHAPTER
17

"Hello," I pant heavily.

"Joanna, are you ok?" Davis' worried tones come down the line.

"I don't know, my wardrobe is open, I can't remember if I left it open," I whisper.

"Come to the door Joanna, I'm outside," he demands and I don't hesitate. I run from my room and pull open the door, letting him in.

"Lock the door behind me and stay here," his brows are knitted together, as he pulls his gun from his holster and moves throughout my apartment, checking each room, leaving the bedroom until last. I wait, expecting to hear a struggle; instead, Davis comes out and holsters his gun.

"It's ok, there is no one there," he sighs, running his hands over his stubbly jaw. I look at him for the first time in seven days, really look at him. He has lost weight too, his eyes are sunken and he is almost sporting a full beard. He looks like he has been to hell and back.

"How did you get here so soon?" I ask.

"I was in my car, I saw your light come on and came straight up," he admits, as he walks back to the door, "lock up behind me."

"Davis," I turn towards him, my eyes downcast again, as I leave his name hanging in the air,

"I can't remember anything good, all I can think about is him and I can't sleep without dreaming about him," my whispering tones are rasped. Davis turns toward the door, but instead of leaving, he locks it before taking my hand and leading me into the living room. I watch as he pulls out his phone, pressing some buttons, before tipping my chin up with his fingers and forcing me to look directly into his eyes.

"I want to share one of my happiest memories with you Joanna, do you trust me?" He asks and I nod, as silent tears burn my eyes. "Close your eyes and listen to me," he urges and I do as he asks. I listen as a familiar song begins to surround us and I recognise it as the song we danced to at Bree and Michaels wedding. He lifts one of my hands to his shoulder and takes the other in his hand, before pulling my body flush with his.

"You looked so beautiful in that pale blue dress with freckles, sprinkled across your face Joanna. I couldn't take my eyes off you; remember our time on the dance floor? You had a life before he tried to destroy you and you can visit happier times when you feel afraid, pick whatever moment shines brightest in your memory and go there when darkness looms." His body sways me gently and I open my eyes, allowing my tears to flow. I lift my arms and wrap them both around his midriff and hug him tightly, resting against his chest. His strong arms come around mine and I feel his cheek on top of my head, as the soft music floats around us.

"I'm sorry I was so mean earlier," I turn up to look into his green eyes. The room is dark, with only the light from the hallway peering through the crack in the door, I feel safe looking into his eyes when he can barely see me.

"It's ok Joanna, I just want to help," despite the darkness, I see the emotion behind his words. I reach up and run my fingers along his bearded jawline.

"I like this," I smile, before reaching up and planting a soft kiss on his lips. I taste the salt from my tears and hold my lips against his, for just a moment longer than I should. When I pull away, he dips his mouth to the crook of my neck, breathing deeply and hugging me hard against his body.

"Please let me stay and keep you safe," his words sound as desperate as his hug and I admit to myself and him, that I need him. "Ok."

Razor

"Hey, Mom said you wanted to talk to me, what's up?" I ask my brother casually down the line, looking over my shoulder towards my Mom, who is eyeing me suspiciously from the kitchen.

"I can't talk for much longer," I hear his teeth grinding

and imagine his jaw twitching.

"Yeah, so what's up?" I continue to act dumb, knowing full well the shit storm that I have unloaded on him and my entire family.

"Clean that mess up for Mom, you hear me?" He whispers low and deathly.

"I'm on it."

"I don't mean tidy things up Razor, make this mess disappear, before the package arrives." "When can I expect it?" I try to gauge how much time I have.

"Three months, maybe four, depending on shipping." I shift my eyes over my shoulder again and as I suspected, my Mom is listening to every word. I move further away, stretching the white telephone line as far as it will go.

"Speaking of packages, looks like the rat will get one soon enough," I swallow, waiting on instructions. I hate the fear my brother elicits in me. He is five years older and has always pushed me around, but I'm just as big as him now and I've promised myself to put my foot down as soon as he gets home.

"How soon?"

"It's hard to tell, maybe six or seven months," I shrug, what the fuck am I? I'm not a fucking Doctor!

"I'll pass it on and Razor?"

"Yeah?"

"If you don't help Mom clean up your mess for good, you won't get to be here when the package arrives," the phone slams down, ending the call and leaving the threat hanging in the air. I knew the moment the news reported the rape, I was in trouble. I was supposed to keep my distance and wait, but I am tired of being the dutiful brother. I clean up my own goddamn mess because I want to, not because some aging prick tells me to.

"FUCK," I yell, slamming my own receiver against the phone hanging on the wall, breaking it, before grabbing my keys and storming out to my van. It has been two weeks now, surely some of the heat will have died down.

Roche

     I log off my computer for the evening and stand, stretching my tight muscles. My days have been too long lately, but I can't justify going home to an empty apartment while unsolved crimes lie on my desk. I'm not the only straggler left behind; other agents, also married to the job, linger on, finishing up on their caseloads. My feet are tired, despite having been sitting the last three hours, but that's what happens when you spend your day walking around a building site. With three out of our targeted building sites visited, we are no closer to pinning down a suspect. The DNA left behind, is still being processed and will take a few more weeks; in the meantime, it's like finding a needle in a haystack. Every builder and contractor that we spoke to, all said the same thing.

"Nah, I don't know anyone who fits that description," they'd shrugged. The FBI are not the most welcomed people in town, but these guys have no tolerance for our presence.

"Most of the lads drive white vans," they'd spouted, laughing at our silliness to assume we could track down the correct van.

"On site, I'm whatever the boss-man wants me to be, glazer, plasterer, cement mixer, plumber, you name it, we do it," they'd announced, proudly, squashing our hopes that it would be a specialised job. With our own investigations falling behind, we have to put a hold on the other two sites for a week or two, but that's no good. Davis, although a pain in my ass at the best of times, is my friend and Joanna means something to him, so while he might not be able to be here putting in the extra hours, I can. I intend to keep on track with this investigation but for tonight, I'm grabbing a beer and having an early night. Building sites usually open around 7.00 a.m. so no harm getting an early start.

Jo

"Wait a second," Davis pulls my forearm as I move to leave his SUV, "do you remember everything I told you?" I look down at his strong hand as it grips me gently and back up to his face. He looks miserable.

"I promise to call or text every hour, I will travel with Eric if I need to go anywhere and I will not leave the building on my own, at any point, for any reason and under no circumstances, will I leave work this evening until you arrive," I roll my eyes, exasperated. He has drilled home his requests, almost every hour, since I told him three days ago that I was returning to work. I have agreed because he is not asking me to do anything I wouldn't have already been doing myself and also, because I thought that he would relax a little. I was wrong, he looks like he is about to have a panic attack.

"Davis, you're going to be late, I'll be in touch soon," I lean back into the car and plant a chaste kiss on his cheek, inhaling his spicy scent. He reluctantly releases his grip and I slide promptly from his car, only to be met by a waiting Eric. Davis has roped him into agreeing to be my security guard while I'm at work.

"Hey beautiful," he hugs me and I pull away, shoving him playfully.

"Less of this mushy stuff please," I joke trying to avoid the, I'm so sorry this happened, conversation. "Where's my coffee?" I narrow my eyes.

"Nice to see you too," he links my arm and walks towards our office, "coffee is on your desk, wench," he purse's his lips. I squeeze his bicep gratefully and he winks, he understands my silent request and I am reminded once again, how lucky I am to be alive. I have continued going to my sessions with Gail but tomorrow evening, she has asked me to join in on a group discussion and it terrifies me. I hardly talk about it with my friends, never mind a bunch of strangers.

"So, what's first on the agenda?" I slide into my red

leather, office chair and lift the coffee cup that Eric purchased to my lips.

"Henry Vincent has his pre-trial hearing in three days, I have prepared all your court documents, but I wasn't sure if you planned to offer him a plea bargain?" Eric is already handing me the manila folder. I open it and familiarise myself with the case. Henry Vincent stalked his ex-girlfriend, harassed her with abusive phone calls, and broke two restraining orders so as to verbally abuse her at her work place, to be finally caught on her premises, in the middle of the night, dressed all in black. A cold shiver runs down my spine when I think of the possible plans he had that night. He was a rich kid, fresh out of college and full of self-importance, he doesn't swallow rejection very well.

"I remember this one, he is a smarmy little shit," I lean back and consider my options, I don't have many. I was a little premature when I pushed for a felony charge, but I was hoping to drag a confession out of him. I'm sure if I pushed him hard enough on the stand, his cool façade would crack and he would reveal his true self to the jury, but I can't risk him walking away without doing any jail time.

"He has been out on bail for almost a month now, has he made contact with his victim?" I call her victim and the word leaves a bad taste in my mouth. I pull over the manila folder again and correct myself, "Grace Rothwell, has he tried to break the terms of bail or the restraining order?"

"No, he has been on his best behaviour, his lawyer put in a motion to have the felony charge thrown out," Eric drops into the seat across from me.

"Yeah, it's a tough stretch, hopefully he will plead guilty, maybe do a year or two for breaking the restraining order," I shrug, hoping that my original plan would still fall into place.

"I'm not so sure that this kid will play ball, there is something overly cocky about him," Eric says, crossing one foot over his knee and removing some fluff from his blue slacks.

"I'll work my magic," I promise. "Next?"

We spend the morning catching up and I am pretty certain that I will be practically living in my office for the next three weeks. Eric went out and got some take away for lunch and we munched at my desk while we continued to work. After lunch, my boss called me into his office to confirm for himself that I was ready to be back on the horse.

"Joanna, you can take more time if you need it." Grayson Bright is the Chief Assistant District Attorney for our jurisdiction and is second only to the head prosecutor of Boston. He was the first person to welcome me into my position as Assistant District Attorney, four years ago and even allowed me to sit second chair with him, on one of the biggest serial murder cases to hit Boston in years. He is a dominant man, not only in his appearance but also in his demeanour. At over 6ft and built like an ox, he has proven to be a force to be reckoned with inside a court room and many defence attorneys, rattle when pitted against him. His success rate is untarnished and he has taught me so much in my short few years here. Since his promotion, his court room appearances have lessened and his once black hair, has now turned grey. I often wonder if the court room trial kept him younger or if the responsibility of his role as chief prosecutor, has taken its toll on him.

"No sir, I am ready to be back," I pull my shoulders back and look him straight in the eyes. I know he can read any man like a book and I am determined to prove to him that I am where I should be.

"I trust you, have the police made an arrest?" He asks firmly.

"No, not yet and I don't believe they have any leads."

"I will put in a call this afternoon, who is the lead detective?" He is not a man to display any kind of emotion, but his eyes reveal a softness that I have never seen before.

"Vic Breen."

"Good detective, I'm surprised that they are so far behind," he clucks, leaning back into his brown leather chair and stroking his chin as he contemplates the situation.

"I'm sure he is doing all he can," I roll my lips together, hoping to be dismissed soon. I'm not sure if this topic is to test whether or not I will break down and I don't want to risk it.

"Is that all sir?" I smile to hide my discomfort and move to stand.

"Yes," he nods and I turn to leave, "oh Joanna, it's good to have you back, we missed you around here," he nods. I say nothing and return his nod with the same fake smile, still planted on my face.

CHAPTER 18

The smell in Bree's kitchen is to die for.

"What's this?" I ask, already lifting the lid and peering into the large metal pot. I look around at all her hard work and feel guilty. "Bree, it all looks beautiful and smells amazing too," I inhale the mouth-watering aromas again.

"Chicken soup for starters," Bree bumps me out of the way and stirs her broth. Michael and Davis have snuck off to watch the football and drink beer before dinner. Thanksgiving has never meant more to me than it does this year. I am alive and surrounded by wonderful friends.

"How was your first week back?" Bree wonders, as she pulls open the oven to check the turkey. She looks radiant in her pregnancy. Her hair is down and flowing over her larger than normal breasts. She is a picture in her loose black, maternity dress and flip flops and I try not to giggle.

"Great, it feels like I'm getting back to normal, how's this little beauty doing?" I move closer and rub her belly, as she leans against the countertop.

"They are kicking the crap out of me on a daily basis, I think it's definitely a boy!" She beams. "I'm so happy that you are starting to feel better Jo, but you know I'm here when you have a bad day, right?" The sadness in her eyes as she switches back to our previous conversation, reminds me of the times I worried about her and I try to put her mind at ease.

"I know Bree, what else are best friends for?" She seems happy with my answer.

"Just don't overdo it in work," she pleads, "I just don't want you to push too hard and then end up like me," she blushes deeply.

"I am doing better, I promise," I try to hug her, but her bump makes it awkward and we both giggle.

"How is living with Davis?" She changes the subject, her eyes lighting up at this topic.

"It's the strangest thing ever," I lean back against the island and cross my arms over my chest, "we get on great, I'm up earlier than him, so I shower first and just as I am finished in the bathroom, he is ready. We take turns doing the dishes and he can cook pretty well," I smile, thinking about how easy being around Davis has been for the last few weeks.

"Where is he sleeping?" Bree asks, making herself busy about the kitchen.

"The first few nights, he slept in my bed until I fell to sleep and then moved to the sofa, but most nights, I fall asleep while we watch a movie and he carries me in, so we haven't been in bed together since then," I tell her honestly. My stomach dips with pleasure and I gasp at the familiar feeling.

"What?" Bree's eyebrows furrow.

"Nothing," I shake my head. Things between me and Davis have been purely platonic since Hawaii, he admitted that he wasn't trying to be my boyfriend and I don't want to indulge in any fantasies. I tilt my head, rubbing my fingers across my head as the realisation that my feelings for Davis are not only still there, they are stronger. The emotion that it spurs, takes my breath away and my chest aches as I try to hold it in, not wanting to cry again.

"Hey, what's wrong," Bree comes around the table and takes my hand in hers.

"I don't know what's wrong with me, I'm going mad," I laugh, blinking back tears.

"Jo, tell me what's wrong, are you having a memory?" I shake my head, no.

"It's not that, well it is, but I'm not thinking about that right now," I stumble over my words, trying to explain what I don't even understand myself.

"Three weeks ago, I didn't want to live, I was broken and even though it's still raw, those intense feelings have lessened," I pull out a chair at the table and plop down in the seat. "Just now, I got butterflies when you asked about Davis and it's the first time I've felt excited," I flick my hair out of my face.

"That's good, why are you upset?" Bree laughs softly, taking a seat beside me.

"He doesn't see me like that and besides, I can't give

him what he needs," my skin heats and I begin to feel nauseas just thinking about sex.

"Jo, a blind man on a horse could see Davis has feelings for you, do you mean...?" Bree shifts in her seat, finding it uncomfortable when talking about sex.

"Yes, I'm still waiting on the all clear and even then, I'm not ready," I nibble my top lip.

"What are you two whispering about?" Michael booms, causing us both to jump up.

"Michael you ass, you scared us," Bree scolds him.

"Sorry Jo Jo, I didn't mean to make you jump," he immediately blurts out, as Davis walks in behind him.

"What about your wife? Don't I get an apology, you might have frightened the babies," Bree whacks him playfully with her dish cloth. I almost miss her words, but Michael's next action confirms what I thought I heard.

"I'm sorry babies," Michael bends, kissing Bree's bump.

"Whoa, whoa, whoa, BABIES?!?" I shriek, springing up from my chair, not sure where I intend to go. Bree and Michael glance at each other and smile guiltily.

"Cat's out of the bag," Bree shrugs to him. Davis comes to my side.

"Are you serious?" He laughs.

"Yep, what can I say, I've got strong swimmers," Michael says, proudly.

"Wait, how many are in there?" I ask, moving to Bree as Davis pats Michael on the back.

"Two, we are having twins," Bree beams happily, I congratulate them both with hugs and more shocked gasps. Twins! I can't believe they are having twins.

"So how will you manage Bree?" I ask after dinner.

"Well, for the first year or two, we are going to hire a nanny to help me, I'm going to leave college and when the business settles for Michael and the children are in school, I might reapply, but right now, I want to concentrate on my family," I look back and forth between them as Bree talks and they seem to have it all worked out. Not only that, they are on top of the world.

"Do you know the sex?" Davis asks.

"No, I wanted to wait," Michael smiles, proudly. I can already tell he is going to idolise his children.

"I still can't believe it!" I laugh, trying to comprehend that in less than five months, there will be two babies filling this house with more love. I think we all enjoy our thanksgiving dinner a little more after their wonderful announcement. It fills me with joy and excitement for the future and for that, I am truly thankful.

Davis and I settle into our usual nightly routine when we get home from Bree and Michaels. I am still buzzing from their huge news.

"Can you believe it, TWINS!" I throw my hands in the air, before plopping down onto my sofa. I look up at Davis as he puts his USB stick into the TV; he has stripped into a pair of black cotton bottoms and a white t-shirt. His hair is still damp from his shower and I don't think I've ever seen him look so good. I smile broadly at him as he nestles in beside me, tucking me under his arm.

"What are you smiling about," he eyes me suspiciously.

"Your big honky feet," I tease him.

"I have great feet," he pretends to be offended and lifts his leg to showcase exhibit A.

"Your second toe is bigger than your big toe," I giggle at how defensive he is.

"That's called Morton's toe, it's completely normal! It's also known as the Greek foot." I sit up and turn to look at him.

"You googled your toes?" I laugh louder.

"Yeah, I was curious," he laughs again, "let's take a look at your feet, Ms Perfect," he pulls my leg up and I fall back against him, giggling.

"See, perfectly straight," I say, smugly.

"They are like two little squares," he sputters and I pull my foot free.

"I have cute feet."

"You have frog feet!" He cracks himself up.

"Ha, says greeky feet," I nudge him in the ribs and he

jumps up quickly to grab my foot again. When he begins to tickle the sole of my foot, I twist and turn hysterically, trying to free myself from his torture. I kick and wriggle and before I know it, Davis is above me as I lie flat on my back, his eyes scorching me with desire. My breathing, already ragged from our play fight, hitches and my chest rises and falls rapidly. We stare at each other for a long moment, before Davis dips his head and takes my lips. My eyes flutter closed as my lips part for him, allowing him access to my mouth. His kiss is deep but soft and for one brief special moment, I forget everything that has happened, I allow myself to taste and kiss him back, until a voice in my head cuts through my happy bubble.

Open your fucking eyes, the memory of his angry words cause my eyes to snap open and I jump up quickly, moving to the other end of the sofa quickly. I pull my knees to my chest and push my hair from my face, unable to look at him.

"I'm sorry, I can't," I fret.

"Joanna, I'm sorry, I should have resisted," the sound of his coarse tones, pull my eyes to him. He is sitting at the edge of the sofa, his head down and running his fingers through his hair.

"You'll cause your hair to go fuzzy," I whisper, I don't want tension between us.

"Serves me right," he tilts his head sideways and smiles at me.

"I don't know if I can ever, you know?" I admit honestly, because he deserves the truth.

"I am a selfish prick; I should have stopped myself."

"Davis, I'm afraid," I whisper.

"I'm here Joanna, you don't need to be afraid," he reaches over, squeezing my hand.

"That's what I'm afraid of."

"What do you mean?" His voice lowers and he tugs on my hand, forcing me to meet his eyes.

"I don't want to become too reliant on you, what if you meet someone? And what about when you want to get back to your own life? That will happen and I don't want to...," his lips turn up at the corners, stopping me mid-sentence, "what are you smiling at?" I frown.

"I thought that you were afraid I'd hurt you, but you're afraid I'm going to leave," his smile widens, his straight white teeth almost blinding me and it's contagious, I can't help but smile.

"Well, yes but only because I don't want to be on my own right now," I roll my eyes in an attempt to burst his gigantic ego.

"Shush, you've made yourself clear, you're mad about me," he begins laughing and I can't believe that two minutes ago, I was huddled away from him on the sofa.

"You're so vain," I join in, his happiness is infectious.

"Yeah, but you love it, get over me already," he flicks his hair dramatically. I have never seen this side of Davis, he is being so playful and it has completely diffused the awkward moment we just shared.

"Come here," he tugs my hand harder, pulling me to his side, "the movie is starting," he bends down and kisses the top of my head, before falling back into our original position on the sofa.

CHAPTER
19

Jo

There is something magical about this time of year that always fills me with joy. I can't help but act like a child and walk on the untouched snow, covering the entrance to my office building. The feel of the snow crunching beneath my shoes and the sounds that it makes, leaves me feeling warm and fuzzy. It is only two weeks until Christmas and despite everything that has happened over the last few months, I'm doing my best to feel excited. Davis is still staying with me; he drops me to work and collects me in the evening. He has been a constant in my life and it terrifies me that when the time comes for him to get back to his own life, I won't remember how to be independent. My feelings for him have grown deeper, but I know my dependency on him, is unhealthy. The old me wants to force myself to ask him to leave, allow myself the opportunity to move past my fears and take back full control of my life. The other part of me never wants to be without him and that side, is winning out. I received news from the hospital last week that my test results had come back clear and with that amazing news, comes the realisation that nothing but my fear of intimacy, is stopping me from taking that next step with him. He hasn't kissed me since that night on my sofa, but there is chemistry between us that can't be ignored forever. He looks at me with want and desire shining in his eyes and it's becoming increasingly hard to deny my own sexual urges towards him. I often wonder how he manages so much control over this electricity that shoots between us, when the only thing stopping me, is the fear of how sex has changed for me. The idea of allowing him to see me naked, to bare myself to him completely, scars and all, causes utter panic to course through my body, quickly stamping down any feelings of desire. I have talked to Gail about this and her advice is always the same.

"When you are ready, you will know. Don't force yourself to feel ok about trusting a man with your body; don't beat yourself up because you want to please him. Trust your own self and when the time is right, you will take that step in confidence."

I hope she is right and that these feelings won't last forever. I shake the snow from my black, beanie hat and jacket when I step inside the building and out of the cold. I received a text message to attend a meeting with my superior first thing, so I nervously make my way to the fifth floor, where his office is located. The last time I was called here was after my attack and I'm hoping my performance hasn't worsened.

Grayson's secretary announces my arrival and a moment later, I am called into his office. He smiles broadly at me, before offering me a seat across from him.

"Joanna, how are you keeping?" He asks, moving to his own chair and sitting down behind his large mahogany desk.

"I'm doing great sir, taking it one day at a time," I cross my legs and rest my hands against the arm of my chair and wait for him to continue.

"I don't want to waste your time so I'm going to get straight to the point. I am sure you aware that Seamus Lynch was granted a hearing to determine whether or not he will receive a retrial. The date has been set for February and I don't need to tell you Joanna, that this is going to get messy," he fixes his red tie and sits back. My stomach turns over, knowing that in two months, Bree and Michael will, once again, be facing the possibility of a retrial.

"I assume our office won't be handling it?" I presume.

"No, we are to have no involvement moving forward and I need you to stay out of this matter, completely. The media are going to have a field day with this one and I don't want to jeopardise the integrity of this office any further."

I feel myself blush at his words, my job is my life and the idea that my involvement in anything, could possibly do damage to all the amazing work we do here, is soul destroying.

"Of course," I manage and he stands, informing me that

our meeting is over.

"Joanna, you are one of my best and I know that these claims are ludicrous. The connections formed after this trial, should not warrant this insanity but unfortunately, it is all a bit too close to home to be ignored," he walks me to the door.

"I understand," I nod solemnly.

He shakes my hand before I turn to leave. My thoughts are immediately with Bree. She is due the babies in March, with the possibility that she could go early, the stress of this impending hearing at the same time, might be too much for her to bear. This was also a sore point for Davis and I and bringing it all back up with him now, is like giving him a reason to leave me sooner.

Davis

I rub the sleep from my eyes and follow behind Roche, into the lion's den. Special Agent in charge, Rick Myers, summoned us as soon as we arrived and looking at his face now, I don't think it was to give us a pay rise. I take the seat across from his desk and Roche sits next to me.

"Morning Sir," Roche breaks the silence.

"Morning," I nod. We watch as he sits forward, resting his elbows on his desk and steeples his fingers under his chin. He is doing his usual routine, before he chews you out and waiting for him to spit out what he called us here for, is agony. I wait impatiently for his customary sigh and like clockwork, it comes.

"Vic Breen from Boston P.D phoned me this morning," he begins pursing his lips. I slide further into my seat; I had prepared for this.

"Yes?" I say nothing else; I'm not sure how much Vic knows about our own private investigation.

"It appears somebody requested that the evidence from the Joanna Carmody rape case, be transferred from the State Police Forensic Labs here in Boston, to the FBI labs in Virginia," he lifts one brow, questioningly at me.

"That was me Sir," Roche confesses too soon, damn him.

"And can you tell me why you interfered in a case that you have no jurisdiction over?" He begins to become flustered.

"I asked him to make the call," I sit up straight, "Joanna is a friend and Vic Breen refused to allow me to help by having the evidence processed sooner, I took matters into my own hand. She is an Assistant District Attorney for goodness sake," I try to remain calm, but the politics of this shit annoys me.

"You have no authority to go over his head, or mine, because you think you know best," Rick's voice booms louder.

"Did you ask him what he has uncovered in the weeks since it happened?" I yell back.

"He said they had some leads, but was mortified when he put in a call to find out about the forensic results, only to be told you had signed off to have them moved out of State!" Rick stands up and throws his reading spectacles across his desk.

"He is an asshole and he knows fuck all about who raped her!"

"And you do?"

"Not yet but we are getting close."

"Seamus Lynch's appeal trial has been set for February and your relationship with Joanna Carmody, is his grounds for dismissal and here you are, interfering in her rape case, are you trying to sabotage all our hard work?" His eyes narrow with unmasked anger.

"I am trying to help a friend and he won't walk free," I growl, I will not have my reputation tarnished on the back of what a career criminal says.

"Do you realise how bad this is?" He furrows his brows.

"Of course I realise, but its bullshit."

"The head prosecutor at Seamus Lynch's trial, was Joanna Carmody's boss. The key eye witness, is Joanna Carmody's best friend and she is now married to the state witness, Michael Ryan! Not only that, but the lead agent in charge of making the Seamus Lynch arrest, was YOU. You were best man at Michael and Bree's wedding and now, you're running around trying to solve the crime against Joanna, so let me remind you that it looks very fucking bad and if he walks, we are all facing a media shit storm."

I run my fingers through my hair, I'm not stupid. Of course I had thought about the links when I heard about Seamus Lynch putting a motion in for a retrial, but our relationships had developed after the case had been solved.

"That was all after the fact," I roll my eyes.

"You and I know that, but if Lynch's defence team twist it the right way Davis," he throws his hands in the air, as if dealing with an idiot, before flopping back into his seat. "I want you two on the first flight to Quantico, you will be training in the Active Shooter programme this week and I'm warning you both now, to stay away from the Joanna Carmody case."

"Can't you send anyone else?" I want to scream, but keep my voice steady; I need to convince Rick to keep me in Boston.

"No, you know about the ALERRT programme, you will be conducting Protocol Training for first response officers, arriving on the scene of an active shooter. There will also be a two day conference I want you to attend while you're out there, Agent Bryce will fill you in when you arrive," he keeps his head down, as he signs off on some document and I practice my breathing, trying to calm down.

"Sir, I can't leave Boston right now, Joanna needs me," I stop myself when I realise that it is exactly the reason I am being sent.

"It's your choice Agents, Vic Breen is leading the investigation into Joanna Carmody's rape, now you both either get on that plane to Quantico or hand over your badges."

"This is a rookie duty and you know it," I growl, before storming out of his office. I have no choice but to go, but

I don't have long to arrange for Joanna to stay with Bree and Michael while I'm away.

Jo

My eyes drift closed again, as I stare at my computer. Davis has been away at Quantico for almost a week now and I haven't slept properly since he left. I look down at the time on my wrist and roll my shoulders back, to ease the knots. I have been in the office since 7.00 a.m. thanks to Michael's early morning routines and although I'm generally an early bird, I don't usually stay in the office until after 10.00 p.m. when I do an early shift. For the past few weeks, I have busted my ass to catch up with my case load, but I'm finally where I want to be with work and I still have another two hours before Michael closes the gym. I don't know how he works such long hours and still manages to be full of energy in the car on the way home. Bree arrives to the gym most nights and travels home with us, but I can't face an hour's drive to Salem. Christmas is in ten days and I have no gifts, no tree or decorations up at home. A little thrill excites me when I think about having my apartment ready for when Davis gets home, God I miss him. I'm exhausted, I need my own bed, a bath and a good night's sleep and then I can start planning for Davis' return. He has been so good to me the past few months, I really want to get him something special to say thank you.

"You look tired," Eric comes behind me and massages my shoulders.

"I think I could fall asleep on a bed of rocks right now," I yawn.

"Get your stuff and I'll drive you to the gym, Michael might close up early," Eric twists me around in my chair and begins to pull me up. I start laughing.

"Well, actually, you could do one better."

CHAPTER 20

Davis

"Michael, what's up?" I walk out of the conference hall to take Michaels call.

"I don't want you to freak out, but Joanna just sent me a text to say that Eric was dropping her home to her apartment, she wanted to stay there tonight."

"No, just drag her kicking and screaming," I run my hand down my face, instantly stressed out.

"Well I called her and she insisted, I came by to talk to her and she is not answering the door, I phoned Eric and he dropped her off an hour ago."

"Kick it down," I order, frustrated that he hasn't already forced his way in, anything could be wrong with her.

"Wait," Michael goes off the line and I begin to pace up and down the carpeted hallway.

"It's ok, she was in the bath, I'm here with her now, I'll have a talk with her."

I puff out the breath I was holding and try to remain calm.

"Put her on," I growl, grinding my teeth in an effort not to scream at her. "Joanna, what the hell are you playing at?" I bark anyway.

"Hi to you too," she smarts and I take another deep breath.

"Joanna, you know that it's not safe for you to be there alone while...," I press my lips together; I don't want to scare her but at the same time, she should know the dangers.

"I know the dangers Davis, it has been seven weeks since I have spent a night on my own and I want to try. I can't live my life like this with constant babysitters. I am not staying with Michael tonight and he is going home to his pregnant wife to take care of her, enough of this nonsense." I open my mouth to speak again but the line goes dead, she hung up on me. Did she actually just hang up on me? Of all the stupid, idiotic things to do!

Jo

I put a hammer under my pillow before I slide into my fresh silk, lilac sheets and pull my heavy duvet to my chin and smile, I feel ok. I feel safe and even though I miss Davis, I'm glad that I took this night to myself. It has spurred me to regain more and more of my independence. I had to practically push Michael out of my apartment and only for Bree agreeing with me, I'm not sure he'd have left. Bree understands my fears and my need to feel normal again. I didn't think it was possible for us to bond any further, but over the past seven weeks, she has been a rock. They all have and I know Davis will be upset. I don't want to fall out with him, I know his heart is in the right place and that his concerns are legitimate, but I need to get on with my life, knowing that my attacker may never be caught. I decide to leave my bedside lamp and bathroom lights on for extra comfort, but my eyes are too heavy to care and I fall asleep straight away.

"Joanna," I swipe away the cold fingers that run along my cheek and turn over in my bed.

"Wake up Joanna, it's me," the familiar voice breaks through my deep sleep and I stir again. My eyes pop open and I feel the weight on my bed behind me. I quickly snap them closed and concentrate on my breathing, moving my hand slowly to grip the handle of my hammer. I feel a hand on my shoulder and without thinking, I swing around, the butt of the hammer raised high.

"Holy FUCK!" I hear a man roar as I scramble to the end of the bed and fall off the edge. I jump to my feet, raise the hammer above my head, my glasses are on my bedside locker and my vision is blurred.

"Get OUT," I yell, hysterically.

"Jesus Joanna, it's me," Davis' voice cuts through my yelling and I freeze, confused and not sure if I recognised his voice correctly.

"Davis?"

"Yep," he groans and I drop the hammer and move to

him.

"What the hell were you thinking? You, asshole!" I whack him across the shoulder or at least I think it's his shoulder. It takes me about twenty seconds to realise that his head is down and he is holding it in his hands. I step back as it dawns on me that I hit him with the hammer.

"Oh shit, Davis," I gasp and grab my glasses.

I gasp again when I register the blood on his shirt and his pale complexion; it's not like him to be so quiet. I lift his chin in my hands and force him to look at me.

"How many fingers am I holding up?" I stick up my middle finger and he smiles.

"Ok, you're alert at least," I smile back, before looking at his head. There is a small gash above his temple.

"Wait here, I have a first aid kit," I rush from the room to the kitchen. I return a minute later, unzipping the bag and taking out supplies. I push his legs apart and stand between them and pull his head up. I press some cotton wadding over the wound and soak up the blood, before looking at it again.

"It's just a scratch," I lie. It's not too deep so I clean it with some antibiotic cream and put some butterfly stitches in place.

"There, brand new," I move to step from between his legs and look down to find him staring up at me, with a smile on his face. He wraps his arms around my stomach and pulls me against him so his head is resting on my tummy.

"I missed you," he whispers. I notice my clothing, or lack of and cringe with embarrassment. I wore a black vest top and black French underwear to bed and only moments ago, I was basically rubbing Davis' face in my unrestrained breasts. My stomach pulls downwards and I feel myself moisten. My breath hitches because with this feeling, comes fear.

"I missed you too," I swallow hard, my throat is suddenly parched.

"You're shaking," Davis pulls back and stands, "are you

cold?"

"No," I shake my head, keeping eye contact, "I'm nervous," I croak.

"I tried to wake you gently," he pushes my hair behind my ear and without thinking, I turn into his hand and kiss his palm. I have no idea if I can go through with what I want to do, but my attraction to Davis right now, is far outweighing my fears and insecurities. I step easily towards him and run my hands up his shirt and over his shoulders.

"Your jacket has blood on it," I whisper, before sliding it off. I take it and fold it neatly on my bed. Davis' eyes follow me, I can tell he is fighting his own demons and struggling.

"Joanna," Davis' voice is a warning, but his deep velvety tones, only further my determination as I step back towards him. I reach up and start to unbutton his white shirt.

"You got blood on this too." His hand comes over mine when I am half way down.

"Joanna look at me," he demands and I look up from under my lashes.

"Are you sure?" He asks, knowing full well what I am asking of him and myself. I nod, "yes" and he dips his head and takes my lips softly. His hands cup the sides of my face as he pulls me back towards the bed.

"Do you want me to turn off the lamp?" I ask.

"No, I want to see you," he smiles.

I bite my lower lip at his boyish grin and lean up on my toes to kiss him again. Davis pulls back my blankets and I help him lose the rest of his clothes, until we are both lying side by side, in only our underwear.

"You need to tell me to stop if it doesn't feel ok, promise me," he pulls my body flush against his, my head resting on his bicep, as he pushes my hair from my face. His eyes are soft and caring and I melt even further at his words. I nod, agreeing and he closes the gap again, kissing me passionately. His hands stay in my hair as he simply kisses me. I know he is delaying doing anything else in case I freak out again, so I close my eyes and enjoy the feel of his mouth against mine, his hands as they caress my neck and cheek and there is nothing, but Davis. I lower my hand to his chest and feel his hard pecs and with my silent invitation, Davis moves his mouth lower, finding my neck first. I moan as my skin prickles with desire, his stubble deliciously scraping along my jaw.

"Davis I'm ready," my tone is laced with fever as I beg him for more. His head moves lower again, his fingers coming to my shoulders and pulling the thin straps of my vest down my arms, releasing my breasts.

"Jesus, you're so beautiful," his eyes meet mine for just a moment, before he dips down to taste my hard nipples. My head falls back and I groan out in pleasure, as my hips jerk upwards, my body begging him to take me. I open my eyes and see the top of his head and my mind races with images of my attacker biting me.

"Davis, stop," I call out and he responds immediately.

"Are you ok?" He's looking down into my now watery eyes; I hate myself for ruining this. "I'm sorry, I was fine but if I close my eyes..."

He quickly wipes away my tears, "Joanna, stop thinking and feeling guilty, trust your body," he encourages me and I nod. I want to get past this; I want to share this moment with him. He sits up and pulls away my underwear, before disposing of his own, his eyes never leaving mine. I'm already forgetting about the attacker, my attention focuses on Davis' amazing body, his compassionate nature and his captivating eyes. He rests on his elbows, before positioning himself at the entrance to my vagina.

"When you're ready, your body will let you know, don't force anything Joanna," he bends again kissing me, his eyes trained on mine, never breaking away. His kiss blows my mind and once again, my body begins to jerk and I feel him enter me, before he slips back out again.

"Davis, I want you," I demand and he answers my call, pushing forward and filling me. He moves his hips slowly and I match his pace as my arousal grows.

"Let me be on top?" I pant, Davis rolls over, taking me with him, before sitting up and wrapping my legs around his back. I move slowly, savouring the connection and allowing the fire to build again. I run my fingers through his damp hair, our noses grazing, as my hips lift and roll. His lips catch mine in soft butterfly kisses, the tip of his tongue faintly meeting mine, our eyes never parting, as we breathe heavier and move faster.

"I love you Joanna," he says and his words push me over the edge of my climax and I fall breathless, against his shoulder. I keep my arms around his neck, squeezing him tightly. The heat from our lovemaking has left us both sweaty and he holds me, allowing me to feel safe in his arms.

"Are you ok?" He pulls back to see my face. I nod, yes, before smiling broadly; I'm more than ok, I'm happy. His words linger in the air between us and I hesitate before bringing it back up.

"What?" He laughs at my cheesy grin, before lifting me from his lap and lying me down to face him on the bed. I pull the duvet over us, the cold air now starting to lick my heated skin.

"Did you just say you love me?" I press my lips together, to stop my Cheshire smile from returning.

"Did you say it back?" He asks, twisting a lock of my hair around his finger.

"No."

"Well then, I'll just have to make you," he leans forward and captures my mouth with a scorching hot kiss before repeating his words. "I love you Joanna," he whispers against my mouth.

"I love ice-cream," I giggle and he repeats his torturous kisses once again.

"I love you Joanna Carmody," he pulls my bottom lip with his teeth, sending a new wave of desire flooding me. I grab his face and force him to look at me.

"I love you too Davis," I say seriously, leaving him in no doubt of my feelings. His own smile spreads further than mine and he moves those lips to my neck and begins his sweet torment there.

I groan. I can't think straight with the sexual haze he is creating in my mind and all over my body.

He cups my breast, sucking my nipple and I scream out in pleasure, as his fingers slip between my folds. My body arches and his mouth catches mine as he enters me again. This time, there is no room for fear, or bad memories, only Davis.

Jo

"Smells good, Mam," I jump up on the countertop next to the cooker, as Davis prepares breakfast. He looks edible himself in nothing but his black boxers and my pink apron. I giggle again at how cute he looks and reach forward to nab a slice of bacon.

"Hands off," he taps my hand with the plastic spatula and I drop the food, laughing.

"Mam?" His right brow lifts quizzically and I laugh again.

"This colour looks good on you," I say, pointing to my apron. He bends sideways and grabs his white shirt that is now covering my naked body and captures my mouth.

"I can remind you of how manly I am, if you like?" He growls, friskily. I grab his face and hold him in place for one more kiss, before he returns to his cooking.

"Nice shirt by the way," he winks, as he flips the bacon over and I lift my hands to my nose, smelling the cuffs of his sleeves.

"Smells like you," I exhale happily.

"It should do, I own it, in fact, I'd like it back please," he pushes the pan aside, turning off the gas and moves between my legs. His fingers move to my face, gently pushing my untamed hair behind my ears and I drop my cheek into his hand. His green eyes have brown flecks and I smile, I've never noticed this about him before. He runs his nose along the tip of mine, before finding my mouth with his. His hands leave my face and begin to unbutton the shirt and I catch them with mine, halting their progress. I still have some marks from where *he* bit me that haven't healed fully and in the bright morning light, he will see all of me, scars and all.

He says nothing, instead he moves his hands to the already unbuttoned part of the shirt, pulls it apart and dips his head and kisses my chest and neck. It's amazing how easily he can make me forget.

"Davis," my voice is laced with need as I call to him, not sure what it is I am asking for.

"I love every part of you Joanna, I want to kiss away the pain and I want you to think of my lips there when you see your scars," his hands run under the shirt, finding my hardened nipples and he squeezes them, causing me to squirm in pleasure.

"Ok," I moan. He is already the only thing on my mind, his lips on my body are all I can think about, his tongue inside my mouth dancing with mine, is all I can taste and when I close my eyes, Davis' forest green eyes and the love oozing from them, is all I can see. He wastes no time with buttons and rips open his shirt, which I find incredibly sexy. I reach under the apron and run my hands down his tight ass, squeezing it and pulling him against my core. He lifts me, now naked, from the countertop and carries me towards the dining room table. He sits down with me straddling him and finds my entrance. I readjust my body and slide down his arousal and begin to ride him once again. I lean back, holding his legs for leverage and allow his eyes to roam my body. He doesn't look disgusted or unimpressed, instead his eyes are ablaze with hunger for me and his hands caress all of me, before resting on my hips and encouraging me to move faster. I wrap my arms around his neck and our tongues tangle around each other urgently. I suck his tongue as I climax around him and he groans loudly, following me over the edge.

"We are going to be late," I say a few minutes later, kissing his neck. We haven't moved our spent and sweaty bodies and I feel him grow hard inside me.

"Jesus Christ, your breath against my neck like that,

feels so sexy," he croaks and I laugh at how easily I turn him on. It feels good, I feel wanted and sexy.

"You need to get ready for work," I rotate my hips slowly and watch as his head falls back.

"I need to stop at mine for a new shirt," he growls out and I laugh against his stubbly jaw.

"You should leave some more things here," I pull his head up, wrapping my arms around his neck, "permanently," I blush. His arms come around my back, before he stands and carries me into my bedroom, kissing me all the way.

"I should," he smiles before lowering me onto the bed and making love to me again.

CHAPTER 21

Jo

For over four years, I have stood up in packed courtrooms and delivered my opening speeches and closing speeches. I questioned witnesses and cross examined witnesses, as well as being pitted against some of the highest paid Defence Attorneys in the state and I never once felt nervous. Tonight, I am sitting in a circle of ten women, all victims of sexual assault and all seeking solace from each other and I have never been more terrified of standing up and introducing myself. I move to a refreshment stand where the other ladies have congregated and pour myself a black coffee. I stand idly by, before moving to another young woman who is standing alone.

"Hi, my name is Jo," I stick out my hand and she takes it nervously.

"I'm Ruth, I'm a little nervous," she admits, her voice shaky and I smile warmly.

"Me too."

"Do you work for the centre?" Her brows furrow, seemingly confused.

"No, I am here for the group support." I watch as realisation dawns on her and can't help but take in the fresh bruising to her cheek. She is a small, frail looking woman, who couldn't be more than a day over twenty five and yet her eyes are dark and sunken.

"I'm sorry, you just look so...," she hesitates again, "... together," she finally whispers, chewing her finger nails.

"I wasn't two months ago, when I was raped," I assure her. We chat for a few minutes until my phone buzzes. "Excuse me please," I apologise, before moving out to the hallway to take the call.

"Hello, Joanna Carmody."

"Hello?" I call down the line again; nobody answers. I listen for a moment.

"Hello?" I say louder and move closer to the reception, in case the signal in the building is bad. Again, nothing.

"Hello, who is this?" I say one more time, frustrated,

there is clearly someone on the line. I am about to hang up when they get there first and I am left staring down at my phone, suspiciously. Maybe it was just a bad reception, I try to explain away the strange call. I put my phone on silent and when I return to the group, they are already seated and waiting for me so they can get started. I apologise profusely for the delay and take the seat next to Gail. I wonder if everyone will now think that I must work for the centre because of my office clothes and my location to Gail.

Some of the stories shared are harrowing and frightening and in the beginning, I fail to see how this can help me to move past my fears, until with each story, I, like the other women in the group, find myself relating to their shame and self-blame. I then find myself wanting to shake each woman and convince her that it wasn't her fault, that she can move on and then it settled with me. If I am giving this advice to others, then I need to give it to myself. I see a few shocked faces when I stand to tell my tale and my suspicions are confirmed, they confused me for staff.

I tell them about the night of my attack, the weeks of sleep after it and then I tell them about Davis.

"He was your guardian angel," one of the women announce and I laugh.

"He is anything but angelic, but he has been my rock," I admit. When I am finished, Ruth stands.

"Hi, my name is Ruth," she pulls the sleeves of her green jumper over her hands as her eyes anxiously move around the group, "I came here tonight to find the strength to leave my husband. He beats and rapes me regularly and I am too afraid he will kill me if I leave." She pulls her shoulders back in an attempt to seem strong, but she is a broken woman and all I want to do is stand up and hug her. She continues. "We have two boys together, my son Blake is four and Evan is two. Three nights ago, Blake woke up and came into the room as his Dad beat me and that was the final straw. I can't have my boys turning out like him," she begins to cry, but holds herself together well.

"Do you have anywhere to go?" I ask first, wanting to understand what her current position is.

"No, my family warned me not to marry him, but I ignored them and haven't spoken to them since," she shrugs, as one of the other ladies hands her a tissue.

"You know that there are shelters for women of domestic abuse," I offer her some information, not sure if she is aware of her options.

"He warned me that if I leave, he will get full custody of my boys, the house is in his name and he works, I don't stand a chance."

"We can set up a meeting with our legal advocacy," Gail offers and I cut across.

"Sorry to interrupt Gail, Ruth, did you ever call the cops?"

"Once or twice, they would haul him away for a day or two, last time they said that if it happened again, the state would be charging him with domestic abuse, with or without my consent, so I never called again."

"Why not?" A red headed lady from the group asks.

"I was too afraid and thought that I could change him, but now I know for sure he is a monster."

"There is proof of domestic abuse, which is one of things considered by a Judge when deciding the best place for the children, so just know that it is unlikely he will get custody. You can get a protection order against him, which means he can't come near you or your children and once the custody is settled, he will be ordered to pay child support."

"Thank you," she smiles.

When the group discussion is over, I hand my card to Ruth and tell her to call me if she ever has any questions or even if she just needs a friend. My phone buzzes with a text from Davis, letting me know he is outside to collect me and I smile like a love struck teenager and make my way to meet him.

"Joanna," Gail calls me just before I slip out the front

door.

"Everything ok?" I smile, as she rushes down the hallway to meet me.

"That advice you gave Ruth was great, thank you," she smiles, "she came into the centre this evening for the first time, so I haven't had a chance to arrange a meeting with Fiona, she is our legal advocacy.

"Anything I can do to help, is worth it."

"Well actually, Fiona can only volunteer three days a week and I was hoping you might consider volunteering on a Saturday, once a month, or more, if you wanted?" She blushes.

"Oh, I had never thought about that," I say, surprised.

"The job is basically to inform rape victims of their rights with regards to civil and criminal justice issues, think about it for a bit and let me know," she hugs me before making her way back to the remaining ladies. I pull my long, clack jacket closed and step out into the cold November air, its freezing. Davis is parked right at the entrance and I hop straight in.

"Hi," I smile and he pulls my orange scarf towards him and kisses me hard.

"Hey beautiful," he winks and I actually gush like a teenager. He is just so manly and sexy and even looking at his bare forearms as they twist the steering wheel home, gives me goose pimples. Who would have thought that a man's forearm could be sexy, I sigh to myself, feeling happy!

"How was the meeting?"

"Gail asked me to volunteer on the weekends, help out with the legal end of things," I shrug, looking out the window and mulling over in my head whether it's a good idea.

"You don't have to do it," Davis squeezes my hand. I turn around and smile at his concerned expression.

"I know, I gave one girl some advice tonight during the group discussion and actually, it felt good to help, I know what they are going through," I shrug.

"Think it over and if it feels right, do it," he squeezes my hand again before returning his to the steering wheel.

Davis grabs my hand as we walk towards my apartment and I think it is the best feeling in the world. I love how long and slender his fingers are and how they intertwine perfectly with mine. I love how his thumb runs up and down my pointer finger and I love how natural it is for him to reach for me. He takes control without hesitation and is so confident about our flourishing relationship.

"So, what do you want for Christmas?" He asks, as he pushes open my apartment door.

"I haven't thought about it," I laugh. It's only a few days until Christmas and for the first year, I don't have my usual Christmas cheer.

"What about you?"

"I have a surprise for you, so close your eyes," he says, pushing open the hall door. I narrow my eyes suspiciously at him, wondering what he is up to.

"Close them," he orders me and I obey, laughing. He keeps my hand in his and leads me the rest of the way. He is leading me to the living room, I can tell, despite being momentarily blind.

"Keep them closed," he warns before kissing me briefly and leaving my side. I laugh as he rummages about. The room fills with the sound of rushing water and birds chirping, which throws me for a loop, I have no idea what he is up to.

"Ok, open up," I stall for a second before I open my eyes and look around at the picnic he has prepared in the middle of my living room floor. We had put the Christmas tree up together the night before and the fairy lights sparkle like diamonds, throughout the room. It all looks so magical and beautiful and I hate myself for how my body is reacting. My eyes fill when I recognise the blanket we used in Hawaii, along with the cellophane sandwiches and the sounds of the waterfall and birds, all combine to make the perfect re-enactment of that amazing day. I have no way of telling him that this memory was what saved me while I was being raped. I have no way of explaining why I am suddenly short of breath and pulling my scarf off to help me breathe easier. I rush from the room and hear him follow behind me.

"Hey, what's wrong?" He pulls my arm, forcing me to face him and I continue to struggle for air.

"Ok, breathe its ok," he rubs my back and I try to concentrate on his face and not the monster in my head, "you're safe," he whispers, understanding without words that I am struggling. I begin to cry out in frustration.

"I'm sorry, it was a lovely idea," I manage.

"Come with me," he takes my hand and moves me into my bedroom. I sit on the edge of my bed and he joins me, wiping away my tears, "can you tell me what happened?" He asks, gently. I turn facing him and decide that he deserves the truth, if we are together, then he needs to know that even though I am moving forward, I won't ever truly forget that awful night.

"When he was raping me, I went there in my mind, to escape what he was doing to me," I sob.

"I thought about you Davis and I remembered that day." His arms come around me, holding me to his chest, as I cry uncontrollably. I feel awful for ruining his lovely surprise and even more when I realise how far I have yet to go in my recovery. I climb into bed without dinner and shut Davis out, I can't look at him without feeling like he deserves better. I can hear him cleaning up and I cry again, ashamed at how I reacted.

Roche

"What I am about to tell you is highly classified," Rick points to the seat in front of his desk and I narrow my eyes, suspiciously at him. It is very rare that I would be called into his office solo and I can't help but wonder why Davis is not present.

"We are setting up a special task force to look into the activities of Seamus Lynch," he blurts out and I sit up straight.

"That case is closed Sir, he is in prison," I say dumbly. He rolls his eyes.

"Seamus Lynch is being monitored in prison. He has received letters from Ireland, some written in Gaelic which have been easy enough to translate. The others are coded and what we can gather so far, is that there will be a package arriving within the next few months. We need to know what that package is and why it's coming from Ireland. His trial is looming and with that, we need to make sure that our security is not compromised."

"What about Davis?" I know he will be pissed off that he is not involved. He had been instrumental in arresting Seamus Lynch from day one and this will not go over well with him.

"Davis is out. He is too close and we can't give Lynch any more rope to hang us with. You will be temporarily transferred to the tech team, as far as Davis is concerned. Roche, this is top secret and your orders are to start after Christmas."

"This package, is it a matter of national security?"

"Yes, we are pretty sure that he is planning some attack. It could be an attempted jail break or a further attempt on Aubrey Richard's life, either way, we can't risk it."

I stand and move to shake his hand, "I'm in," I say, before turning to leave.

"Finish up whatever cases you are working now. You won't be assigned anything further for the rest of the year and remember, Davis is to be kept in the dark about this," he warns. I nod again and leave.

I have enjoyed working with Davis for the past few years and although I don't like lying to him, I know that he would want me to take this case on. This is something that we both worked together on and I'll be damned if I'm going to stand back and wait for this fucker to pounce again. Christmas can't be over soon enough for me.

Jo

I stare into the glass window of the department store and sigh. I have wracked my brain to try and come up with the perfect gift for Davis and yet, here I am, on Christmas Eve, with an hour to go before the shops close and I still have nothing. My bags are filled with small things, like a goofy jumper and a James Dean poster, but they are stocking fillers, not the kind of thing you give to your boyfriend on your first Christmas together.

"Jo," I hear my name being called and turn to see Jake standing behind me, with his arms outstretched, waiting for a hug. I hesitate for a moment, our break up had been bad, but with the time of year that it is, I forget about the past and embrace him.

"Jake! How are you?" I sound surprised. He was the last person I expected to run in to.

"I'm great Jo, I'm sorry I didn't get in touch, you know, after the attack," his eyes shift away from mine and my heart sinks. He can't look at me and although I shouldn't care about his reaction, I do. I don't want people to see me differently or to know me as the girl that was raped. I was a person before the attack and I'm still that same person, it hurts that he can't see that.

"Oh, I didn't realise you knew," I'm suddenly warm despite the cold snow that whips around us.

"I heard the news reports and although they didn't mention you by name, I looked up the hospital charts," he has the decency to look embarrassed, "I planned to phone you but I could never find the right words, I'm sorry," he finishes. I try to remain calm, to not let this chance meeting rock me but my insides are shaking. I feel sick, angry and confused by his admission and yet I feel sorry for him, all at the same time.

"It's ok Jake, really, have a happy Christmas," I move to leave and feel his hand on my elbow.

"I could call by over the holidays and check in?" He offers.

"I'm seeing somebody Jake, but thank you for the offer, goodbye," I smile and rush into the store. I walk around in a daze, unable to concentrate on what I can get for Davis and when the store lights flash, I leave, empty handed and with a hollow feeling in my soul.

Davis meets me outside with all his bags and a huge smile on his face. The look on his face cheers me up and I try to shake off my encounter with Jake. It shouldn't matter; I know that these things will continue to happen so I take Davis' hand, with the intention of looking forward to our first Christmas together. Nothing can ruin it.

CHAPTER
22

Davis

Things have felt a little strange between us since I fucked up the other night. In hindsight, trying to make Joanna remember happier times is forcing her to look back and I want her to keep moving forward. I made a serious note to myself, no more trips down memory lane. It worries me that one day she will look back at this time, the time when we began our romance, that it will be tarnished with the memories of her attack. Relationships don't usually start out under such stressful conditions and no matter how afraid I am that it is wrong to start anything serious now, I can't stay away from her. I want to be the good in her life, I want to make her happy and I am miserable when I'm away from her. My time in Quantico was like torture, all I could do was think about her and returning home, to her home. Her eyes have lost some of their sparkle over the past few days and I don't know how to make her feel better. On the surface, she is smiling, cheerful and even loving towards me, but I see the distance in her eyes.

"Did you get everything you need?" I ask, taking her hand and making my way to the metro. We decided to leave the car at home and venture out into the cold weather. She looked too adorable in her red hat and scarf to deny her request and insist on driving. Her nose is now as red as her hat and scarf and I want to bend and kiss it. Instead, I catch her lips and feel them stiffen beneath mine.

"You ok?" I pull back and search her eyes for what I know she won't tell me.

"Yes, I'm great," she smiles, but as I thought, I see her truth. She is shutting me out and I have no idea how I can help her. I nod and look away; I can't help but feel rejected. I know it's irrational and unfair to feel anger, but I wanted this day to be perfect. I feel a tug on my hand and turn to see that she has stopped walking. Tears brim her eyes.

"I'm sorry, I know you deserve better," she sniffles and my anger dissolves immediately.

"Joanna, don't get upset, I don't deserve better. I just want you to talk to me," I wrap my arms around her.

"I bumped into Jake and he looked at me like I was diseased," she admits and I feel that anger rise again.

"What did he say?" I try to keep my cool. I can hardly ask her to open up and then blow my lid when she does.

"Nothing, just how sorry he was, but it was how he looked at me. I don't want people to know, or to see me differently. I know people in work whisper, I heard Eric defend me the other day and I try to ignore it but...," she wipes her own tears and starts walking, "...I'm sorry, forget it, I'm being ridiculous. I don't want to ruin this day," her cool façade comes over her again. I take her hand again and with my free hand, I lift her chin, forcing her to look into my eyes.

"What do you see when I look at you?" I ask.

"Love," she whispers, her eyes pooling again before a wide smile spreads across her face.

"I do love you and everyone else can fuck off! They don't matter, we matter and you need to know that you can rely on me and you can talk to me, no matter how ridiculous it may seem," I say, determinedly.

"I have a confession," she chews her bottom lip.

"What?" I ask warily.

"I didn't get you a proper gift, I looked and I couldn't find you anything good enough and now I have a few miserable gifts," she pouts, looking guilty and I laugh.

"Jesus, I thought you were going to tell me you wanted Jake back," I laugh, "I have you for Christmas, besides, I bought my own gift," I wink. She leans up on her tip-toes and catches my mouth with hers. I melt into her kiss, deepening it when I feel how soft and welcoming they are. When I pull back, the sparkle has returned and I pull her under my arm and hold her close, as we walk through the snow storm home.

Jo

Davis was very enthusiastic about his small gifts, so much so that I laughed along, forgetting my embarrassment. I am sitting on the sofa with my hands out and eyes closed waiting for him to give me my gift. I feel the package being place in my hands.

"Ok, open up," he says and when I do, he is sitting next to me, with a bag of gifts at his feet.

"These are yours, but this is the most important one," he smiles and my attention shifts to the small box in my hands. My throat dries as I look at what I suspect could be an engagement ring and my stomach recoils, it couldn't be! I try to reign in my thoughts before I shakily pull away the red gift wrap. I lift the lid slowly and the first thing I see, is the sparkle. I snap the lid shut and stand up.

"Davis, it's too soon," I push the box back into his hand. He looks up at me with a bewildered look, before he begins to laugh. He almost doubles over, his eyes watering with delight before he catches sight of my confused face.

"Joanna, it's not a ring," he takes a deep breath, before laughing again. He pulls my hand and forces me onto his lap.

"Open it," he says, pushing it back into my hand. I take the box, my pride a little wounded that he has found this all hilarious, but that is quickly replaced by wonder when I look at the beautiful sparkling angel that winks at me from the red velvet cushion. My mouth drops open and I turn to him.

"Davis, it's beautiful," I whisper, before throwing my arms around his neck.

"It's a guardian angel, to watch over you when I can't be there," he smiles and I kiss him. My kiss is deep and urgent; my desire for him is so sudden that I begin to lift his red reindeer jumper over his head. He is happy to comply and lifts his hands, before pulling at my red dress and removing it in one swoop. Our mouths clash in a lust filled hazed, as we rip the clothes from our bodies. I feel desperate for skin on skin, wild for his touch. He shifts me beneath him and makes love to me on the sofa, hot and fast. My legs wrap around his back, pushing him deeper as he thrusts with the same ferocious need that I take him, clenching and milking him, as my body explodes with ecstasy.

"Do you want the rest of your gifts now?" He says, a while later. We are both still naked and lying in the same place. His hands are running through my hair and I feel too cosy to move.

"Hmmmmm," is all I can manage and when I feel his body sit up, I groan in displeasure. He pulls me up with him and smiles, no doubt at my wild and messy hair.

"I thought you might want to wear these," he winks, handing me a flat box. I open it, removing the pink tissue paper and smile at the black laced underwear.

"I take it this is the gift you bought for yourself," I smile happily, lifting the expensive lingerie up to admire it.

"Damn, skimpy." I lean into him and tilt my head to look up at him. "Thank you, they are beautiful," I smile and he drops his lips to mine, delivering a chaste kiss.

"You look so beautiful right now," he smiles. "Ok, get dressed, we have an hour before we are due for dinner at Bree and Michaels and you are tempting me to stay home," he demands, moving away from me and dressing himself.

I pin the angel to my dress and run my fingers over the delicate brooch. We leave for dinner and I feel like the luckiest girl in the world today.

****

"10, 9, 8, 7, 6, 5, 4, 3, 2, 1, HAPPY NEW YEAR!" Cheers ring out amongst us, as Auld Lang Syne fills the room. Davis pulls back, ending our kiss and I lean against his chest as we sway to the festive tune. Bree and Michael agreed to attend Eric's annual New Year's Eve party with us and even Roche has tagged along. It feels amazing to see in the New Year with the people I care most about in the world. "Here is to Roche's new position," Davis lifts his champagne flute a while later, as we all gather in the living room and we all join in to celebrate Roche's department change.

"It's only temporary, I'll be back before you know it," he rolls his eyes at Davis, but I can tell he is touched all the same. Davis was annoyed initially, but having had time to mull it over, he knows his friend and partner will be back at his side in no time. I think it's great that he cares so much, not just for Roche but for all those closest to him; it's part of the reason I love him.

"Michael, I think the children have had enough for one night," Bree yawns and leans back in Michaels arms and I smile at her. She wanted to stay home this year, but kindly agreed to tag along.

"Thank you for coming," I reach over and hug her goodbye.

"We had fun," she yawns again, unable to stop the onslaught of exhaustion and it must be catching because my mouth opens wide as I join in.

"I think we should maybe call it a night too," Davis announces.

"I think I'll hang back," Roche winks. He hugs me and Bree goodbye, before moving to the beautiful blonde lady he had been chatting up all night.

"Have fun," Davis calls after him, laughing. We say our goodbyes to Eric before all four of us leave together. Michael offers us a ride home which we gladly accept. There is a slim chance that we will get a taxi on New Year's Eve.

The lights on the Christmas tree guide us through the darkness as we arrive home. I lift up my long navy dress and kick off my heels, before reaching up to free my hair from its pins. Davis' green eyes catch mine and he pulls me silently into the living room.

"10, 9, 8, 7, 6…" what are you doing. I laugh as he pulls me into the same embrace he held me in earlier in the night.

"I'm not ready for the night to be over, 3, 2, 1," he whispers, before catching my mouth in his and kissing me deeply. When he comes up for air, I gasp for breath, "dum, dum, da dum, dum dum, dum dum...," he begins to hum Auld Lang Syne, as he unzips my dress at the back.

"Davis," I laugh as his mouth drops to my neck, his stubbly beard tingling my heated skin.

"I wanted to do this earlier," his voice is coarse and filled with need. My head falls back and I grab hold of his biceps to steady myself.

"You looked so sexy with your hair up, your neck looked good enough to eat," he growls, as my dress drops in a pool at my feet. His arms come around my waist and legs, as he lifts me up and carries me to bed.

****

The cold air whips around my face as I step out of Davis' SUV and walk into the gym. This is the first time that I have returned since the attack, but it is the first time that I have felt ready to begin training again. All over Christmas, Davis harped on about how important it was that I continue with the self-defence classes, I knew he was right but I couldn't face it. On New Year's Day, he came up with a great idea, to invite the women from the crisis centre for a trial class. His plan is to teach the women everything they need to know about protecting themselves in the future and I couldn't say no after that. I think it was part of his plan, but it worked and I agree with him. It is more important now that I am prepared, I don't ever want to be vulnerable again. With Davis by my side, I feel safe, but we can't keep living in each other's pockets. Davis wants to continue dropping and picking me up from work, but already I am beginning to feel suffocated by this. It is too co-dependant and I don't want our relationship to ever be unhealthy. I pull open the doors and am delighted to see that at least ten women have shown up, including Gail. I walk over and greet them all and receive a few elbow nudges, when Davis lines us up.

"Holy smokes, he is a hotty," Ruth blows out in appreciation, her eyes roaming up and down Davis' body and I begin to giggle.

230

"Silence," he barks at me, I had forgotten how serious he can be and I find it sexy. I wink to Ruth whose eyes have now landed on Michael.

"What are the membership fees?" she asks and I begin to laugh again.

"Ok Joanna, as you have already done a small intro into this class, you can come up to the front and demonstrate for the ladies some of what you know," Davis waves me beside him and I am mortified. It has been months since I have done this class and I can't remember a thing.

"Ummmm...," I mumble, unsure what he wants me to say, "...the first thing is prevention!" I announce, happily. I try to recall what the steps for prevention are, but Davis takes over for me. We all practice moves on each other and at the end of the class, we are sweaty and laughing, I think we all found it cathartic. Gail moves to stand beside Davis and calls us all to attention.

"Ladies, I know this is a little unusual in terms of a therapy session, but I think this is an amazing example of taking back the control of your own life. I hope you will all appreciate the time Agent Davis has dedicated to this class and the kindness of Michael for allowing us the use of his gym, free of charge. I for one will be back," she smiles at us, before turning and clapping her hands towards Davis and Michael. I watch them both blush as all the ladies join in and I feel so proud of the most important men in my life.

"Thank you," I reach over, kissing Davis' cheek as we pull out of the car park an hour later. He turns to me and smiles, his eyes alight with love and humour as he watches me. I feel exhilarated and just as Gail said, I feel like I am taking back control of my own life. I am ready to take the next step to being independent.

"You're welcome, I think it went great," Davis changes gear before grabbing my hand and linking it with his as we drive.

"It went better than I could have imagined Davis, the ladies loved it and I feel empowered," I sigh, happily. I'm not sure if it's the endorphins from our work out or if I am just in a happy state of mind, but I feel like a weight has been lifted from my chest. I feel like I can breathe easy for the first time since the attack.

"Davis," I pause, chewing my bottom lip as I figure out just how to say this.

"Yes?" He takes his eyes from the road to look at me. When they narrow suspiciously, I decide I better spit it out before he starts to worry.

"I think I'm ready to drive again." His hand leaves mine and changes gear again but when he makes no move to reconnect and remains silent, I try again to talk to him.

"Davis?"

"Joanna, I'm struggling right now," his sad tone, tears at my heart strings, "I listened to Gail tell you all to regain control of your lives tonight and I knew that this was coming soon, I just thought I might get another week," he shrugs.

"I know it's scary, but we need to have a healthy relationship, not one that means my very existence relies on you. We can't control what happened in the past or what might happen in the future, but I want to be a healthier, happier person, for myself first and then, for us and our future," I say, softly.

"I know and I don't want to stifle you, but I am afraid to let go of that control, I am afraid that he is waiting for me to slip up, so he can come back."

Guilt and shame are my first reaction to his words. I have been so consumed by my own pain and my own struggles with the rape, I have never taken a step back to think about how Davis copes with it all. His coping mechanism has been to protect me, to be by my side, to stop my attacker from getting to me again. I have no idea how these changes that I insist on making will unravel, or how he will cope when the only thing that he has to feel better about all of this, is taken away from him. It is a frightening thought, but we need to push ourselves to face these realities and if we come apart because of it, then we should not have been together in the first place.

"Davis, I love you and I am afraid to change things. I'm afraid to burst this little bubble of love and security, but we need to live in the real world and it's not sustainable for you to constantly be at my side. You have a career that calls you away at times and my career, means that I can't live in Salem every time you're gone. I know he is still out there and I know why you are afraid, but you can't carry that burden or it will drag you down and our relationship won't survive it," I reach for his hand and he reconnects with me, linking our fingers.

"I am going to find it hard Joanna, you will need to have patience because I will probably be calling you to make sure you arrive ok and to make sure someone walks you to your car," he pulls into our parking space and turns to face me, "is there security that can walk you to your car?" He asks.

"Yes, or Eric but I will be parking in front of my building. It is well lit up and pedestrianised so it is always busy, I promise I would never take silly risks again."

"Ok, I want this for you, so I'm going to be as supportive as I can," he smiles. It doesn't reach his eyes, but I don't expect him to be overly happy about the situation. We hop out and he wraps his arms around me as we walk inside and out of the cold.

CHAPTER 23

Davis

I twist and turn all night while Joanna sleeps peacefully beside me. I can't believe I have agreed to allow her to drive to work on her own. I must be mad, that animal is still out there. Even though myself and Roche are investigating the case whenever we have any free time, so far nobody of any interest has turned up from the construction sites we have managed to visit. It's tedious work to get the men to talk to us, let alone snitch on one of their work colleague's. We have no warrants, because this is not our case, so we can't demand the names of any employees. Sometimes we may get lucky and the foreman doesn't want the hassle of us coming back with a warrant, so they give up the information, but the empty threat has only worked once. I sit up and pull my phone from the bedside locker. It is 4.00 a.m. and I'm pretty certain I will get my ear chewed off me tomorrow, but I can't relax enough to sleep, so I fire off a text to Roche. He is a light sleeper, the man could be deep in sleep and would hear a pin drop three doors down, I know he will get my text straight away.

Joanna is driving to work alone tomorrow. She will be leaving about 8.00 a.m. can you park on the street and follow her there? She will know if I do and I won't rest until I know she makes it to work ok.

I wait a few minutes for a reply and smile when my screen flashes and his name appears;

I am not your partner anymore, dickhead! Yeah, I'll be at the office tomorrow for tech training so I'll call by. I wanted to touch base on what we are doing about Joanna's case. Don't text me again, I have a friend over.

I smile at his reply and debate if I should reply with some joke about how there is no way he has any friends other than me, but then I never was any good at cock blocking. I relax and fall asleep soon after.

Jo

I park my car right outside my building and press the button for the central locking, before walking through the now slushy ice, into work. I loved every minute of being back behind the wheel, I listened to the radio and like old times, I raised the volume and sang along to the tracks. My phone beeps and I look down to see a text from Davis.

*You get there ok?

I roll my eyes; he must be psychic.

*Just walked in the door, I'm fine, go to work and stop bothering me ;) I will see you this evening x

His reply makes me giggle.

*One text and I'm already a pest! Have a good day, love u x

I pop my phone into my handbag and get to work. I don't check it again until lunch hour and notice that I have three missed calls from a private number and another text from Davis.

*My parents want to meet you. Dinner tonight????

My eyes almost pop out of my head and I quickly type my reply;

*They know about me? What have you told them?

I feel a little shaky as I wait for his response. He had visited with them over Christmas and I refused to join him. I didn't want to impose and just landing on their door step over the holidays was a lot to ask. He has told me a little bit about them but ashamedly, I don't even know their first names, worst girlfriend ever!

Of course they know about you, I take it yours have no idea about me! I told them that you are a crazy, wild haired banshee who refuses to take no for an answer, so I eventually caved.

My parents are divorced, I don't speak to my Dad so you won't ever meet him and my Mom is currently backpacking in Peru in search of herself. Very funny, I'll be sure to throw my hairbrush at you later. I want to meet them, what if they don't like me?

Joanna they will love you, I'll call them now and tell them we will be there for 8.00 p.m.

*Aaaaarggghhhh, I'm nervous now, but excited too.
I miss you, see you later x*

My phone vibrates in my hand as soon as I press send and the private number flashes up on my screen again. I hesitate before answering it, but decide that it could be someone important, after all, this is the fourth time they have tried to call me today.

"Hello," I answer.

"Is that Joanna?" His voice is strangely familiar and not in a good way. A cold chill runs down my back, causing the hairs on my neck to stand up.

"Who is this?"

"An old friend."

The line goes dead and I fall into my office chair, shaking. I contemplate phoning Davis and telling him, but I know he will freak out. I don't want to ruin our dinner plans, so I decide to wait until we get home tonight, before I tell him about the strange call.

We drive over the Chelsea Bridge and out towards the suburbs. My feet ache from standing in court all afternoon, so I take this opportunity to slip my heels off and stretch my legs. I am still a little shaken up from that disturbing phone call at lunch, but I try to be upbeat about meeting Davis' folks. I pull down the visor and groan at my appearance in the mirror.

"I wish I'd had more time to change," I pout, wiping the black mascara smudges from under my eyes. I was late leaving the office and arrived home with little or no time to spare. Thanks to me, we are already ten minutes late.

"You look gorgeous, relax, they will be in jeans and tees, they aren't the fancy type," he smiles, clearly amused at my worried expression.

I roll my eyes. "Sweet talking won't make my hair any less flat or my eyes less tired," I pinch him playfully, "you need to tell me everything I need to know about your parents, ASAP."

"Ok, here is the Davis family rundown with all the vital information that you will need, are you ready to absorb?" He jokes and I can't help but smile. Damn it, I'm so whipped!

"Hit me with it."

"Mary Davis is 60 years of age and goes by the street name, Mom. She is 5ft 5, with brown hair, but her appearance can change if she misses a salon appointment. She makes a killer cheesecake and has been known to throw shoes at my head, if I leave them lying around the house. Lance Davis, aka Dad, is 6ft 3, balding and broad. He runs in Mary's crew and can be seen driving her around town on errands. He is ex-cop turned house husband, Mary is the boss and she runs a tight ship. They have a dashing son who would be a great catch for any lucky girl and an annoying but lovable daughter, Blaire."

I giggle at his description. "they sound perfect," I am genuinely excited to meet them now. We drive into a beautiful suburban neighbourhood in Saugus. The footpath is littered with fallen leaves from the trees that line the wide roads, but the streets are clean and the gardens well maintained. I can tell that people take pride in their homes and their country, with an American flag attached to a spinning pole, on their porches. There are no fences between the raised gardens and no lawns unkempt or uncared for. What if they hate me? My eyes widen with fear as we pull into the drive of Davis' parent's home.

"They are going to love you," Davis answers my unspoken question and I take a deep breath to steady my nerves, before opening my door and stepping outside. I stand waiting for Davis to come around and join me, taking in the house he grew up in. I love it, the top half of the house is white and panelled and the bottom half, red brick. Like every other house on the block, an American flag, hangs proudly above the porch, with a warm glow coming from the rooms upstairs. I turn to face Davis and catch sight of something that throws me back in time and out of this moment. A white van passes us by slowly and I freeze, staring as it picks up pace.

"Joanna," Davis' expression becomes concerned when he sees my face.

"There was a white van," I point to the empty road and shake my head to try and compose myself.

Davis turns around and narrows his eyes at the empty street, "I'll go after it," he moves to jump back into the SUV and I grab his arm frantically.

"No, it was just a van Davis, you can't chase after every white van," I beg him to see sense, regretting having mentioned it.

"I can and I will if it helps to catch him," he pulls me into a hug.

"I know you would, but tonight, I want to meet your parents," I grip his green flannel shirt and he wraps one arm over my shoulder, leading me into his family home. He looks over his shoulder onto the dark street, one last time, before he closes the porch door behind him.

I get a little misty eyed as I watch Davis' parents greet him with such joy. My own family dynamic leaves a lot to be desired and I can already see that his parents are good people.

"Introduce us to your girlfriend Willie," his Dad bellows,

as Davis hugs his Mom and I step forward, offering my hand.

"I'm Joanna, you can call me Jo," my voice is shaky, I can't believe how much I want them to like me. He takes my hand with a firm shake before pulling me into a hug.

"How did my clumsy kid land such a knockout?" He jokes and I laugh along, relieved that they are easy going.

"Paws off Lance, let me say hello," his Mom steps forward, brushing her husband aside to hug me. Her embrace is less intense, but just as warm and inviting.

"I'm Mary, lovely to meet you Jo," she smiles before taking my hand and leading me to the dinner table.

Throughout dinner, the conversation flows as well as the wine and before I know it, I find myself teasing Davis and laughing along to his father's tales of a young, clumsy, Will Davis.

"He was still playing cops and robbers with Blaire when he was seventeen," Mary interrupts as Lance talks about Davis and the fact that he always wanted to be in law enforcement.

"I DID NOT!" Davis splutters, mortified and I use my napkin to hide my laughter.

"As in running around the house with a fake gun?" My eyes water, imagining a gangly Davis, forcing his younger sister to play along.

"Yes you did, he said it was practice," Lance backs Mary and we all laugh, except for Davis, he narrows his eyes at his parents, but they are having too much fun goading him.

"Remember when Sheila Harris' house was broken into and he went door to door, doing his own investigation," Lance holds his stomach laughing and I fall over the table, shaking my head in an attempt to ask them to stop.

"That's enough of that, I'm showing Joanna around," Davis comes around the table and pulls me, still laughing, from my seat and towards the hallway. We walk upstairs and down a narrow hallway and into what could only be his old bedroom. The blue walls are hidden behind posters of movies, cars and models and I look around, trying to imagine a teenage Davis spending time in here. A poster facing his bed catches my eye and I move closer, smiling at the handsome James Dean who smoulders back at me.

"I knew you fancied yourself as James Dean," I turn back, pointing my finger and narrowing my eyes at him. He catches my out stretched hand in his, before lifting it up and twirling me around.

"I prefer my new poster," he dips me and kisses me softly.

"What are you doing?" I laugh.

"Admiring my beautiful girlfriend," his hands grabbing me at my waist and his mouth drops to mine. His kiss is full of fire and I pull back, fanning my face and puffing for air.

"Your Mom and Dad are downstairs," I remind him, as he kisses my neck, causing all rational thoughts to quickly disappear.

"Davis, you need to stop," I push weakly at his shoulders.

"Jesus, you're so sexy," his hands come under my skirt, squeezing my ass and pulling my moist core against his hard length. My head falls back, his tongue gliding along my collarbone and I groan out in frustration, as he inflicts his delicious torment.

"Davis, your parents," I remind him again, but doing nothing to stop him.

"I'm just kissing you," he says against my neck, his warm breath sending tingles all over my body. I pull his mouth to mine and kiss him hard, before pushing him backwards and holding my hand up between us to allow me some breathing space. He takes my hand and sucks my index finger, his eyes burning with desire and causing an inferno inside of me. My knees are weak: I can't think straight. My breathing becomes ragged, what is he doing to me? my scattered mind wonders, before I step forward, wrapping my arms around his neck and kissing him hurriedly.

"Joanna, we need to stop, my parents are downstairs," he pulls away, his eyes riddled with mock disappointment and I blink twice, confused. A victorious smile begins to creep across his face, confusing me further.

"I don't understand," I step away and he laughs.

"You teased me, so I teased you back," he continues, cracking himself up and realisation dawns.

"You play dirty Will Davis, we will see how that pans out for you later tonight," I fix my skirt, pull back my shoulders and walk, seductively, out of the room. No matter how much I want him later, he will have to beg for it and the look on his face as I leave, tells me that he knows it. Fight desire with desire is my new motto, well, for tonight anyway.

The car heater buzzes and I rest my eyes as we drive home a few hours later. I had two glasses of wine and that, mingled with the warm air, is making me sleepy. I hear my phone buzz from the dash and ignore it.

"Should I get that?" Davis asks and I nod, keeping my eyes closed.

CHAPTER
24

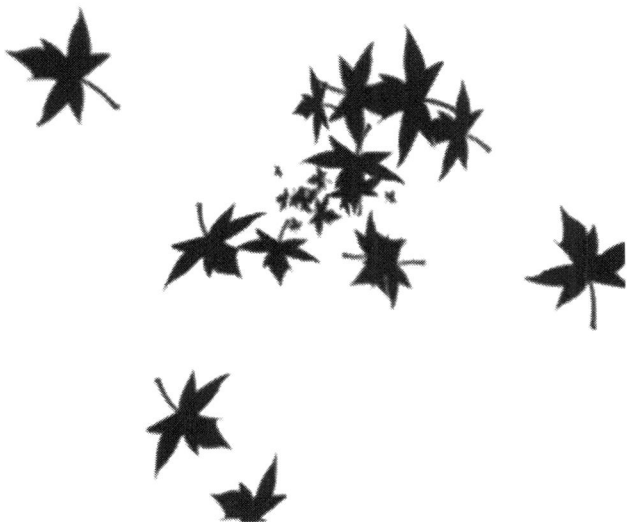

Davis

A loose strand of hair, falls over Joanna's face as she curls up into the seat beside me. Her long eyelashes are splayed across her cheekbones as she rests her eyes, she is tired but I can tell she isn't sleeping just yet. Her mouth pops open just a fraction, when she is fully asleep. Her phone shrills and I pick it up, ready to hand to her and watch as her little nose scrunches up, in distaste.

"Should I get that?" I nudge her gently and she nods her approval. I look at the blocked number and press the button to answer.

"Hello?"

"I would like to speak to Joanna," a male voice that I don't recognise comes down the line.

"Who's speaking?"

"This is her boss, it's important," he says gruffly and I bite my tongue. I hope he doesn't use that tone with her in work, but out of respect for her career, I say nothing and nudge her.

"Joanna, it's your boss," I hand it to her and she sits up immediately to take the call.

"Hello Sir, is everything alright?" She asks.

"Hello?" She calls out again and looks at the phone. The time is ticking away on the screen, indicating that the call is still active. She puts it back to her ear and I can vaguely hear him talking. I glance at the road in front of me and turn back to see her pale and shaking. The call has ended and the phone is now resting in her lap.

"Joanna, what's wrong?" I ask urgently.

"He wants me dead," she whispers, her face contorted with fear.

"Who was that on the phone Joanna?" I pull over into the hard shoulder and shake her. She is staring into space, her eyes dazed and unresponsive.

"It was him, he said he misses me," her eyes well up now and I pull her against my chest. My blood begins to boil and I seethe with rage.

"He phoned me today," she whispers, her words almost inaudible and I push her back from my body. I grip her arms and stare into her eyes.

"What do you mean?" I try to remain calm, but I feel my nose flare as my rage simmers, dangerously close to the top.

"At work, I was going to tell you tonight, but I wanted to wait until after dinner," her eyes plead with me to understand, but as ridiculous as it may seem, I feel betrayed. It was her first day back out there on her own and he made contact. She promised to keep in contact with me all day and she kept this from me. She might as well have taken a knife and ripped through my skin. The fact that she didn't call me straight away, is too much to bear. I push her away from me and restart my engine. I need to call Roche and I need to calm down.

Jo

Davis climbs into bed beside me a few hours after we arrive home. He had phoned Roche who came over and both men sat for hours talking, while I "slept". I could hear Davis' frustration as he and Roche hashed out ways to get ahead in the investigation. I eventually pulled the pillow over my ear, unable to listen any further as they talked about me like a victim. I know that what happened makes me a victim of that crime, but Davis was supposed to be the person who could see beyond what happened. I wait for him to pull me closer and hold me. I wait for him to ease the worries that have tormented me since his reaction to the phone call earlier. A silent tear rolls down my cheek when he doesn't reach for me. Instead, he turns away from me, leaving a gaping hole between our bodies. I could see the change in him the minute I told him about the phone call and I could feel the shift between us. It swooped in and ruined everything without warning and all it took was for my demons to come calling. I pull back my duvet and sit up in the darkness.

"What's wrong?" He asks and my back stiffens as he makes no move to come closer.

"I'm fine," I lie.

"Joanna, what's wrong?" He ignores my response and asks me again. His tone is hard and uncaring, affording me the opportunity to be honest with him.

"I could see it in your eyes tonight," I croak out, not sure if I'm ready to face the ugly truth. There is a long silence before he responds again.

"Joanna, what are you talking about?"

"I could see your disgust at what he did and I felt your distance straight away," my voice is low but heavy with emotion.

"Joanna," he scoots closer, his hand coming to my shoulder, "I was angry about him calling you, I am disgusted and angry and enraged that he put his hands on you and I want to kill him! I can't pretend that I am not hurt that you kept his earlier call from me, I need to figure this out in my head." I turn and look into his green eyes and see the truth in his words.

"I know you're angry with me Davis, but you don't want to touch me, there is a two meter gap between us, but it might as well be a mile," another tear dives over the edge, gliding down my cheek.

"That's ridiculous," he splutters.

"Don't lie to me," I yell, "don't treat me like some charity case," I cry.

"Ok, Joanna, I won't lie to you," he sticks out his chest, his own anger rising up, "I hate what he did to you. I want to erase the memory of him from your memory. I want to kill him for raping you and tonight, I can't have sex with you because all I can see in my mind, is him attacking and invading you. All I feel is anger when I look at you because you kept that call from me!" He is breathing heavy as he finishes and although I asked for his honesty, pushed him to be truthful, his words are like a dagger to my heart. He realises straight away his error and reaches for my hand.

"I'm sorry, I didn't mean that," he tries to retract his

words, but I jump up and move away from the bed. I turn to face him, at a loss for words, I'm not angry with him for feeling the way he does, but I'm angry that he fooled me into believing that he would never see me that way.

"I want you to go," my chin wobbles. I cross my arms over my silk nightgown and cover my breasts, looking away from him towards the white walls of my bedroom.

"Joanna, listen, I'm sorry, I didn't mean that," he moves from the bed, putting his hands on my hips and turning my body so that I am facing him.

"Go Davis, my bed was cold with you in it, I won't miss anything," I spit, before locking eyes with him to send my spiteful message home.

"I'm not leaving," he grinds his teeth and I push past him, climbing back into my bed.

"You know where the living room is. You can stay until you catch him and feed your ego but after that, I want you gone from my home," I turn away, dismissing him.

"You are twisting my words out of your own insecurities," he reefs a pillow from the bed and storms out, slamming my door behind him.

Davis

I can pinpoint the exact moment this doubt crept into my mind, but at some point during the night, I gave it power. Trying to be the perfect boyfriend, wanting to be her hero, has rightly backfired on me and now, I am left feeling bitter. I resent the fact that I don't get to have the Joanna I met two years ago, all of the time. She can be happy for days, weeks even, but every now and then, I catch her staring into space and I know he has her. I know he still visits her mind and taunts her, pulling her from me when he does. Our sex life is amazing and the connection I feel to her is unlike anything I have ever felt before, except for the nights when she looks lost afterwards. Those nights, I know that I lost that connection somewhere during our love making and again, he is there between the sheets with us and I hate him. I hate him and I hate myself for being selfish enough to indulge in these thoughts. I feel twisted with rage, like a bull teased and taunted with a red cape, but never charging. Last night, I wanted so much to pull her body against mine and lose myself in just her scent, but I held back. I stopped my hand reaching across for hers and lay there wondering if I was good enough for the job of looking after her. How can I protect her when she won't even tell me when he makes contact? I have tried to be strong and to support her emotionally and I've tried to be patient and understanding. She has just been through a violent attack, violated by some scumbag. Doesn't she know the pain I feel for her? Can't she see that it tears me up inside to know that she suffered at his hands? Still suffers! I listen at night to her nightmares before gently nudging her in her sleep to wake her from his grip, once again. Am I fool to believe that I can provide that safe haven, a place where he can't reach her? I want her to continue her counselling and I encourage her to work through her grief, but when I show her my weakness, my anger and pain, she turns me away so coldly. Even admitting to myself that I struggle to be her rock and admitting that I too am suffering, shames me. I hate myself more than I hate him, for feeling this way. The realisation that this will always be there in our relationship, whether it is sexually, mentally or emotionally, for the rest of our lives, frightens me. I want to kill him and I want to protect her, but I am so fucking worried that in time, when she relives these moments, suffers flashbacks and shuts me out, I won't be strong enough to stay. I started something that I'm not so sure I can finish anymore.

I lift my forearm to wipe the dripping sweat from my brow, before going at the black leather punching bag again. I came straight here this morning after I dropped Joanna to work. That was one of the most uncomfortable car journeys I've ever sat through. The silence between us was as cold as the weather and I couldn't bring myself to apologise. Why the fuck should I? I duck my head lower and punch harder and faster, the air in my lungs wheezing out through my clamped jaw. I haven't been to the gym in weeks and my muscles are burning with the intensity of my workout. Michael has hovered around me a few times, eyeing me suspiciously. I am trying to work these cancerous thoughts out of my mind, before I succumb to them and forget the reasons why I am fighting for her. I know that mostly I'm afraid, I'm afraid that she meant every word last night. I am afraid that when I do catch him, and I will, that she won't need me anymore. I am afraid that through her counselling, she will realise that our relationship is no good for her recovery and she will let me go and it scares the shit out of me. I feel a hand on my bicep as I ferociously expel this pent up self-pity and turn quickly, my fist comes with me. Michael ducks, avoiding my power punch and I pull off my headphones.

"Shit, sorry man," I apologise, immediately.

"What the hell has gotten into you today?" He scowls, crossing his arms at his chest.

"I have a lot on my mind," I reach for a towel and wipe my sweaty brow.

"What's up, you and Jo Jo fall out?"

I sit down on the small bench, throwing my face into my towel and groaning. The small wooden bench dips, when Michael takes a seat and I worry it might snap with the weight of both of us.

"Thought so," he sighs and I turn to look at him, feeling heavy with emotion. When my eyes well up, I twist the towel until my hands hurt.

"I'm not sure I can cope with it all," my voice breaks and I clear my throat, mortified.

He nods with understanding, not needing me to explain any further and for that, I am grateful.

"I don't really talk about the bad things in mine and Bree's relationship, but it's not always perfect. I can be a real controlling jerk at times and she nags me to no end about chores and coming home too late. I don't talk about them because they don't matter and I realise that some relationships struggle with much bigger challenges and a lot of heartbreak. We are lucky and maybe it took all of those bad things to happen for us to know that, or maybe we would have always felt lucky anyway, but either way, you gotta cherish what you have. You know Bree still has bad days?"

I shake my head, no, because just like Michael said, they always only ever seem happy and I haven't seen Bree upset since she found out she was pregnant.

"She has been having nightmares about Seamus Lynch, now that this hearing is looming. I hate myself every day for what I put her through all those years ago. I met her and fell in love and when I thought loving her was hurting her, I allowed her to believe I was dead. I thought leaving her was the right thing to do. I was so fucking wrong mate, loving her is all that she needs from me. She doesn't ask me to be a robot and not feel my own pain and shame at what I put her through. She doesn't blame me and that angers me, still to this day. My point is that Jo Jo doesn't want you to feel guilty over what he did and she doesn't want you to fix it! She wants you to love her and to be there, through thick and thin and if you think that you might walk when the going gets tough, then you don't deserve her wounded soul," he pats my back firmly and his words hit every nail on the head.

"She is shutting me out and I don't know how to break through this barrier," I break down, like a baby, the anguish I feel is for Joanna, for me and for us.

"You can't erase this Davis, you just learn to cope with it, as best as you can. You forgive her when she is cold and distant and remember that this was never her fault. You remember that the good days are not far away and you treasure those days when you have them, because life is too short to spend it worrying about when she might have a bad day. You two are perfect for each other man."

I wipe my red eyes, "I would never think that this was her fault," I say, horrified that he could think that.

"I know mate, Joanna relies on you to be her strength

but look at you now, when you don't have her there to be strong for you, you're a blubbering mess," he teases me and I laugh.

"Asshole," I look down at the gym floor and shake my head, surprised by this release of emotion.

"On a serious note, this has been a very taxing time for you both, of course you are going to feel beaten at times, but that doesn't mean that you are! You are one hell of an Agent and you're going to catch him, he won't even see you coming!"

"Jesus, you should get a degree in psychology," I laugh, before standing up. He joins me and I hug him. "Thanks Michael."

"Ok, calm down, this is getting a bit weird now," he pushes me away, laughing.

"What the hell is going on in here," we both turn to see Bree, waddling through the doors. I smile warmly when I see her swollen face, pregnancy suits her.

"There's my woman," Michael walks over, bending down to kiss her and I watch them, remembering everything that they went through and I feel like a fool.

"How much longer have you got left?" I ask her, before giving her my own hug.

"Two months, but the doc reckons I could go sooner," her shoulders slump at the idea of another two months of pregnancy, "I just put an ad in the Boston Times for a Nanny," she lets out a deep breath.

"Ok kids, I am meeting Roche in a few minutes, so I better dash."

"Oh, do you and Jo want to eat out tonight," she calls, "I could do with a night off from cooking."

"Not tonight Bree, we fell out so I have some serious grovelling to do," I admit to her, before kissing her forehead and running towards the showers. Roche and I are meeting outside the final construction site in one hour and I feel pumped to not only make up with Joanna, but to look at this case with new eyes.

CHAPTER
25

Davis

The location we arrive to, could hardly be described as a building site anymore, despite the amount of men walking around in hard hats. The skyscraper building, will soon be an upmarket apartment complex for Boston's elite.

"There is a guy in a blue hard hat over there," Roche points to a chubby man who is holding a clipboard and running his mouth off at some poor schmuck who arrived late. We both roll our eyes and walk towards him.

"FBI," we both flash our badges and watch as his already red face, turns purple, "we need to ask you some questions." Roche nods, while folding his badge back into his suit pocket. I decide to stand with my legs spread and my arms crossed, assessing this mans every move. I have a knack for seeing through somebody's bullshit and today, I am in no mood to be running around in circles chasing my tail. I want to know who this fucker is. His DNA didn't match with anyone already doing time, leaving this avenue as the only lead in the case.

"What's your name?" I ask.

"Gary Thurlow, I'm the foreman," he snarls and I lift my brows, my eyes darkening in warning.

"We are looking for a man; we think he may have worked here," Roche takes the lead on the questioning, "he would have worked on panelling, specifically with white cement."

"We used white cement in all the bathrooms, rich folk's, ey?" He blows out a nervous breath and I wonder why he is on edge. I know for a fact that he didn't commit this crime, but he is hiding something and that just might work in our favour.

"Yeah, crazy," Roche agrees, mollifying him, "how many men would have overseen the interior building?"

"We have had numerous contractors coming on site the past few months, you would be looking at near two hundred men," he slams his hands on his hips, his eyes rolling upwards as he thinks.

"We are looking for someone who would be about 6ft 3, crooked teeth with a scar above his left eyebrow," Roche reads out the description from his notebook, but I keep my eyes trained on him and because of it, I spot the slight twitch in his eyes.

"Sound like anyone of your workers?" I ground out sharply.

"No," he shakes his head adamantly, "I hope you find him," he moves to leave and then I see it, fear. He is afraid and he knows exactly who I am looking for.

"Wait," I call out and he turns back. "You know it's against the law to withhold information, don't you?" I try my own fear tactic.

"I do," he nods his head, before looking down to kick the dirt.

"I can have a search warrant within the hour to close this place down," I whip out our only bluff.

His eyes flare up in anger. "Now wait a minute, I don't have time for your lot coming around here and delaying this project," he waves his rolled up blueprints at us.

"I know you're hiding something from me," I cross my arms and stare him down.

"Jesus Christ," he rubs his jaw, clearly conflicted. "Ok, but first, I want you to guarantee that none of what I tell you, can be held against me and that you won't investigate my company further," he stutters, confirming my instincts that he was hiding his own dirty dealings.

"How about you tell me and I won't close you down today," I counter.

"Guarantee my company is left out of this shit and I can lead you straight to him," he crosses his arms, knowing full well he has some ammunition.

I take him up on his offer because today, whatever crap he has going on here, doesn't mean shit to me. I'm here as Joanna's boyfriend, my badge might as well be from the dollar store. We are breaking all the rules and Roche is the only person who I trust enough to have my back.

"Deal," Roche cuts in once again, risking his career to

help me.

"There are some workers that I might take on, that aren't exactly through the books," his face flushes red. "This one guy came to me through another contact, he is a good worker, keeps his head down, but he's tough, not the kind of person any of my men would mess with."

"A name," I growl.

"I don't know his full name, but the lads call him Razor."

"That's not good enough."

"All I know is that he arrives on time and leaves when his work is done, he never gave me his surname and I never asked for it, I didn't need it," he shrugs.

"What does he drive?" Roche asks.

"A white van."

"Make and model?" I snap. I should probably go easy on him considering he is risking his business to help us, but I'm too impatient. There is a fire in my belly; it's a familiar feeling to me. I get it when I know I am close to closing a case.

"It's a ford transit, that's all I know about him," he becomes flustered, waving his hands and looking beyond us.

"Is he still working here?" I hear Roche ask, but I don't hear his answer as the hairs on the back of my neck stand up and a cold chill runs down my spine.

As if in slow motion, I turn around towards the gates into the building site. The sun is low and blinds me. I lift my hand to shade my eyes and sitting halfway through the entrance, a white van comes into focus. I stare at it for just a moment before its engine roars and it reverses at speed. I run in its direction, unbuttoning my holster and grabbing my gun as I go. I watch as it crashes into the parked cars on the street, one of which is my SUV. I reach the entrance as he accelerates past me. Our eyes meet for one split second and I know that this is the man that raped Joanna. I raise my gun praying for a clear shot, but the streets are too busy and the sun is too low to risk it. Roche reaches me as it turns the corner and out of sight. We run for the SUV, but the driver door is jammed shut, causing me to have to climb over the passenger seat and I curse in frustration, this is slowing me down.

"Call it in," I direct Roche, before giving chase. We turn the same corner and there is no sign of the van up ahead. There are two turns just up ahead and we stop, looking left and right and again, we can't see the van in either direction.

"How the fuck could he have disappeared so soon," I roar, punching the steering wheel.

"Highway 89 is to the right, he might try to head out of the city," Roche reasons, but I turn left.

"He isn't leaving," I turn on my lights and siren and rush towards Joanna's office.

Razor

My heart is racing; the thrill of outsmarting him and getting away, is electrifying. My dick is hard just watching them speed past me and I know exactly how I want to build on this ecstasy. I pull out of the warehouse I hid in and head to the site; I need to know exactly what that fat bastard Gary told them. I always knew that they would catch up with me; I had been sloppy when I left Joanna alive, but I'll finish what I started before skipping town. I don't plan on coming back or ever facing the wrath of my brother. He and his new boss can find themselves a new spy; I'm done being their babysitter. I have dreams of my own, fantasies I want to carry out on the road. The next few days are crucial, I need to cover my tracks and get out of Boston undetected, before they finally identify me.

Jo

Maybe I over-reacted? I question myself again, before fixing my lipstick. I lean over the sink, closer to the bathroom mirror and catch sight of the black rings under my eyes and cringe. I hardly slept a wink last night after I kicked Davis out of my bed. I lay awake, terrified that he is going to do what I told him to do and leave. I dab some foundation around my eyes before heading back to my office.

"Where is she gone?" I turn the corner to see Davis and Roche standing in the entrance of Eric's office. As I move closer, I realise that Davis sounds frantic.

"What do you mean you don't know, how long is she missing?" He yells. I rush over to stop this madness.

"What the hell is going on?" I look between all three men. Eric is standing up, his hands on his hips and looking unimpressed at the fact the Davis is screaming in his office. Roche has the decency to look embarrassed while Davis continues to look pissed off.

"Where have you been?" He snaps and I narrow my eyes at his tone, before turning to Eric,

"I'm sorry about this Eric," he smiles sympathetically, "get out of here now!" I bark, before I turn on my heels and leave Eric's office, knowing that Roche and Davis will follow me. I sit down at my desk, just in time for them both to barge into my office.

"Gentlemen," I smile tightly, before looking back at my keyboard.

"Joanna," Davis growls at me, but I continue to ignore them both. I have already asked them what is going on and I refuse to explain that I was in the ladies' room, without some explanation as to why they are at my workplace, screaming at my friends and colleagues.

"Joanna," Davis' raspy tones plead with me to look at him, so I turn facing him, but keeping my expression blank.

"Something has happened today, we got a huge break in your case," he sits across the desk from me, his eyes never leaving mine.

"Did you find him?" My stomach twists violently and the need to throw up assails me. I try to swallow past the dry lump that has lodged itself in my throat, but instead, I'm forced to take a drink of water. Davis shakes his head, no, as I lift the bottle to my mouth. I look up at Roche who is standing behind him and he too looks worried.

"No, we know he goes by the name Razor and that he works construction across town. We don't have his real name yet, but we are already working on it. The thing is, he saw us and fled the scene, in a white van."

"You saw him? How did he get away?" I ask urgently.

"The SUV was damaged when he was fleeing, it slowed us down," Roche interjects.

"Ok, so how will you catch him?" I link my hands, squeezing them hard. My body is trembling and I need to try get myself under control.

"I don't think he will leave Boston, not until he finishes what he started with, you," Davis comes around and hunches down beside me, "I won't let that happen," he promises. He reaches for my hands and covers them with his own. Their warmth soothes me and I twist in my chair to face him and nod.

"So, what's the plan?"

"We need to fill Vic Breen in on what we have so far, he needs to be the one making the arrest. I need you to stay here and I will pick you up on the way home, no going to the bathroom alone, don't leave the office for anything and don't answer your phone," he demands softly and I agree. I'm not stupid, if my attacker is running scared, then he is unpredictable. He is more dangerous now than ever before.

CHAPTER 26

Davis

We arrive to the Police Department and fill Vic Breen in on everything. To say that he wasn't pleased to see us, is an understatement. This case is close to home for all of us, so his happiness at our new lead, over-ruled his other feelings. I know that we over stepped our boundaries by interfering in his case, he is a good detective but on this, he was too slow.

"Ok, so we had our tech team email us a list of men, aged between twenty and forty five, living in Boston and driving a white Ford van," I pull out my phone and begin to scroll through my email.

"Send it to me, we can print it off," he pulls out his chair and sits down at his desk, firing up his computer. We wait patiently for his internet to load.

"I can just send it to the printer from my phone," Roche offers.

"I don't have time for all this modern technology crap!" He huffs and we both roll our eyes. He is the one wasting time by being so stubborn and set in his historical ways.

"Now see, almost done," he clicks the internet icon and again, we wait, as the page loads.

"Jesus, send it to the printer already Roche," I run my hands through my hair, frustrated with this ridiculous scenario. A few seconds later, the unmistakable sound of paper being drawn into the printer, sounds out and I thank God for small mercies.

"Didn't quite get there fast enough boys," Breen smiles triumphantly, as if winning some battle against technology and I ignore him and begin scanning down the list on my phone, as he scans his paper list.

"How many names have we got on here?" He asks a few moments later.

"About three hundred, just see if any name stands out," I pull up a seat next to him. I don't mind admitting that this is one area that Breen will have better Intel. He has worked the streets of Boston for over thirty years, he knows them like the back of his hand and with that, he knows the people who walk them. He finishes one page and lays it face down on his desk before starting the second.

"Ok, here we go," he pulls his reading glasses down and looks over the rim, towards us.

"You got Richard Casey here, I think he is the younger brother of Nate Casey," he begins to type the name into his computer screen and we all hover around it, waiting for the information to load.

Richard Casey, I say the name over in my head, trying to find some connection to Joanna, but nothing comes to mind.

"Nate Casey, currently serving twenty five years for armed robbery," Vic taps the screen where siblings are listed, "he has a younger brother, Richard Casey and a younger sister, Yvonne."

"Who is this guy, Nate?" I ball my fists in an attempt to quell the bile, rising in my throat. My gut is telling me that we are on to something.

"Who prosecuted him?" I ask, waiting to hear her name.

"I can look into that, but he is ten years into his sentence, long before Joanna, so I doubt that is the connection. He was a mean son of a bitch; I remember him well."

"So, what have we got on the younger brother?" Roche butts in.

"Let me run a search now on him," Breen says, typing away, "ok, so he is thirty five, single, lives two blocks from Roxbury Crossing, unemployed."

"Look up his previous work history," I interrupt Breen again. "Son of a bitch."

"What?" I snap, not close enough to read the screen myself.

"He worked for Beck and Smith Construction for five years, before they went out of business in 2009."

"Ok, so this has to be our guy, Roche, see if you can get any images of him from the tech team," I look to Roche, who already has the phone to his ear. I listen as he calls out Breen's email address and then hangs up.

"They are sending his most recent drivers licence photo," Roche informs us. I begin to tap my foot impatiently and when both our phones beep simultaneously, I know the emails have come through. I quickly open the attachment and stare down at the face of Joanna's attacker. There is no doubt in my mind that this is the face of the man who assaulted her and tried to murder her and my blood boils with rage.

"That's him," I snap.

"We need to be sure, let's go show Jo the picture," Vic stands.

"No, we don't have time, I know it's him!" I grind my teeth, impatiently.

"This is my case and I'm not arresting someone without more proof than your hunch," Vic growls back and I turn away from him to gather my thoughts. I need to tread carefully.

"Hold on a minute," I take out my phone and dial Joanna's number.

"Hello," her voice is shaky and I feel awful for what I am about to do to her. She is alone and afraid and I'm about to ask her to face her fears.

"Can you do something for me?" I ask, softly.

"Do you know who it is?" She returns.

"I think so, but Vic needs you to identify him before they can make an arrest, if I send you a photo."

"Send it," she answers quickly.

I nod to Roche who closes his eyes, not wanting to be any part of this. I watch him send the image.

"Did you get it?" I ask a moment later.

"Yes. It's him," she manages, before I hear her weep and my heart clenches.

"I'm sorry, I'm coming to get you as soon as I take care of this," I promise.

"Ok," her voice is muffled before she hangs up and I feel like shit.

"Let's go get him," I stand after a moment and face both men.

"No, you can't be present at the arrest, Davis!" Breen slices his hand through the air, before taking his cream, suit jacket that is hanging on the back of his chair and putting it on.

"What the hell do you mean?" I growl.

"Do you want this fucker behind bars?" Breen snaps back. I clench and unclench my fists, trying to distract myself from this burning desire to hunt and kill.

"Don't talk shit, you know I do."

"Then you can't be anywhere near this arrest, this is not your jurisdiction and I won't have the case thrown out on a technicality," he walks away, before turning back, "I will have your badge if you try to involve yourself here Agent, go home and wait with Joanna, I'll call you when he is in custody."

"Davis, I know you don't want to hear this, but he is right," Roche pipes up, a few seconds after Breen disappears behind his Superintendent's door. I stand, unmoving, allowing my brain to digest the information. I could ignore all protocol and just go and pull this scumbag out of his house and kill him or I could give Joanna's case the best chance in court and walk away. Walk away, the idea of leaving here and doing nothing is too disturbing, but being the person that fucks this up, is even worse. I can't bear the idea of letting her down, but I'm pretty certain that either way, I could potentially be doing just that.

"What if he gets away from them and we aren't there to stop it?"

"Technically, he warned you away, so I could still follow them out there and keep my eye on everything," Roche smirks.

I nod, saying nothing and everything with one gesture, before we walk towards the exit. We drive back to the Bureau where Roche collects his car and we part ways. I trust Roche will keep me up to speed on any and all developments.

Roche

I wait in my car as Vic Breen and his team, descend on the house. The targets white van, is parked outside and it looks like somebody is home. There are flashing blue lights everywhere, hardly a covert operation but technically, they're only taking him in for questioning. My head is pounding as I sit here, feeling helpless. We should be there to question the scumbag; after all, if it wasn't for our work, they wouldn't even know where to be looking. I pull out my phone and text Davis to let him know they have gone in, before turning my attention back to the small white house in Roxbury. The neighbourhood isn't bad, but there is something about this particular house. It looks unloved and uncared for. The garden is overgrown and even from where I sit across the street, the white paint around the small porch looks to be chipping. After another thirty minutes, Breen walks out with a woman in handcuffs. Fuck this shit! I decide to step out of my car and walk over.

"Jesus, I should have known one of you would show up," Breen curses, but he seems more amused than angry.

"What's going on?" I ask, twisting my head to see past him and into the house.

"He came home two hours ago, dropped the van, told his Mom he was leaving town for a bit and packed a rucksack," he shrugs, before talking into his radio.

"Why are you arresting her?" I wonder.

"She was burning clothes out the back when we arrived, looks like a work blanket and some other things, so we are taking her in to see what else she is hiding."

"We should put an APB out on him, get officers to every bus station, railway station and taxi company in Boston, find out how he left," I suggest.

"Already on it, we found this," he holds up a plastic bag with a passport in it, "he won't be leaving the country any time soon, unless he has a fake."

"Get some men on the airports anyway, ok, good job,"

I shake his hand before jumping into my car and heading straight to Joanna's to fill Davis in. I know he will be walking the floors waiting on news and although this is not necessarily good news, its progress.

Jo

The same silence from this morning, accompanies us on our journey home. Even worse, I can't distract myself from driving because Davis had to return his damaged SUV to the Bureau and insisted he drove. I feel alone and afraid and he doesn't seem to be aware or even care. I wrap my arms around myself and try to hold in my tears.

"I'm sorry about last night," I gulp, looking away from him and out the window.

"This doesn't ever leave us, does it?" He asks and I turn to face him, but his eyes are on the road ahead of him.

"No," I answer honestly, because he deserves the truth. I am broken inside and it won't heal overnight or maybe ever, "you should probably just go, sooner rather than later, I don't want to drag this out," I sniff.

"I'm not leaving," he barks, his nostrils flaring in anger, but he still refuses to look at me, "I'm going to catch him and then, we are going to figure this out Joanna."

"I don't want to be a burden, I don't want you to feel guilty, Will, you can go and I wouldn't blame you, this is too fucked up to ask anyone to put up with," I find a tissue in my bag and blow my nose.

"Don't ever talk about yourself like that again Joanna!"

"Like what? You can't even look at me," I yell, frustrated with him. I feel confused and exhausted and alone. We pull into a parking space outside my apartment and I jump out. The cold air is a welcome change from our heated discussion and I fall against my car. Davis steps out and looks over the hood at me.

"The reasons I can't look at you are because I don't feel good enough right now. It doesn't mean that I want to walk or that I think I deserve better; it means that I think you deserve better!"

His soft admission causes my vision to blur. He comes around and takes my hand, leading me into the building.

"We have a lot of talking to do Davis, I'm not sure we can get through all of this," I say, regretfully.

"Not tonight, let's take a day or two until they catch him and then, when things aren't so emotionally charged, we can figure it out," his thumb slides across my cheek, wiping away a tear and I nod.

The strain between us has lessened but once again, Roche pays a visit and informs both of us that Richard Casey, aka Razor, is on the run. Davis sleeps on the couch again, insisting that it is to keep an eye out for any intruders, but I just can't be sure that it's not more to do with not wanting to be intimate with me. I try to rid my mind of negative thinking, but it plagues my thoughts until I fall asleep in the early hours.

CHAPTER
27

Bree

"Michael, I'm getting stretch marks," I climb into bed and plop down heavily, beside my hunky husband. My tummy has grown so much that I can only sleep comfortably on my side or back and I can't wait for the day when I can roll onto my stomach again.

"You literally have two stretch marks Bree," he laughs and pulls up my top to kiss my belly.

"I still have two months to go Michael!" I sulk, sticking out my bottom lip and he laughs at my childish behaviour.

"Women!"

"Listen up Mr. Ryan, you are not allowed to give out about my womanly complaints; I'm friggin seven months pregnant with twins! I think my feet are swollen but I wouldn't know, because I can't see them anymore, my back aches and my face is puffy and unattractive," I continue my pity party, while he turns out the bedside lamp.

"You have never looked more beautiful," he pulls me into the crook of his body and kisses my cheek.

"My back is sore babe; can you rub it?"

I hear him chuckling softly, as he runs his hands along my tender muscles.

"You are such a crank today," he says, as he kneads my lower back. I can't even deny it, I have moaned every minute of the day and Michael has graciously taken it in his stride.

"I know, it's my hormones," I turn onto my back, my big belly sticking up into the air and turn my head to face him. His beautiful blue eyes are smiling at me in the darkness and his hands run over my bump slowly.

"Do you want to divorce me?" I joke.

"You mean I can," he laughs, before reaching forward and kissing me. A sharp pain shoots across my back and I wince.

"You ok?" He freaks, sitting up immediately. "Is it time?"

I begin laughing at his reaction. "No Michael, the midwife said I would get these cramps, remember?"

"But you looked in pain Bree, maybe we should get it checked," he is so serious and I can't help but laugh again. All evening, I have been getting a dull ache in my tummy and back, but this is the first serious cramp that I have experienced.

"Jeez, will you relax Michael, this is all normal, I have a check-up in two days, we will speak with the nurse then," I reassure him.

"If you're sure," he says, reluctantly, before lying back down beside me. His arms come around my tummy, as he cradles his family. We fall asleep, snuggled up together.

I wake when I feel a warm gush of water between my legs. My first thought is that I wet myself, but before I can process what exactly is happening, Michael jumps up.

"What the hell?" His sleep laden voice croaks out, as he bends to switch on the light.

"I think my waters just broke," I say dumbly, before becoming frantic with worry, "it's too soon," I fret, as I move out of the wet. A sharp pain crosses my stomach and I begin to cry.

"Michael, this is happening, I'm not ready! What if something is wrong with the babies?" I clench my teeth together, talking through the pain.

"Bree, practice your breathing, everything is fine," Michael comes around the bed and tries to reassure me.

"I'm calling an ambulance now, just remember your breathing exercises," he kisses my lips, before talking down the phone to the emergency operator. Michael dresses quickly.

"I don't have my hospital bag ready," I cry, feeling like the worst mother in the world already. I should have been more prepared to go early.

"Bree, that's not important, I'll throw some things into a bag now," Michael hurries about, doing just that.

"You need two sets of everything and put my nightgown in there too," I call after him, as he leaves to fetch things from the nursery, "and bring some blankets, oh and their bottles," I call from the edge of the bed, as another pain takes hold.

"MICHAEL," I yell in agony and he rushes back to my side.

"I'm here, stay calm," he speaks low and easy to me, as he pulls my wet nightgown over my head and replaces it with a clean one. He bends and removes my underwear and again, replaces them with a fresh pair.

"Thank you," I cry because he is being so attentive.

"The ambulance is here," he says, at the same time, I hear them arrive.

He leaves my side and rushes to let them in. When the paramedics help me into the ambulance and my care is in their hands, Michael then allows himself to worry.

"Will I call Jo?" He asks, holding my hands. I take another deep breath as a stronger, more intense pain crosses my back and tummy.

"YES," I answer loudly, I need Michael, but I also need my best friend because I am scared shitless.

Jo

My flashing phone lights up my room in a blue hue. For a split second, I freeze, before reaching over to my locker to look at who might be calling at this hour. I have been unable to sleep. I miss Davis beside me and I wish I could just go out and tell him how much I love him. I want so badly to take back the things I said earlier and promise him that we can get through anything together. Every time I stepped out of my bed and my feet touched the cold floor, I jumped right back under the covers where I'm safe, where I don't have to bare myself to him in the hopes that he won't reject me. He wants to wait until they catch Razor, but that may never happen. I keep telling myself to go to him, tell him that I'm sorry and maybe he too, will feel relief. I tell myself over and over that he loves me, I just wish I believed it was enough.

"Bree," I answer the phone immediately when I see her number on the screen.

"Jo Jo, it's Michael," I sit up when I hear Michael's concerned voice come across the line.

"Michael, is everything ok?" I switch on my bedside lamp and pull back my covers, ready to leap from my bed if they need me.

"The babies are coming, Bree is calling for you," he sounds as shocked as I feel, the little rascals are early. The noise of the ambulance in the background begins to sound down the phone.

"We are on the way, tell her to hold on!" I say, excitedly.

I hang up the phone and call out to Davis. He is in my room in no time and looks surprised to see me smiling, as I pull on some jeans.

"Get dressed! Bree is in labour," I chirp, pulling my favourite grey knitted jumper over my head.

"Is Bree ok?" His fretful expression is so endearing, I love how much he loves Bree. I don't think I could love somebody who didn't find Bree as amazing as I do.

"I imagine she is in the worst pain of her life, but she will be ok," I laugh.

I pull on some shoes as he leaves my room to get ready. When I'm good to go, I stand by the front door and call after Davis to move his butt. He eventually comes out of the bathroom, looking like he is going to a party, with his hair slick and his favourite cologne wafting from his skin.

"It's not a fashion show," I roll my eyes at him, while throwing him my car keys. He catches them with one hand and cocks a smile.

"You can never look too good baby," he winks and I roll my eyes again.

"Out," I point to the door and he walks past me, laughing. I'm happy that there is an easy atmosphere between us, at least for tonight.

We are met at the entrance to the hospital by Michael who brings us straight up to Bree's suite. When we walk in, she is lying on her side and sucking gas and air from a tube attached to the side of her bed. I rush to her side, pulling off my jacket and taking her hand.

"You're doing great," I murmur softly and watch as her face contorts in pain and she moans out loudly.

"MICHAEL," she cries in agony.

"I'm here," he comes behind me and I look over at Davis, who is standing very close to the exit.

"I can't do this, I'm going to die," she cries again and I try to soothe her.

"Bree, you aren't going to die, practice your breathing and remain calm," I take a warm towel and wipe the sweat from her hair.

"What's your birthing plan?"

"I didn't want any medication, but if they don't give me an epidural soon, I'm going to kill somebody," she squeezes my hand and the nurse that is in the room, moves me aside to check the babies' heartrates.

"Bree, I am going to see how far along you are and then we can discuss pain medication," she smiles, warmly.

"Ok, I'm outside," Davis hurries to Bree's side, "good luck, you'll do great," he kisses her cheek before rushing out of the room.

I look up at Michael who is pale and completely out of his depth.

"The good news is that you're ten centimetres Bree, the bad news is that it's too late for pain relief," the nurse pulls off her latex gloves and stands up from the bed. She moves to the wall, pushing a red button before moving away. My eyes follow her, shocked, before I turn to Bree who seems just as bewildered.

"No, I can't be, ahhhhhhh," she tries to dispute the nurse's findings, but a new contraction silences her.

"Bree, you can do this," I lean forward and kiss her forehead, "Michael, you take her hand here and I'll move around the other side of the bed. I pry my hand from Bree's deathly grip and allow Michael closer to her. She keeps her eyes closed as her face turns purple, I can tell she is trying to hold in her screams.

"Good Bree, you're being so brave," I try to praise her. I don't think I'm much use right now, all I want to do is take away her pain. A moment later, two female nurses and a doctor, walk into the room, bringing with them two incubators.

"Ok Bree, this is the moment that you have waited for," the doctor speaks to her as she checks the reading from the heart monitor and Bree's vitals.

"After the next contraction, we are going to start pushing," she smiles warmly, before moving away to prepare for delivery. The nurse who has been in the room all along and whose name tag reads Sophie, lifts up stirrups from the side of the bed.

"Let's get your legs up here and we will try pushing with you lying down first," she smiles.

"I can't, my legs are too weak to lift," Bree's eyes are heavy and she seems to be falling asleep.

"Oooouuuuucccchhh," she whimpers again, turning towards Michael.

"It's ok Babe, I'll lift them up for you. I am so proud of you Bree, you're doing a great job, let's see this through, ok," he whispers lovingly into her ear and I watch as her eyes pop open. She smiles at him weakly and nods. My eyes well up as he lifts her legs before returning to her side.

"Ok Bree, when I tell you to push, you push down into your back side, with all your might, ok?" The doctor comes and sits at the end of the bed. When he sees the signs of her contraction reappearing, he calls for her to push.

Bree and Michaels first baby is born twenty minutes later.

"It's a boy," one of the nurses announces before quickly holding him up for Bree, Michael and myself and rushing him away to be cleaned up.

"He is not crying," Bree frets, but her worries are soon put to rest when his first little squeal rings out around the room.

"Ok Bree, your job isn't over just yet," the doctor reminds her and two minutes later, another baby boy arrives. They are both wrapped in blue blankets and brought over to meet their parents. I stand by watching, as this family meet each other for the very first time and feel overwhelmed with pride and love for them all. It was the most magical thing I have ever witnessed, once again reminding me that there is beauty in this world, you just have to be open to receiving it.

Davis comes back into the delivery suite when the nurses have finished cleaning Bree up.

"What are you going to call them?" He asks, bending over me to get a closer look at their scrunched up little faces.

"We have each chosen a name," Bree keeps her eyes on her little bundles of joy. "I'm calling this little guy, Daniel and Michael is calling this little guy, Rohan," she leans over, kissing both their foreheads.

"Perfect" I croak delighted they have given each child their own individual identity.

"Ok, we need to take the babies to ICU, just to monitor them over night," the doctor cuts across our moment, "they are quite big for premature babies, but we need to make sure they are breathing for themselves. It's only precautionary."

"We will go and let you rest," Davis taps my shoulder and I nod in agreement. It is almost 6.00 a.m. now and we both need to work today.

"I will come back this evening," I promise, before kissing both babies on the forehead and hugging Bree and Michael goodbye.

CHAPTER 28

Aisling

"Hi, Michael, I'm your little sister, surprise!!!"
Maybe I shouldn't drop that bombshell straight away. I
close my eyes, take a deep breath and begin again. I look
straight into the small square mirror and my blue eyes
stare back at me. "Hi Michael, guess what? We have the
same Da," I keep my voice low, in case someone is waiting
outside to use the toilet. Jesus, I sound like an absolute
eejit! I groan inwardly at my ridiculous introductions.
Granted, it's not easy to travel halfway across the world,
track down the brother you never knew you had and risk
being turned away. I chew my thumb nail nervously, while
thinking harder for the perfect introduction. Ah come
on Aisling, cop on, it's not bleedin' rocket science! You
can think of a better way to introduce yourself to him,
I become frustrated again when nothing comes to mind.
I run my hands through my long, sleek auburn hair, just
as we hit some turbulence, which causes me to fall back
against the toilet. I steady myself before unlocking the
door to return to my seat. I'm met with the angry face of
another passenger, alright mate I'm done, I roll my eyes.
I sit down just as the seatbelt light comes on and can't
help the little surge of excitement that courses through
my body. I am giddy with anticipation and can't wait to
set eyes on my handsome brother in person. I have seen
newspaper clippings of him and his beautiful wife Aubrey
and I just know I will love them both. He has kind eyes,
that's the reason I worked up enough courage to make this
trip to visit him. Leaving Dublin, was easy enough. I have
no ties, except my best friend Kate, to keep me there and
I long to be part of a family again. It was getting up the
cash to get the hell out of there, now that was a struggle.
Working in a crèche is rewarding. but not very lucrative.
The plane wobbles again and my stomach dips once more,
just my luck, crash into the Atlantic before my feet touch
American soil, I fret.

"Ladies and gentlemen, we have a bit of turbulence

up ahead, please remain seated until the seat belt sign is switched off," the pilots voice booms over the speakers. I lean over the Priest who is seated next to me and catch sight of the dark clouds.

"Looks like we will have a bumpy landing," he smiles.

"Jaysus, Father don't go administering the last rights or anything," I joke.

"Ah no, sure I'll only do that when we are nose diving into the ocean," he quips back and I laugh out loud. I love a good sense of humour.

"If that happens, do you think I'll get into heaven by association?" I giggle, but it turns into a full laugh when the priest howls louder.

"I can't promise you anything, but I'll have a chat with himself when we arrive at the gates."

"Thanks Father," I smile warmly, before settling back against my chair.

"You going on a holiday?" He asks and I turn with my full smile still remaining. I feel so happy right now that even grey clouds or potential imminent death, can't drag me down.

"No, I'm meeting my brother for the first time, I'm so nervous and excited all at once."

"Marvellous dear, I'm sure he is feeling the same way, he will love you," he pats my hand.

"Well Father, maybe you could pray that he will want me to be part of his family," I ask him, seriously.

"Of course dear," he promises, before returning to his book.

We land two hours later and I walk through Boston airport, in awe. I'm sure to everyone else, I look like a total moron as I walk about with a grin as wide as the River Shannon. I collect my baggage and stop myself from squealing with delight when I walk outside and hop straight into the back of a yellow taxi, or is it a cab?

"What part of Boston can I take you to Mam?" The driver asks and I get all tingly. I just love the way he says 'part', 'paht'!

"I'm staying at the Day hostel, I think it's...," I pull out the print off that I brought with the address of my hostel on it, "...it's 2230 Sycamore Avenue," I beam.

"You got it," he says, before pulling away from the airport. I stick my face up close to the window and try to get a better view of the city. Unfortunately, the weather is crap so I can't see much but it doesn't matter, this is my new home, I have enough time to see it in full colour.

Jo

At one point during the day, I think I fell asleep with my eyes open. How I managed to make it through the whole afternoon on no sleep, is beyond me but by the time I was leaving the office, I had a new burst of energy. It may have had something to do with the fact that I was visiting Bree and the babies. We stay with them for over an hour, before I begin to feel nauseated with sleep deprivation and bow out. Davis looks like the walking dead and because we both look a mess, Michael insists on taking us home in my car before getting a cab back to Bree and the babies. We don't bother with food and fall straight into bed.

I sleep all through the night and wake up to the sounds of Davis, snoring lightly beside me. I turn around and face him as he sleeps, his mouth is propped open a little and I smile at how cute he looks. I am happy that he stayed with me last night, but I wish we were on better terms. The alarm clock sounds and his eyes pop open and meet mine.

"Hey," he sits up, still dressed in his jeans and shirt from yesterday. I, on the other hand, had managed to slip into something more comfortable.

"Morning," I stretch my arms above my head and roll onto my back. I'm aware that the blankets have been pulled down, revealing my lace camisole. Davis' eyes travel up my torso before landing on my breasts and I feel my nipples harden at his perusal. His hand pulls the blanket lower and he takes in my black lace French knickers.

"How did I miss this last night?" His husky voice causes my skin to prickle with need.

"We both hit the pillows hard," I say, moving to sit up.

"No, stay lying down Joanna, let me look at you," he orders me and I must admit, I like when he is bossy. I fall back into my staged pose and when his head dips and his tongue slides across my tummy, I groan loudly.

"I've missed you," I whisper honestly and his eyes come up to meet mine.

"I'm going to show you just how much I have missed you Joanna," he says, before pulling the blankets completely from the bed and sliding lower between my legs. Spreading me wider, he stares appreciatively, before running his fingers on the inside of my underwear. He slides up and down my folds without parting them and it is torturous.

"Jesus Davis," I writhe beneath him and he smiles seductively, before pulling away the lacy barrier and finding my core with his tongue. I thrash about beneath him, my hips taking on a mind of their own, as my body moves to the rhythm he has set. It is heaven and hell all at the same time and when I finally find my release, it is off the Richter scale. I sit up, pulling at his blue shirt as he removes his jeans and like wild animals, we attack each other's mouths. He pushes me back down and falls with me, before finding my entrance and coming home. His body against mine, our mouths clashing, his pelvis as it thrusts deeper, all combine to drive me over the edge again and we both convulse together.

"Now, that's what you call make up sex," he laughs softly, his head still nestled between my breasts.

"I'm sorry that I was so distant and cruel," I croak and again he leans up, looking into my eyes.

"This is not going to be easy Joanna, I don't feel good enough to help you through this and I am afraid that you won't need me forever, but right now, all I know is what I am good at."

"What's that?"

"Loving you, I can do it like nobody else can and even

though I might say stupid shit, or put my foot in it, at least you will know that I'm here and I'm not leaving, even if I do have to spend a few nights on the sofa," his face turns upwards in an easy smile.

"Davis," my throat constricts as I try to open up and let him in, so that he knows how much I need him and how much I care. "I have days when I feel sick and afraid, I worry that this horrible thing could happen again or that worse things could happen to me, because I don't feel invincible anymore and on those days, I go into my little shell and I hide, but please know that when I'm ready to come back out, it will only ever be to you," warm tears run down my cheeks.

"I'm here on those days if you need me, but if you need space, I will respect that, but you need to understand that I hurt for you and with you, so as long as we respect each other, we won't need to worry that the other will flee." He runs the tip of his nose against mine. I wrap my arms around his neck, feeling like we can get through anything together.

"I love you so much," I kiss his cheek.

"Ditto," he pulls my waist and holds me tighter against his chest.

****

If Dick does not let us pass the security gate, I think I will throw my first ever hissy fit. Bree and Michael are due home from the hospital within the hour and we convinced them to give us a set of keys to prepare a small welcome home party.

"What is taking him so long?" I moan to Davis, while we sit waiting on Dick to return from his booth.

"He is on the phone, probably to Michael," he shrugs, seemingly relaxed.

"Ok guys, go on ahead, sorry about that," he comes back a minute later and waves us through.

"Can't resist your charm," I nudge Davis and he turns

with a wicked smile on his face.

"He's not the only one babe."

"Call me babe again and I'll rip out those sexy eyes of yours," I laugh as we climb out of his now repaired, SUV. We haven't talked much about my attacker over the last few days. I know that Roche and Davis have had numerous conversations with Vic Breen and that Roche is keeping close tabs on the investigation. He has been over to our apartment almost every night, to fill Davis in, but I refuse to listen in. I only want to know vital information; I'm trying to be upbeat and positive. I have group therapy this evening and I'm really looking forward to getting all of this off my chest.

We hang banners and dress the kitchen with blue balloons and decorations.

"Joanna, what the hell?" Davis runs his hands through his hair, looking bemused.

"What?" I say offended, as I look around at my creation.

"Did you buy all the balloons?" His eyes widen, as they roam around the room, causing me to laugh.

I don't have time to answer him because the front door opens and in walks Bree, Michael, Daniel and Rohan. I run from the kitchen, my heels clicking against their oak floors to meet them.

"Oh, give them here," I lean over the car seat Michael is holding, before turning my attention to Bree. She looks tired and pale, so I reign in my excitement and shower her with attention first.

"You go have a bath and then we can have some cake," I usher her towards the stairs a few minutes later and smile, as she hesitates about leaving the babies. Michael is holding baby Daniel.

"Will you check his diaper?" She calls over her shoulder to him.

"Sure babe, I'm on it," Michael smiles, before standing up and while still holding the baby, crosses the room to plant a soft kiss on her lips. "Go relax for an hour, we have this," he smiles and she relaxes.

"The nurses taught me how to change a diaper, I'm kind of glad she isn't around to see me mess up first time," he admits to us when Bree is out of earshot.

"You are doing so good Michael, don't doubt yourself," I encourage him. I am actually pleasantly surprised to see him taking it all in his stride. It's like water off a ducks back.

"You guys going to follow our lead?" Michael winks at me and I splutter my water.

Both Davis and I turn to each other in horror. That is something we have not discussed and really, it is way too soon to even contemplate having a baby.

"Maybe in ten years," I joke and Davis smiles, seeming happy with my response.

Baby Rohan begins to moan from his basket.

"Will I feed him?" I ask Michael, who is re-doing Daniels diaper.

"Sure, his milk is prepared in the bottle warmer in the kitchen," he directs me.

I go grab it and return to find Davis has lifted Rohan out of his basket and is sitting, holding him, on the sofa. He looks so cute that I take a few seconds to admire them both, before Rohan moans again. I nervously take the baby and begin feeding him, he is so tiny and fragile and my heart melts. I don't think I will wait ten years to have my own children, maybe two or three.

CHAPTER
29

Roche

I check in my weapon and pass through a metal detector, before being allowed access. The guard who is escorting me along with Agent Leah Greg, pulls out a large ring of keys, finds one and unlocks the gate for us to enter. He leads us down a long, white corridor, away from where the prisoners are held and towards the interrogation room. Seamus Lynch is housed in this high security prison and today, an inmate has agreed to give us some information. The guard unlocks a metal door and we both step inside, to find an anxious Nate Casey. When we got the call that he had requested an interview with the FBI and that I was to lead the questioning, a dark reality began to dawn on me. This is the brother of the man who raped Joanna and also the same man who is housed in the same wing as Lynch. I was firstly annoyed at myself for missing the connection and for not looking further into his criminal background and prison connections. When I did, I found that the guards had named him as one of Lynch's confidants. I have only been working with Leah for two weeks, but I like her. She is focused, strong and dedicated to her career; she takes a seat next to me across from Nate and smiles warmly at him. She is attractive and the hope is that he will open up more.

"I'm Agent Roche and this is Agent Greg," I introduce us.

"Where is Davis?" He snaps, his eyes to Leah and dismisses her angrily.

"Davis is out of town," I lie and watch his eyes narrow in suspicion. His nostrils flare before he settles back in his seat, resting his cuffed hands on the table in front of him.

"Have you caught my brother yet?"

"No, do you know where he is?"

"I hope he was clever enough to get out of town," he shrugs, "so here's the deal Agent," his eyes roam leisurely to Agent Greg and he scans her body greedily. She recoils and he smiles.

"My brother won't last pissing time in this prison when

you catch him, there is already a mark on his head and if you guarantee that you will transfer him out of state when he is caught, then I will tell you some things I think you will find interesting."

"No," I say and stare him down.

"Look, they are going to kill him in here, he stands a better chance somewhere else," he sits up and glares back at me.

"Tell me what you know about Lynch and this package and I will discuss it," my gut squeezes. It goes against everything to make a deal with these scumbags, especially the brother of Joanna's rapist, but I need to know what Lynch is planning so I can stop anything else from happening.

"I will tell you this much for now. Lynch asked me to find someone on the outside that could follow Michael Ryan and his wife. I asked my brother, he was supposed to takes notes of their routine and report back to me, but his dick had other plans and now he has fucked over Lynch and I'm not the most popular guy on the wing at the minute. I can take care of myself, but I can't stop what they will do to him if he gets sent here. There is a package arriving and it is due real soon and trust me, it's going to fuck with your friends more than my brother has, so if you want to know more, make it happen so that he goes somewhere else."

I had surmised that Joanna's rape was somehow connected to Lynch as soon as I heard that Nate Casey wanted to talk with us. Joanna had been caught in the crossfire and proving Lynch's involvement, would be tough. I weigh up what Davis would do if he were in my position and decide to agree to his terms.

"Tell me about the package and it's a deal," I say and watch him sigh with relief. It's not just Lynch who you have to worry about catching up with your brother, I keep this thought to myself. Davis won't hold back if that animal comes for Joanna again and I wouldn't blame him.

I leave an hour later, knowing that the 'package', is no longer in transit and has arrived on American soil. With no clue of how to track it down, or even where to begin, I rush back to base and inform the rest of our team. We are a four man squad, well, three men and one woman and our sole purpose now, will be to find it and stop it before it destroys everything that Davis and Michael worked so hard to protect.

Jo

I look over my shoulder everywhere I go and the anxiety about my rapist's whereabouts, is beginning to take a toll. He has been on the run for over a week now and with little sightings and no updates from Vic Breen, the cold reality that he might still be here waiting to pounce, is unsettling. Davis has been by my side and I have tried to be upbeat around him the last few days, but the cracks in my façade, are beginning to show.

"What are you thinking about?" Davis tugs on my hand as we sit watching a movie. We have had a busy few days, both of us in work and then, with the twins arriving early, everything has just been so hectic. I'm exhausted physically and emotionally and I know when I'm quiet, he worries. I smile up at him.

"I'm so tired," I yawn, as if on cue and he smiles, pulling me tighter against him.

"Let's get you to bed," he kisses the top of my head, before switching the TV off. The faint sounds of a car alarm can now be heard instead. I sit up, listening more intently, recognising it as my own.

"That's my car," I move quickly to the window and draw back the curtains. Sure enough, in the car park below, my beautiful car is screaming for help as a young thug smashes the window.

Davis is immediately at my side.

"Little shit, call the police," he rushes to the sofa, pulling on his boots.

"Where are you going?" I squeal.

"To catch the little fucker," he growls. He reaches for

his holster that is still resting on the coffee table and takes his gun from it, sticking it behind, in the waistband of his dark jeans.

"Davis, just wait for the police to come," I beg.

"Joanna, lock the door behind me and call the police," he barks, rushing out and closing the door behind him. I rush over and twist the key, before searching through my bag for my cell phone. It vibrates in my hand just as I reach it. I look down at the unknown number and answer quickly.

"Hello," I rush, anxious to tell the caller that I can't speak right now.

"Go to the window Joanna," his voice creeps down the line. I stand, frozen to the spot, a cold sweat breaking out all over my body. I can't speak and although it is only a few seconds, it feels like a lifetime before my feet move towards the window.

"Why are you doing this?" I croak.

"I can't see you fully, pull back the curtains," he whispers maliciously and instead of fear, I feel disgust. The memory of his breath, his eyes, cause me to recoil and anger becomes my driving emotion.

"What the fuck do you want?" I ask again and my eyes catch Davis as he crosses the car park and it dawns on me. He looks up at me and I begin to wave erratically at him.

"I wouldn't do that if I were you Joanna," he laughs down the line when Davis waves back and continues on to my car.

"You have one minute to come out here or I'm going to put my knife through his heart," his whispered threat is laced with deadly intent. I consider my options, do I run to Davis. I make a snap decision and hope that it is the right one.

CHAPTER
30

Richard

I slip in the door as he runs out to be the hero. Little does he know, he just gave me the entrance I need to get to her and she just told me which apartment I would find her in. Fourth floor, first apartment to the right.

Davis

Joanna waves at me from the window with the phone to her ear, letting me know that she has called the police. I move to the car quickly and press the alarm off, my phone buzzes in my hand and I look to see Joanna's name flashing on the screen. I turn and look up to the fourth floor window where she still stands, again, the phone to her ear.

"Hey," I answer, while dropping to the ground to look under the cars for feet.

"He is here, he is outside and he has a knife. He said he will kill you if I don't come down," her frantic screams have me jumping to my feet. I look around at the empty parking lot and decide not to risk Joanna's safety.

"STAY THERE! I'm coming up, hang up and call the police NOW."

I push the phone into my back pocket and scope out the area once more, before running back towards the exit. My main priority is to get back to her and get her out of here. I type in the security code and make sure to close the door fully behind me, before taking the stairs two at a time. I don't have time to wait for the elevator. I turn and rush up the final flight of stairs, my body was moving too fast. My mind focused only on getting to Joanna, that I missed him as he stepped out of the shadows. It was the glint of his knife as the dim lights of the stairwell reflecting off it, which caught my attention in the end, but it was already too late. He drove it straight into my gut. I look up from two steps below him and squeeze his hand, biting down hard on my teeth to quell the pain. His dead eyes stare into mine, expressionless. He doesn't move for a moment, choosing to watch me as he tries to take my life and I know that in his hands, Joanna will suffer. A slow smile creeps over his face, as I break out in a sweat.

"Thought you could stop this, didn't you? She was special and I want her to come with me and you can't be there when it happens, that's our time," he pulls the knife quickly from my body. Without it, my body slackens and I tumble down the stairs. I press my hand to the wound, trying to stem the flow of blood, but already, I am dizzy. I watch through blurred vision, as he pulls open the door to the fourth floor and walks through it.

"Joanna," I call out weakly, before all I see is black.

Jo

My hands tremble, as I punch in 911. I stare at Davis, with tears streaming down my face as he rushes back across the parking lot and back into the building. My eyes are pinned to the entrance of my apartment block, making sure that he does not get in. I call out my location to the operator and give her a brief history of what is happening. A few moments later, I hear Davis bang on the door and rush over to open it.

"My boyfriend is FBI Agent Davis, he is here now," I say, pulling open the door. Without warning, my body is thrown back against the wall, landing painfully on my wooden floors. I scramble to get to my feet, only to feel a foot on my back, pushing me back to the floor.

"HELP, HE'S HERE," I scream out, looking for the phone. I see it across the room and try to crawl towards it. A large black boot comes down hard on it. My eyes travel up his leg and over his long body until I look into his dark, evil eyes. He hunches down, pushing my hair from my eyes and I recoil at his touch. His nostrils flare in anger before he pulls me to my feet to face him. I close my eyes, begging my mind to focus, to recall my self-defence training, so that I can get enough time to run. *Using the palm of your*

*hand and shooting it upwards, aim for his nose. If you
use enough force, you could not only break it, but water
their eyes and again, giving you a chance to escape,* Davis'
words come to the forefront of my mind.

"This time you will look at me Joanna," his twisted
words break through my clarity and I realise that he thinks
I am hiding from him. I snap open my eyes and glare back
at him.

"You are nothing but a coward, I'm not afraid of you,"
I spit.

"Your boyfriend is dead Joanna," he taunts.

I realise that Davis still has not returned and immediately
begin to struggle from his vice like grip. He drops my
left hand, my weakest considering I am left handed and
begins to drag me towards the living room. I take my only
opportunity. With my palm facing up, I turn back into his
body and with all my might, push up towards his nose.
His hand drops away from my restrained arm, as he bends
over, grabbing his nose. I don't wait, my legs feel like lead
and my body is shaking like a leaf, as I rush for the door.
The door is closed with the bolt in place and already, he is
screaming behind me. I turn over my shoulder to see him
storm towards me, with his knife raised.

"You fucking bitch," he screams.

The police sirens howl in the distance and I know help
is on the way, but they still seem too far away to make it
in time. I have no choice, but to rush into my bedroom. I
make it through the door, only to feel his hands grab my
blonde locks, once again, hurling me across my bed like
a rag doll. I roll off the other side, landing on my back. I
turn and look under the bed to watch his feet as he moves
towards me, but I also see the hammer I stored there a
few weeks ago. I reach under, grabbing the leather handle
tightly and wait for the perfect moment to strike. I close
my eyes, playing dead.

"Joanna, I wanted to have so much fun before we left
this world together, but hell will be fun."

He kneels down over me. I turn my head and open my

eyes at his words, to find him with his knife raised, ready to plunge into me. I hear a loud bang ring throughout my apartment and I waste no time in swinging my hammer, connecting with his head. He topples slightly, but not enough to take his weight from me. He drops his knife.

"DIE, YOU FUCKING BITCH," he screams, his hands finding my neck again as he squeezes. I turn my head away from him; I don't want his face to be the last thing I see. My eyes look under the bed and when I see another set of feet appear, I find hope again.

Davis

I wake with a start and sit up straight. My hand finds my wound again before my memory returns.

"Joanna," I call out, my voice echoing throughout the empty stairwell. I need to get to her. I turn onto my knees and crawl to the top of the stairs, each step is hell. By the time I reach the landing, I am sweating and depleted of energy. My mind fogs and my vision blurs again as I pull myself from the floor. Using the wall as leverage, I slide against it and pull open the door to the fourth floor. I do the same and make my way to the closed apartment door. I turn the handle and find it locked. I groan in pain as I push against the door with my shoulder. I know that I am not strong enough to bust through these doors. I can hear the police arrive outside, but she doesn't have the luxury to wait. I pull out my gun and shoot out the locks. I can hear her screaming from the bedroom and my heart stops beating.

"Joanna," my voice is a ghostly whisper as I rush to help her. With my gun raised, I step into her room and blind rage becomes me. I can see her feet at the end of the bed, kicking out as he bends over her on the floor.

"HEY," I yell loudly to get his attention and when he looks up. I fire one shot, straight at his head.

Jo

He falls on top of me, his hands, now limp, are still around my neck. I begin coughing as I scramble to get out from under him, all the time trying to catch my breath. When I manage to throw him from me, I push back on my heels across the floor. My eyes search my room for Davis and find him slumped over on my bed.

"Davis," I scream, my voice still hoarse from his attack. His gun is on the floor, his hand dangling above it from the bed. I jump to my feet and rush to his side, shaking him. His eyes are closed, his skin grey and when I look lower, I see his blood soaked t-shirt.

"Jesus, Davis, wake up, please wake up," I cry, just as police officers barge into my room.

"Mam, let us help him," one officer pulls me away and I begin kicking and screaming. He pulls me from the room.

"Let us do our job," he repeats over and over, as I refuse to relent.

"Let me see him, please, I need to be with him," I beg, watching an ambulance crew arrive. They bring in a yellow and black gurney and wheel it into my room. A few minutes later, they come out with Davis strapped in. I rush towards the door to follow them out.

"Ok, you can travel with him, just let them get him into the ambulance," the officer comes behind me again. They are moving too quickly for me to hold his hand and when the elevator is too packed, I am forced to run down the stairs. I meet them at the doors.

"Is he ok?" I ask the paramedic who ignores me and pushes forward with the gurney into the ambulance.

"Someone tell me something," I cry out impatiently.

"He is critical, we need to get him to the hospital," the female paramedic finally says. Fresh tears stream down my face.

"Please keep him alive," I sob, stepping into the ambulance and for the first time, taking his hand. "Davis, I'm here, I love you, please don't leave me," I sniff.

The male paramedic continues to squeeze oxygen into

his mouth before switching it over to the oxygen tank. An officer closes the doors of the ambulance when they are set and taps loudly when they are secure, signalling for the ambulance to take off.

"I love you Davis, please fight," I repeat over and over, until we reach the hospital.

CHAPTER
31

Jo

It has been twelve hours since we arrived at the hospital. Davis was immediately rushed to surgery so the doctors could take a closer look at the damage. After surgery, they informed me that they could not find any "severe" intestinal injuries. They had cleaned and stitched his wound and would monitor him for the next forty eight hours. I had phoned Bree and Michael as soon as I arrived and Michael had stayed with me until an hour ago. Bree was anxious for him to come home and take over care of the babies so that she could be here. I take a seat by his bedside and listen, as his heart rate beeps steadily. My eyes are heavy with exhaustion, but I can't sleep, I can't close my eyes until I know that he will be ok. I reach forward and take his hand, silently praying that he comes through this ok. We deserve a chance at happiness, we have been through too much for him to leave me now.

"It's not fair," I well up again and squeeze his hands. He is breathing on his own which is a good thing, but the doctors have warned me that there is still a risk of infection. A nurse has already come in to clean and change his dressings, twice. I twist my head, resting it on the bed as I continue to hold his hand. My eyes refuse to remain open any longer and just as I close them, his voice brings me back to consciousness.

"Is he dead?" He mutters, sounding parched and in pain. My head snaps up, my eyes finding his.

"Yes," I manage, before bursting into tears. I stand up from my seat and lean over him, kissing his lips gently. "I love you, I'm sorry for all of this," I cry softly.

"Joanna stop," he winces and I step back.

"I'm sorry, did I hurt you," I fret immediately.

"No, it hurts when I breathe deeply, I mean stop talking like this is your fault. It's over now, I'm fine."

"You are not fine, you almost died and you will have a scar," I wipe my running nose with my tissue, before taking his hand again and sitting back in my seat.

"I have never felt better knowing that fucker is dead," his eyes turn to me again. I stare back and for the first time, I allow the relief of his death to sink in.

"Thank you for saving me," I whisper because my voice will not allow me to speak any higher.

"I'm sorry I didn't get to you sooner, did he hurt you?"

"No, he had only gotten to me when you arrived," I tell a small white lie, because I know he will torture himself otherwise.

"You are to stay with Bree and Michael until I get out of here," he warns me and I giggle, I think he is going to be just fine.

EPILOGUE

"There is no way you are keeping this jacket!" I try to pull Davis' worn leather jacket from his hands, but he holds fast, refusing to let it go.

"Joanna, I swear, if you make me choose between you and the jacket, you are gonna lose," he laughs.

"It's old and battered, why are you so attached to it?" I roll my eyes, letting it fall from my hands. He drops it to the floor and wraps his large arms around my body, entrapping me. He kisses me softly before walking me backwards and falling on top of me, onto the bed. I begin to giggle; I love when he is like this.

"I've had that jacket for years, it's cool," he growls against my neck. His stubble scrapes along my jaw, sending delicious tingles all over my body.

"Ok, keep it," I exhale deeply.

His chest rumbles above mine as a deep chuckle escapes his mouth.

"You mean to tell me, all along, all I needed to do to get my own way, was kiss your neck."

"I secretly love the jacket," I laugh. He lifts his head and peers down into my eyes.

"You enjoy tormenting me, don't you?" He narrows his eyes, suspiciously. I wriggle beneath him, thrusting my hips against his erection.

"Yep," I grin, biting my bottom lip seductively. He growls once again before dipping his head and with his own teeth, he gently frees my lips from my hold. His lips crash against mine then, his hands moving up the inside of my tank top.

"Davis, I'm all sweaty from the move," I remind him. We have just spent the afternoon moving all my belongings into his duplex.

"You look too sexy for me to care," he continues to push my tank top over my head, revealing my naked breasts to him. His warm mouth covers one of my nipples, sucking it deep into the confines of his mouth. I thrust against his hips once again, before finding the hem of his t-shirt and disposing of it straight away.

"We should be unpacking," I pull at his belt.

"You're doing a great job of it right now," he winks and I laugh out loud before freeing him into my waiting hands. Our mouths meet again in a lustful kiss, devouring each other with hunger. He quickly rids my body of any remaining clothing before pushing deep inside me. Like always, I gasp when he fills me completely and allow my body a moment to adjust to his size. I wrap my legs around his back and ass, holding him where he belongs and run my fingers through his hair, as we race over the finish line. Our bodies dive deep and take everything the other has to offer, before pushing us both over the edge, into ecstasy. I tremble in his arms, while he continues to pulse in and out of my body, slowly.

"That was some welcome," I smile lazily a few minutes later.

"I think I'll let you live here, rent free, in return for sexual favours," he jokes and I smack his arm, playfully.

"How's your stomach?" I suddenly remember his wound and move him, so I can assess it.

"Its fine Joanna, it's been two weeks, its healing fine," he rolls his eyes. We made love every night since his hospital release, but even still, that was the first time we had forgotten ourselves.

"As long as you don't hurt yourself," I wrap my arms around him again, breathing deeply, remembering the night I almost lost him.

"I'm ok woman," he shakes his head but deep down, I know he loves the attention. My stomach rumbles with hunger, triggering my memory.

"I brought something for you," I say, jumping up and rummaging through the boxes. When I find what I am looking for, I turn around and throw it to him. He laughs, holding up my pink apron.

"I take it you're hungry."

"Famished and I like nothing better than watching you cook in that," I wink.

"I'm ordering pizza, but just to make you feel welcome, I'll pay for it wearing this," he smirks. "If I do, you have to wash the dishes for the week," he challenges.

"And if you don't, you're my sex slave for the week," he canters. "Deal," he slaps his hands together, it's too late when I finally realise that for him, it is win, win.

We eat pizza, watch an action movie and then fall into Davis' bed. I rest my head against his chest, feeling safe, loved and knowing that I am right where I want to be.

"We will get somewhere nicer soon," Davis kisses my forehead.

"This is perfect," I smile, before snuggling into him and falling into a deep sleep.

EXCERPT FROM
BOOK 3
SUSPICIOUSLY
UNDONE

Aisling

Give me a laptop, internet access and one hour and I can find just about anyone. Many friends have asked me to help them track down their elusive crushes, the 'cool' kids that are too cool for social media, so to speak. Within the hour, I can usually reel off the most obscure information about said crush, like their mother's maiden name or what dentist they visit. I can find their home town, their siblings and this one time, I even managed to find out how much a person had earned the year before. The information is always there, no matter how much people try to hide from the big bad internet; like DNA, once you touch it, you leave behind traces of yourself. I have no formal education, no degree in computer science and I definitely don't ever remember joining the Gardaí.

I do, however, have cop on, street smarts, social intelligence, call it what you like but the point is, that with all my stalking experience, I am left stumped. I can't find a trace of Bree or

Michael, other than their connection to Seamus Lynch, I've got nothing. I did find an Aubrey Richards registered with a college to study English Lit, only to further discover that she had dropped out of the course. My brain is fried and I am so close to packing it all in and heading home to Dublin. I have come to this café day after day and I have run out of search options. I lean back in my chair to ease my stiff back and catch a glimpse of the TV. I look closer and see Seamus Lynch's mugshot on the screen. The volume is low but it's subtitled and I read every word, eagerly. My excitement levels rise and rise, as each new line appears across the screen. Seamus Lynch will appear before the Criminal Courts of Justice tomorrow to appeal his sentence. I literally jump up and down, clapping my hands, until I realize that a red headed, Irish girl, jumping for joy about the fact that an Irish mobster had won a re-trail hearing, looks a tad bit suspicious. I sit back down, pull my chair closer to the computer and type 'Seamus

Lynch hearing,' into the search bar. The time and location both pop up straight away in the results and I jot them both down.

"Mam, I'm afraid the public dock is not open for this hearing, you will need to move along," I throw my head back in frustration when the female court clerk, ushers me out of the building. Maybe I was a bit naive to think that I could walk into one of the most high profile hearing Boston has seen in years, but God loves a trier. The steps leading up to the grey courthouse, are crowded with news reporters, police officers and bystanders, all waiting to find out the fate of Seamus Lynch. I try to stay on the side-lines, with a clear view of everyone that goes in and comes out of the building, but the crowds are like crazed fans, hungry to catch a glimpse of their favourite rock star. I am pushed and pulled deeper into the rungs of people until eventually, I am on the outskirts, nowhere near the entrance and with little or no view of anyone arriving. I look down on the clean grey pavement, hoping to kick a can in disappointment, but it's spotless. Do they actually wash down the paths? I wonder to myself, there is not one speck of dirt on the footpath. I distract myself with this quandary for all of thirty seconds, before remembering the task at hand. I'm like a bloody magpie, I scold myself, before looking up with a new resolve to get back to the top of this growing crowd. I fix the straps of my backpack and redo my ponytail, before looking around once more for a chink in their armour.

They are all mashed together, shoving and pushing each other out of the way, trying to claim their position in the mosh pit. I look back over my shoulder in search of a snow plough; I could just scoop them all up and toss them behind me. Drastic I know, but they didn't mind outing me. I freeze when I see the most handsome man I have EVER laid eyes on, step out of a black SUV.

Draped in brown leather and wearing aviator sunglasses, this God among men comes round to open the passenger door. I see her long, slender legs first before Joanna

Carmody slips out of the car. She is stunning; her wild blonde hair is loose and whipping around her face as the breeze catches it. She leans into the absolute ride and kisses him tenderly and then I recognize him. Agent Will Davis, Michael and Bree's friend, Joanna Carmody's sexy boyfriend and the man who arrested Seamus Lynch. They both pull their shoulders back, neither hiding their relationship, despite the fact that this trial all hinders on the suspicion that the DA's office, had somehow stitched up Seamus Lynch. It was so far-fetched and ridiculous that Lynch's attorney, might just pull it off. I watch, in awe, as this power couple walk straight into the media frenzy, ignoring the questions fired at them and manage to make it to the entrance in one piece. Davis protects her all the way in and my heart flutters at how sexy he is.

They both look so much more attractive in person; there is an aura about them both that makes you mad with jealousy. When I grow up, I want to be like Joanna Carmody and I want the full shebang, hot boyfriend included. She is not only intelligent and beautiful, but she is also a survivor. I read about her rape in the newspapers and seeing her today, I can tell he didn't break her. Davis saved her life when her attacker came back; japers, he is too much! I will need to keep my crush on him to myself when I meet them.

A buzz of excitement seizes me; I will get to know these people if Michael accepts me as his kin. I squeeze my eyes and lift my shoulders, expressing my utter joy at the prospect. I change my tact now; I will keep my eyes focused on the road. Everyone that is arriving will be pulling up here first. My eyes scan the parked cars across the street and one in particular stands out. I pass it, before my eyes snap back to take a closer look at the external advertisement that is affixed to the black SUV, "MCR GYM," I mumble to myself before looking closer to the passenger seat. My eyes widen when I see a man sitting there, wearing shades and a baseball cap. His eyes are narrowed and his nostrils flared, as he stares across at the courthouse. I follow his line of vision and watch, as Seamus Lynch is escorted by armed guards inside. When I turn back, he is already pulling away and I dash across the road to try stop him, but I'm too late. I watch him speed away, throwing my hands up in frustration, as he disappears around a bend. I stand there, deflated and it's only when a large horn beeps behind me, do I realize that I am still in the middle of the street. I jump with fright and notice that a few faces from the mosh pit, have dragged themselves away from the show to see what all the fuss is about.

MCR Gym, I remember the car advert and pull out my notebook, jotting it down. I keep a diary of my search, I want to make sure that I don't forget any important information that I might pick up along the way and this is definitely note-worthy.

Roche

I look through the lens of my camera and zoom in on all the faces that surround the courthouse, from across the street. The media coverage of this pre-trial is intense, but there are also random citizens, taking time out of their day, to come here. Mostly, these will be nosey busy bodies, wanting to see what all the fuss is about, then there will be passers-by, who will stop out of curiosity. Everyone else interests me and I want to know who they are and if they are the package. I pass over the crowd with speed until flame red hair, catches my eye. I stop and zoom in on her face, for a moment, I just look, my mind wiped of all thoughts.

This stranger is the most attractive woman I have ever set eyes on. She is like a small child at a parade, trying to see over all the adults' heads and I want to go over and lift her onto my shoulders, just so she doesn't miss anything. Her rich dark hair, is pulled back into a ponytail, highlighting her pale skin and piercing blue eyes. I am captivated by her beauty, my mind imagining how good it would feel to kiss her plump, pink lips. She looks adorable in her jeans and sneakers, as she hitches up her backpack and tries again. I keep my camera trained on her and notice her attention drift to the side street. Her eyes widen with lust and a pang of jealousy rushes through me. I need to know who has affected her like this and move my camera to see Davis. I roll my eyes, he's taken sweetheart, I smile, triumphantly. She follows their progress all the way into the courthouse, before squeezing her features in delight.

"Who are you?" I say aloud and begin to take snaps of her. She is now looking anywhere, but at the courthouse.

"Trey," I call to another colleague, who is watching the courthouse from a different angle across the room. "Keep your camera on Lynch and everyone around him as he arrives," I direct him.

Something about this girl, feels off and when her eyes land on Michael Ryan's car, her attention remaining solely with him as Lynch arrives, my curiosity peeks. I continue to snap pics of her pretty face and when she runs out into the road after Michael's car, I know that she is here for more than idle curiosity.

"I have something here," I call out, keeping my eyes on her at all times, "red headed female, on the corner of Washington and Rosemount, blue jeans, yellow jumper and blue backpack. I'm going to follow on foot. Garcia, take over here....."

57387958R00202

Made in the USA
Charleston, SC
11 June 2016